THE
STAGER

THE
STAGER

SUSAN COLL

SARAH CRICHTON BOOKS
Farrar, Straus and Giroux
New York

Sarah Crichton Books
Farrar, Straus and Giroux
18 West 18th Street, New York 10011

Copyright © 2014 by Susan Coll
Printed in the United States of America
First edition, 2014

Library of Congress Cataloging-in-Publication Data
Coll, Susan.
    The stager : a novel / Susan Coll.
        pages   cm
    ISBN 978-0-374-26881-7 (hardback) — ISBN 978-0-374-71072-9 (ebook)
    1. Home staging—Fiction.   I. Title.

PS3553.O474622 S83 2014
813'.54—dc23

                                                                2013049020

Designed by Abby Kagan

Books published by Sarah Crichton Books / Farrar, Straus and Giroux may be
purchased for educational, business, or promotional use. For information
on bulk purchases, please contact the Macmillan Corporate and
Premium Sales Department at 1-800-221-7945, extension 5442,
or write to specialmarkets@macmillan.com.

www.fsgbooks.com
www.twitter.com/fsgbooks • www.facebook.com/fsgbooks

1 3 5 7 9 10 8 6 4 2

For Sophia Musleh,
eternal childhood

4.5BR SINGLE FAMILY HOUSE–BETHESDA

This elegant 4.5 bedroom, 4 full and 2 half bath Flemish Villa sits on 1.5 meticulously landscaped acres in the private, gated enclave known as The Flanders! Overlooking the 8th fairway of a premier golf course, Kew Gardens Country Club, this home provides gracious entertainment spaces as well as comfortable rooms for everyday living! You will have sweet dreams in the 1000–sq. ft. master bedroom suite with ensuite bathroom featuring imported Italian marble, his and her sinks, designer toilets, sunken tub with Jacuzzi! Unwind in the gymnasium or cozy up to the magnificent stone fireplace in the living room or enjoy a gourmet meal in the expansive cook's kitchen with all new stainless steel appliances! With 6,200 sq. ft., there is no lack of space to enjoy in this home! Only minutes from the area's finest restaurants in close by Potomac Village or Bethesda! Feast your eyes on the gorgeous grounds featuring a swimming pool, beautifully landscaped stone terraces, private putting green, 3-car garage, and spectacular views of the golf course!

OPEN HOUSE SUNDAY: NOON TO 4 P.M.

PART I

THINGS FROM YOUR LIFE

ELSA

There is a skinny lady with bright red lipstick and purple nail polish standing in front of my refrigerator when I get home after field-hockey practice. Dominique is cradled in her arms, and in her hand is a crooked nubby carrot with the bushy leaf still attached. She is trying to get Dominique to eat the carrot, but he won't open his mouth.

I don't know who this lady is or why she is standing in my kitchen holding my rabbit, but since the first FOR SALE sign went up in front of our house three months ago, I've gotten used to finding strangers in random places, doing random things: Once, I found a lady sitting on my bed with her shirt unbuttoned, nursing her baby; another time, I saw a man going through my mom's dresser drawers. One lady even went around the house flushing all the toilets while her husband sat in my dad's favorite chair in the living room, reading a book.

But no one has ever tried to feed my rabbit before. Dominique doesn't even like carrots. Also, he looks kind of sick. I'm surprised to see him, since he's been missing for a couple of days, so I reach for him. At the same time, Nabila walks into the kitchen, sees the lady, and screams. In the chaos, Dominique winds up getting dropped. He hits the ground headfirst, and for almost an entire minute he doesn't move. I worry that he's dead, but then, just when I'm about to tell someone to call the police, or the fire department, or my mom, he lifts his head, pricks his ears up straight, looks around the room, and hops out the back door, which is propped wide open—I'm guessing because of the bad smell in our house.

We spend an hour walking around the neighborhood, calling Dominique's name. We see about ten different rabbits, and even though they all look sort of like Dominique, none of them is him.

LARS

Were Bella narrating this story, she'd lean in confidentially, in a manner that would make you feel that you alone are privy to the secret of my unraveling.

"Lars has been sweating and tossing and pounding his pillows for seven nights straight," she'd say, "and the dreams he recounts, sometimes shaking me awake at three a.m., verge on harrowing noir."

Bella actually speaks like this, tossing out phrases like "harrowing noir" with the casual ease of a crack dealer counting hundred-dollar bills. Her thoughts line up in smooth, neat sentences replete with proper punctuation, with just enough emotion to be suggestive of fonts. Without your even noticing, a mini-thesis takes shape, with topic sentences and closing arguments that loop back nicely to echo her chief points. No "um"s or "like"s spill from her lips; her speech is the grammatical equivalent of a military cot.

Don't get me wrong. I'm not suggesting my wife is robotic: even in her sleep-deprived fugue, she shows interest in my dreams, asking questions that go right to the heart of complicated narratives that have mostly to do with animals: beaches full of toxic fish, weaponized penguins, a plague of crustacean-like parasites that have invaded our house and cannot be eradicated.

On the fourth day of our trip to London, I awake with a nightmare about a rabbit whose cigar ash has set our house on fire. Later that same afternoon, when we're doubled down, dealing long-distance with the Dominique debacle, I am troubled by the coincidence; concerned there might be some weird rabbit mojo amok in the atmosphere. Bella explains patiently, as if I am a child, that rabbits are prevalent figures in popular culture, appearing in books and advertisements more frequently than most people realize, and that my dream was likely inspired by Dominique's destructive habits. He has been quietly ruining our house for years, she reminds me, and this coincidence is surely meaningless.

It can be exhausting to live with someone who always has the answer. I shoot her a withering look. Or at least I mean to; I am no longer sure if my facial expressions convey what I intend.

BELLA HAS HER own theory about what is going on with me: Buried in the fine print of the three pages of disclaimers that accompany the latest addition to the cocktail of medications she insists I take is the possibility of disturbing thoughts, hallucinations, vivid and unusual dreams, and episodes of psychosis. I've always been plugged into the flotsam and jetsam of the universe, and, spouselike (Bella might say witchlike), into my wife's brain. Some of this manifests as normal, déjà-vu-y stuff, like dreaming about rabbits just before our own disappears, but sometimes I simply *know* things. And lately I know even more, because things are crystallizing. My eye has become such a finely tuned instrument that I can actually see a ray bounce off the surface material and calculate the degrees of the arc at which it is about to bend back to me. Light carries energy in discrete quantities, and now that I have learned to harness this, it gives me strength.

We argue about this frequently. Bella is a pragmatist. She insists these nocturnal animal visitations, as well as my ability to see, and channel, the light, are merely chemically induced side effects. But she's wrong: I've never felt clearer, and I am finally beginning to understand. I am not as articulate as my wife, and although I am completely fluent and from a highly literate family (my late father was a well-known Swedish mystery writer; you are probably familiar with the whitewashed landscapes and his rugged, brooding, chain-smoking detective, Jesper Johanson), English is not my first language; so when she asks me what it is, exactly, that I am beginning to understand, I cannot explain it to her satisfaction. Only that it has to do with the light. Seeing the light, grasping the importance of diffraction and absorption, embracing the beauty of transparency.

This is something Bella ought to understand better than she does, transparency being the centerpiece of her new professional life. You might think I am just casually tossing about metaphors, but four months ago she was actually named the Vice-President for Transparency for Luxum International, the world's second-largest investment bank. Their new television commercials run in a seemingly endless loop on the cable news networks: "Luxum International = Transparency + Efficiency + Accountability." Bella had been Luxum's Vice-President for North American Equity Derivatives for the previous five years, commuting from our home outside Washington, D.C., to New York most weeks, until the company became the subject of a long cycle of unflattering headlines touched off by losing a class-action lawsuit for defrauding investors in risky mortgage loans. This they might have overcome—everyone was defrauding investors, so that was no big deal—but then, that same week, a trader went public with the fact that his team had been siphoning funds to build an underground pleasure palace in Dubai, the sordid details of which were tabloid fodder for weeks and involved underage girls without visas and a room full of goats. Yes, it sounds over-the-top, but I'm telling you, I don't know what kind of mind could make this stuff up. Part of the recovery involves a massive rebranding effort, and Bella—my personable, articulate, beautiful, brilliant wife, my Bella, who inspires trust among her colleagues—is going to be Luxum's salvation. The job comes with a mid-six-figure salary, stock options, and the potential for (but not the promise of) astronomical bonuses. The only downside of being Luxum's VP for Transparency is that we need to relocate to their London headquarters.

Personally, I find this rebranding campaign a bit elliptical. If you aren't already doing business with Luxum International, you will likely view these commercials with great puzzlement. You might guess that Luxum is in the business of tailoring the sharp Italian suits the actors wear on the commercials, or that they manufacture those slim computers, illuminated with the Luxum logo, that appear on the background desks. Whatever it is that actually occurs beneath the veneer of transparency + efficiency + accountability (and, to be honest, I'm not entirely certain myself), they want Bella badly. They upped the initial offer after she said no on the grounds of not wanting to disrupt Elsa, although I suspect she is really more concerned about disrupting me.

You are only as sick as your secrets. This phrase has lodged in my brain like a splinter, even though I can't remember where I picked it up. Twelve years into our marriage, four days into our trip to London, to borrow from the lingo of my wife's former profession, we are so far removed from the lede that we are buried in the jump. We pretend the secret away; we placate it, medicate it, tiptoe around it, construct overpasses and back-road arteries, and we are now in the part of the story that lands in newspapers beside advertisements for convertible sofas and wooden fences and is used to line birdcages or start fires or wrap fish at the dock.

I shake Bella awake and narrate the arc of another hideous dream.

I am trembling so badly I may be convulsing. My wife urges me to take another pill. The management of symptoms further erodes the memory, which may in fact be the point. While the sumptuous blue molecules dissolve in my bloodstream, she calls my doctor back in Washington and leaves another voice mail.

ELSA

The lady with the purple nail polish suggests we go to my room to play with the dolls. Maybe she thinks this will make me feel better about Dominique disappearing.

"Molly and Kaya look kind of bored and lonely," she says, which is of course ridiculous, since they are inanimate objects. But it's true that they've been sitting at their little dining table for more than a year, staring at their kebobs, wearing bathing suits. They are having a luau. The same luau for a year. They are covered in dust, and Molly has slumped into her dinner plate.

The lady picks up a skewer of pineapple. One of the yellow plastic chunks is dented at the center; if you look closely, you can see teeth marks.

"It looks like you have some hungry mice!" she says.

"No, that was probably Dominique. He likes to chew on things. I mean he *liked* to chew on things."

Now she looks worried, like she's waiting for me to cry.

Poor Dominique. I hope he's found someplace warm to stay. It's starting to get dark outside, plus it's colder than it's supposed to be in

April, and I *think* about crying, but I don't. Maybe I'm less upset
than I should be about him being gone. Dominique was an unhappy rabbit who never seemed to like me very much. He bit whenever I tried to pet him. He didn't seem to like our house. He gnawed
on the legs and gashed the fabric of an antique velvet chair that was
some sort of family heirloom. We found him hanging from the
living-room curtains like a monkey—he must have leaped up and
gotten his claw stuck in the lace, which he shredded in the process.
He bit my parents and they took him to a doctor, who said he didn't
like being cooped up in our house. Then my mom bought a cage,
but I let him out whenever they weren't home. Instead of being
grateful, though, he just destroyed more things—like, last week,
he'd eaten a hole in the living-room carpet and thrown up bits of
white wool, which was weird, because rabbits aren't supposed to be
able to vomit. Before my mom left for London, she'd asked me if
I was trying to make it so that no one would want to buy our
house, which hadn't occurred to me at the time, but was not a
bad idea.

The lady finds the box with all the toy food in it and dumps it on
the floor. She then sifts through the enormous heap of stuff, stopping
to study the sushi platter and the hamburger buns and each little
cereal box like these are the most amazing things she's ever seen. She
gets all excited about the chicken-noodle soup, for some reason, and
then she digs around until she finds the tiny can opener. She's really
into this, the way she clamps the blade onto the side of the can and
turns the handle and pretend-pours it into a small plastic bowl. Then
she takes a spoon and blows on the invisible soup and feeds it to Kaya,
who is wearing the same blue-and-white polka-dot bikini I'd changed
her into a year ago. I prop Molly back up in her chair so she can eat
some soup, too. She's wearing a tie-dye one-piece under a sarong. Her
hair is in two braids, one of which is caught in the strap of her bathing
suit. As I fuss with her, I stir up so much dust I'm embarrassed. People
clean my room once a week, but my mom told them never to touch

the dolls. That's because the cleaning lady who used to work here before we got a new cleaning lady once dusted Molly's horse and his saddle fell off. When she tried to fix it, a stirrup broke, and then the cleaning lady had to leave the country. I'd asked my mom if she had to leave because of the broken stirrup, but all she said was "Don't be silly, Elsa!"

WE'VE ONLY BEEN playing for about ten minutes when the lady looks at her watch and says, "Oh my! It's later than I realized, and your nanny said you had homework to do. Plus I need to get home to walk my dog."

I don't understand who this lady is or why she's here, playing with me. I'm not even sure if I like her, but I don't want her to leave. "I don't have that much homework," I lie, "and anyway Nabila is not my nanny. She's my friend, plus she does my laundry and drives me to school and stuff. But . . . wait, who are *you*?"

"I told you when we were downstairs, remember? I'm the Stager. I work for Amanda."

Amanda is the Realtor. She is helping us sell our house so we can move to London. She always dresses perfectly. Her business card says *Amanda Hoffstead Always Cinches the Deal!* We are all afraid of Amanda, but my mother says that her being intimidating is possibly a good thing: maybe people will be frightened into buying our house this time around. A different lady already tried to sell our house, but no one wanted to buy it, so after three months, when her *exclusive* was up, we had to *relist*.

"I know you are the Stager, but what are you actually *doing*?"

"I'm just fixing up your house to get it ready to go on sale, to make it so other people can imagine themselves living here. Nothing too major. Your room is fine, really—it's actually perfect, the best room in the house—so all we need to do is tidy it up a bit, put the dolls away for starters."

"Well, if that's all you're going to do, then it sounds like you're just a cleaning lady."

"*Touché.*"

"What does that mean?"

"It means you have a good point. But I'm meant to do a little more than put things away. It's actually a creative job."

"It is?"

"Well, it's more creative than you might think. I'm kind of new at this; I'm just doing it on the side. I'm really an artist. Well, I *was* an artist, before I became a journalist. Now I'm . . . Well, I don't even know what I am anymore. An unemployed journalist, I suppose."

"No way! My mom used to be a journalist! She wrote about money. But now she makes money. Or helps other people make money. Or helps people behave when they make money. That's why we have to move to London."

I don't want to move to London, but no one seems to care. Everyone keeps saying how exciting it is, and that soon I'll be speaking with a British accent. And drinking tea and eating scones. I'm really tired of the whole London thing and we haven't even moved yet.

"Well, I'm not exactly a journalist anymore, either. I was running a magazine until a few months ago."

"Oh. Like *People*?"

"No. It was a shelter magazine."

"A *what*?"

"A magazine about homes."

"I didn't know there were magazines about homes."

"Not so many anymore, which is why I'm sitting on the floor playing with dolls!"

"So what else are you going to do with my house?"

"There are lots of little things I need to do. And I have to work very quickly, since your open house is on Sunday."

"But it's only Tuesday."

"Yes, but there's a lot to do."

"Like what?"

"Oh, nothing too radical, just a bunch of little stager tricks. Mostly just depersonalizing. People want to imagine their own families living here, and it's hard when they see all of *your* things, like your toys or your pictures."

"What are some of the 'tricks'?"

Before the Stager can answer, we hear voices moving up the staircase, and then, all of a sudden, there are three people standing at my door. One of them is Amanda, the Realtor. She is in the middle of a sentence about the square footage of my bedroom, but then she sees me and the Stager sitting on the floor and she stops talking and says, "What are you doing, Eve?"

The Stager puts the little spoon down and says, "I'm helping the child clean up her room."

Amanda says "Oh," and then turns back to the people she is with, who are both very large. The man is wearing a blue suit but no tie, and the lady has on a dress with orange flowers. I can't tell if the flowers are enormous or if they just look enormous because of the size of the lady. I also can't tell if the man she is with is her husband or her father.

"We could paint, maybe knock out those bookshelves, change the carpet, and turn this into Toby's room," the man says.

"Or we could put Briana in here and keep the décor," the lady replies.

"No, I think we'd need to paint, no matter who goes in here. These colors are pretty hideous."

It's true; we decorated my room three years ago, back when I was in second grade and was really into pink and purple. But I would like these people to get out of my house. The idea of Toby or Briana living in my room, whoever they are, makes me want to scream.

"By the time you come back on Sunday, these colors will be gone. You're getting a sneak peak," says Amanda. "This is the first showing.

It's not technically listed yet. We're cleaning and painting, so it will be spick-and-span by Sunday."

No one has said anything to me about painting my room.

"Wasn't this already on the market?" the lady asks. "I looked at a couple of other places in The Flanders and I'm pretty sure I noticed a sign out front, but, if my memory is correct, it was out of our range, so I hadn't bothered to look."

"Do you smell something funny?" the man asks, making a sniffing noise. He looks at the lady, who is his daughter or wife, but she doesn't say anything. Then he sniffs again, twice in a row, more conspicuously. Amanda walks over to my window and pulls it open. A gust of wind makes the lace curtains puff out, and we watch as they slowly settle back against the wall. Then the people come into my room and walk around, inspecting things, like we aren't even there. The lady opens the closet and looks inside and pushes my clothes to the back of the rack. The man walks over to the window and stares out at the pool. Then he taps on the wall behind my bed and says something about its being "load-bearing." They all go into the bathroom at the same time, and I hear the cabinets being opened and closed and the sound of the water running. Then they come back out and stand in my room again.

"We're giving this a little TLC and a fresh start," Amanda says. "The market has been pretty volatile, and the last Realtor priced it wrong, plus it needed a bit of sprucing up. But this neighborhood is dynamite, and things are getting better every day—as I'm sure you know, since you're shopping. Home prices in this area rose by seven percent last year."

"Really?" says the man, surprised. "What about that new development right behind here—that Unravelings place I keep hearing about? I thought it was in foreclosure, and bringing the whole neighborhood right down with it."

"Unfurlings," says the lady, who is maybe his wife.

"That's an unfortunate situation, but it's had no impact on values in this area, generally," says Amanda. "It was a poorly conceived idea for some New Age baby-boomer living concept. Unwind, unfurl! Live like hippies, raise llamas, grow your own vegetables, listen to NPR, and live in three-million-dollar dream houses."

Amanda laughs, but everyone else is silent, like maybe they don't get why that's funny. "They've organized the place like it's a college campus, or a library, or some Marxist commune," she continues. "Each according to his interests! They have fiction and nonfiction enclaves, a history enclave, music, visual arts, etc. Great idea, apart from the fact that no one can afford to live there. Or maybe it's just that the people who can afford to aren't the ones who want to live like hippies, if you get what I mean. The people with hedge-fund money want to live like hedge-funders!"

It's not clear what the people think of this, or if they are even listening. The man knocks on the load-bearing wall again and says something about maybe knocking it down after doing some reinforcements. Amanda says that's surely doable and a great idea. Then they turn around and walk back into the hallway. Amanda follows, and I hear them talking about replacing the carpet as they head up the next flight of stairs and into my parents' room.

They don't even say goodbye.

The Stager picks up the spoon again and blows on it before putting it to Molly's mouth. "Have some yummy, yummy soup," she says.

"They're going to knock my wall down? And I didn't know you were going to paint my room. I thought you said it was perfect!"

"It *is* perfect," she says. "Amanda is crazy."

"Well, then, what *are* you going to do? What are some of the tricks you were talking about?"

"Well, 'tricks' might not have been the best word, but you can do little things; like, once, I staged a house where there were a lot of holes in the wall, and I patched them up with toothpaste, then slapped on a coat of paint, and it was as good as new."

"With toothpaste! That's so funny! I hope not the kind with blue or red stripes in it! Why were there holes in the wall?"

"Lord knows. The woman was a little crazy. It almost looked like she'd been playing with a nail gun."

"Really? *My God!* She might have hurt someone!"

"Well, no, I mean, I don't think she was actually playing with a nail gun—that's just what the wall looked like."

"Oh, I see," I say, although I'm not sure that I do. Now I am confused about the nail gun and whether the owner is crazy, or the Stager is crazy for saying that woman is crazy when she isn't, and also if Amanda is crazy for saying that my room needs to be painted, or if the Stager is crazy for saying that it does not.

"Also, there are a couple of things that are sort of like tricks, like the Rule of Three."

"What's that?"

"Well, you know how things come in threes?"

"No."

"Like the Three Little Pigs."

"Oh! Or the Three Blind Mice?"

"Exactly. And there's this stager trick that says you should always cluster things in groups of three. Like, on the counter, you should have three asymmetrical objects."

I know the word "asymmetrical." It means "uneven." I'm in the advanced honors reading group. I'm the only one from fifth grade in with the sixth-graders. I get to walk across the tennis courts every day and go to the middle-school building for reading. "What kind of asymmetrical objects?"

"It depends on what room you're staging. Say, in your front entranceway, you've got that pig, and that bowl of tulips, and that African statue. That's a good cluster. The pig is very small, the tulips are medium height, plus the flowers splay out nicely, and then the statue offsets both of them, tall and thin."

"The African statue?"

"You know, that tall wooden figure?"

"Oh, the naked starving person?"

"I guess."

"I don't know if she's starving, actually. She might be pregnant."

"I hadn't really focused on that possibility," the Stager says.

"But that's already a cluster of three objects, so maybe we don't need you to be the Stager."

"True. But there are other rooms, and anyway, even though that's a good cluster, it's probably a little too specific to your family's tastes. A little too . . . ethnic. Not everyone likes that."

"But I love that pig."

"I love that pig, too," she says.

"If you shake it, it sounds like there's sand inside."

"I know. But the rule isn't just about objects. It's about things like color. You want to have three different things going on—say, one shade on the wall, another on furniture, and a third for accents, like throw pillows."

"There were also Three Bears and Three Billy Goats Gruff."

"Very good. Listen, sweetheart, I really need to go now. Let's just put the dolls away and clean up all this food."

"No! We can't put the dolls away!" I say. "Let's just feed them some dessert before you go." I dig around and find a Key lime pie. It's chewed up pretty badly, too. We both stare at it for a moment.

"He'll come back. I know he will," she says. "Rabbits have an amazing sense of smell. They can find their way home from hundreds of miles away."

I'm pretty sure she's making this up. "I think dogs are the ones with the good sense of smell, not rabbits."

"Oh, I don't know, I wouldn't be so sure. Rabbits are pretty remarkable creatures. Just think of all the books about rabbits. I wouldn't be surprised if Dominique shows up at the door any minute."

I want to believe her. But anyway, if she's right, Dominique probably ran away on purpose because of the bad smell in our house!

"What rabbit books?" I ask.

"Well . . . let's see. There's a rabbit in *Alice in Wonderland*, right? And there's Peter Rabbit, and there's . . ."

"Oh! I know, there's these ones that I love about a rabbit brother and sister named Max and Ruby," I said.

"I know those books! I love them, too!"

"My favorite is the one about the egg," I say. *"Max's Breakfast."* I stand up and walk over to my bookshelf to find it.

"I remember that one," the lady says. "'Eat your egg, Max,' said Max's sister Ruby. 'BAD EGG,' said Max."

"I can't believe you remember that!"

"My nephew was obsessed with those books. I used to babysit him a lot when he was little."

I flip the book to the page where Ruby is standing on a chair. She's wearing a pink dress and tasting the egg. "Here's my favorite part: 'See, Max?' said Ruby. 'It's a YUMMY YUMMY EGG.'"

The lady starts laughing, and I do, too. Soon I am laughing so hard I'm having trouble breathing, so I stand up and go over to my night-stand to get my inhaler.

"Are you okay?" the lady asks. "Should I get your nanny? I mean, Nabila?"

"No. I'm fine."

"Okay. Well, tell me if you're having any trouble breathing, okay?" She looks at her watch again. "I hate to leave, but my dog . . ."

"What's his name?"

"Moses. She's a girl."

"A girl dog named Moses?"

"Yeah, it's actually kind of a funny story," she says. She unloosens Molly's braids, finds a brush, and starts to run it through her hair. "The dog was supposed to be named Moose. That's the name I decided on when I brought her home from the pound. I don't know what kind of dog she is exactly, but she's big and a couple of different colors, mostly brown, probably part Lab and part some sort of terrier, and, well, she actually looks a little like a moose—her ears are so big they reminded me of antlers. So, anyway," she says, "I sent my husband an e-mail at work and told him I thought 'Moose' was a good name . . . But when he got home that night, he said, 'Hi there, Moses,' to the dog, and I said, 'No, it's Moose.' And he said, 'No, you told me it was Moses,' and we had this fight. Well, 'fight's the wrong word . . .'"

"Was there shouting? Or crying? Did your husband lock himself in his room?"

"No, no. I guess I didn't mean to use the word 'fight.' Anyway, we just went back and forth about this for a while, and he was really insistent. It started to become kind of absurd, so we went into the office to pull up the e-mail on the computer."

"Don't you have an iPhone?"

"Well, yes, I do now, but this was a long time ago. So I found the sent e-mail and he was right, it actually said 'Moses.' And then I realized that my spell check must have changed 'Moose' to 'Moses.'"

"I don't think it would do that. Maybe you just made a mistake typing."

"I don't think so," she says. "Well, maybe. But anyway, then he . . ."

"He? You mean your husband?"

"He's my ex-husband now, although we never bothered to actually get divorced, and believe it or not he's very expensively on my COBRA right now . . . Go figure! Sorry, that was sort of inappropriate of me."

"You have a cobra?"

"No, no, COBRA's what you call it when you lose your job and need to extend your health insurance for a while."

"But I thought you had a job. I thought you were working with the Realtor."

"I am now. But this is a new job. It's not really a real job. Well, it's a real job, but . . ."

"My mom's phone did that once."

"What?"

"Her phone changed a bunch of 'xoxoxo's to 'socks.' I didn't know why she said 'socks' at the end of her message. So I asked her, and she said she didn't say 'socks.' And then it happened again! Do you and your mom text?" I ask.

"No. My mom's been gone for a long time. Before there were cell phones, even."

"*My God!* That's so sad! My grandma died last year—my mom's mom, not my dad's mom. My dad's mom lives in Sweden. But my mom's mom didn't have a cell phone, either," I say, hoping this might make her feel better, although my mom says two wrongs don't make a right, so I suppose a second person being dead and not having a cell phone doesn't make it less bad about the first person.

"She died? I'm so sorry to hear that. Had she been ill?"

"She had Alzheimer's. She was sick for a long time."

"Oh my. How rough! It must have been especially hard for your mom, having her in California."

"We brought her here and had a nurse stay in the house. Her name was Lucy. The nurse, I mean. Not my grandma." I'm surprised that she knows my grandma had lived in California, but I'm surprised by everything lately, because no one tells me what's going on. They don't want to bring up the subject of moving, because they think I'll get upset, so instead weird stuff like this kept happening—strangers coming into my house, bad smells, and now my rabbit runs away.

"Anyway, it's become a joke with me and my mom. Instead of saying 'I love you,' we just say 'Socks!'"

"That's sweet," she says, but I'm not sure she really thinks so.

"Do you think the girls might want to change into their pajamas after they finish dessert?" I ask.

Before she can answer, Nabila appears at the door. "Elsa," she says, "it's time for dinner. Plus, don't you think you should begin your homework?"

"I don't have homework today."

"Elsa, sweetie, I don't think that's true."

Of course it's not true. I always have so much homework that I can spend my entire life doing nothing but homework. But I don't want the Stager to leave. I have more questions about her dog; also, the thing about the American Girl dolls is that you can let them sit there like this and not play with them for a really long time, but then, once you get started again, you remember how much fun they are. For a while I was so into them that for every birthday all I wanted were things from the catalogue, and then I ended up with so much stuff! This is a little embarrassing to admit, but at one point I think it might have been true that I had everything there is to buy in the catalogue. I think my mom bought me everything she could, just to make up for the fact that she wouldn't let me have a dog.

The lady stands up and adjusts her skirt, which has crept up and is wrinkled. Also, her shirt has come untucked.

"Listen to Nabila," she says, stuffing her shirt back inside the skirt and yanking the skirt around so the zipper is back on the side, where it belongs. "You should do your homework. I'll be back tomorrow. If we have time at the end of the day, we can play a little bit more."

"Do you promise?"

"Absolutely."

"What about if we bake? Or paint? I have an easel and I have a really nice box of art supplies that I've never even opened. Can you paint?"

"Absolutely. Yes. I used to paint chairs."

"Chairs? Like, you painted the actual chairs, or you painted pictures of chairs?"

"Pictures of chairs. I illustrated furniture."

"Was it in museums? My dad likes art a lot. We bought a really famous yellow painting in Spain last year, for his birthday. He says it's his favorite painting in the world and it makes him happy every time he walks in the door because it has such nice bits of light."

"The one downstairs in the foyer?"

"Yes. Did you paint like that?"

She laughs. "No. I mean, I did just for fun, but for work it was more straightforward illustration."

"Let's paint some chairs!"

"Okay, come on, Elsa. Stop being such a chatterbox and let the lady go home." Nabila has her hands on her hips. "Who did you say you were again?"

"I'm the Stager."

"I know you are 'the Stager,' but do you have a name? What are you doing in here, playing with Elsa? She's supposed to be doing her homework, and you are supposed to be . . . Well, I don't know what you're supposed to be doing exactly."

"Nabila, don't be mean. She's really nice and she has a dog named Moses and we were just feeding Molly and Kaya some pie."

"Nabila is right. You should listen to her and do your homework. I'll be on my way."

The Stager runs down the stairs quickly, like she's frightened, and I hope I haven't said anything wrong. I hear the door slam and I go to the window and see her pull her keys from her pocket and get in her car and drive away.

"The lady forgot her bag," Nabila says. This is true. We both look toward the spot in the corner where she's left a big orange bulging bag. It's open, and her things are spilling out of it onto the floor. A hairbrush, a notebook, a French fry.

"I guess she'll be back."

"I don't know," says Nabila. "I'm going to ask your mom. Something about this smells a little fishy to me."

LARS

On our way to meet the Craigslist contractor, anxiety attacks me. That's really how it feels, like I have been jumped from behind in a dark alley and anxiety is tightening his meaty, angry fist around my throat. Although, in this case, to be more precise, he grabs me as we emerge from the taxi on East Heath Road. I begin to sweat, even though there is enough of a chill in the morning air so that Bella and I are wearing coats. Apart from the malaria-like delirium in which I've spent the last few nights, I'm not generally a spontaneously sweaty kind of guy, but as soon as I glimpse our new house again, I experience an episode of real physical panic, animal in its pureness and intensity. By the time we get to the front door, I must be a mess, because Bella unwraps the scarf that is draped artfully around her neck and hands it to me to blot my excretions.

She looks at me less as a husband than as a lab rat in a cage, with a sort of morbid curiosity.

"You okay, Lars?" she inquires casually, as if I have merely stubbed my toe getting out of the cab.

"Fine," I say. "It was just a little suffocating in there."

The ethos of our marriage demands that I always say I am fine even when I'm clearly not. I'd say I was fine even as my fingers fell off from frostbite, fine as I was being burned to a crisp in a fire, fine as I bled internally, which in fact I fear I am doing right now—which is to say, I am unsure of my answer, and wonder if I am possibly on the verge of a catastrophic event.

Bella thinks the problem, or at least the part of it that involves the light, began when I first saw the house three days earlier. And though it's true, that visit marked the first time my anxiety manifested as a physical thing—it felt as if my heart were being squeezed, or crushed, or pulped for juice—the matter of the light is nothing new; it has been growing inside of me for the last three years, ever since I swallowed, inadvertently, the first seed of truth. Or maybe since I swallowed the first blue pill, the one meant to cast some shade on the brightness. (I don't mean to be obtuse, but it's hard to separate these events entirely, because they were roughly simultaneous.) (Truth and light are roughly simultaneous, too.) (Or maybe what I mean is that they are close relations.) There is even a passage in the Bible about this— "Whoever lives by the truth comes into the light." I would tell this to Bella, but she is not easily impressed by religious symbolism. Still, you don't need religion or symbolism or truth or pills to appreciate that the darkness in the house we have just purchased is a tangible, toxic thing, like mold.

Poor Bella. That look of desperation three days earlier, when I first explained the problem of the light! She always thinks it's about her, but it's not. Not always. I'm not trying to punish her, although my forgiveness is something she regards with suspicion. Because I can see the light now, I can also see that there is so much to be gained in forgiving her that it actually constitutes an act of selfishness on my part to let go of her mistake, which I have, at least to the extent that I can when the past is present in my everyday life.

Anyway, there is no need to be dramatic about the fact that the house is deficient in light. Some houses simply are, the way some people are short, or bald, or too fat or too thin. It is almost certainly on the top-ten list of complaints a potential home buyer might have when inspecting a property for purchase, and it is offensive to insinuate that the person observing the gloom is demonstrating signs of mental illness or experiencing an adverse reaction to the pharmaceuticals his wife insists he take. Besides, all I really said on that first visit was that the place might benefit from a good washing of the windows. It was on the second visit that I had the idea that we should hire a contractor to put in a skylight.

It only took an hour to identify a carpenter on Craigslist. He was willing to begin right away, and to do it for cheap, so there was really no need for Bella to make this a bigger issue than it was. But she began to obsess on the subject. She said she knew it had been a mistake to buy the house without me there, to believe me when I insisted that anything she chose was fine, to think I was *better*. Every little thing in the present, it seems, goes straight back to the past, becomes a low-hanging fruit, ripe with significance, when really, seriously, all I want is a little more light!

I told Bella that I was willing to take full responsibility for the problem, and that I would be in charge of the fix. I was the one who had refused to go on the house-hunting trip three months earlier, after all, and I'd insisted that what she'd shown me of this house via e-mails, photographs, phone, and Skype was sufficient. It wasn't as if the decision had been rash: she'd described the floor plan to me in detail, right down to measuring the insides of the kitchen cupboards to be sure there was enough depth to accommodate our oversized dinner plates, the ones with cabbage roses that had belonged to her great-aunt Mae. And she'd been honest in her own assessment that although the house was lovely, with recent updates including a large two-story addition on the back, it was, after all, just a house. She wasn't doing cartwheels over it, she'd said. (I had pointed out to Bella that she wasn't a woman who would ever do cartwheels over a house, espe-

cially not in the wrap dresses she favored, and we'd both laughed.
I did not insert the thought that she might do cartwheels over Raymond Branch, yes, but over a house, no, because I did not want to mar
what seemed a sweet, and rare tender moment, even if it was occur-
ring by way of a transatlantic phone call that was racking up massive
roaming charges.) I was reminded, during that call, that we knew each
other well, or, to be honest, that we once had (which is to say, I understood that she wasn't the type to stick Post-it notes in the Crate &
Barrel catalogue, to create a wish list of sofas and coffee tables with
the hope of plugging, with furniture, some hole—well, really, for Bella,
a specific hole—in her emotional life. She wasn't a woman easily seduced by advertisements for sectional sofas or wing chairs, even if the
raffish-looking man who was sitting in one, holding a brandy snifter,
appeared to be reading from a book of poetry while watching an NFL
game on TV. His wife, perched on the ottoman, stared at him ador-
ingly. I think Bella envied this woman, but not for the reasons the
advertisers supposed. It could be exhausting to be Bella, and I think it
would have given her some solace to be made happy by the things that
money can buy. (The ability to find happiness in the acquisition of
consumer goods, or in fashion, or in spa weekends, or in mindless
television, is seriously underrated and unfairly mocked and I think
ought really to be more widely celebrated as evidence of a person's
ability to experience happiness at all. (Whereas I had once thought
it an indication that I possessed a certain shallowness because of the
degree of pleasure I took in my putting green and the new set of golf
clubs I purchased to celebrate its installation, I have since come to
believe that it is a sign of strength. Better to be satisfied by what you
can get, rather than striving always for the unattainable and intan-
gible. To be able to move from thing to thing and continue to find new
pleasure, over and over and over, in the unwrapping of cellophane, or
the snipping off of price tags, is a gift. The high from the new elliptical
machine lasted three long months, the flat-screen TV—the largest on
offer at Best Buy—nearly half a year. The thrill from the authentic

Wassily chair I found on eBay might still be with me had Bella not hated the thing so much. Even the fact that it had once belonged to three-time Wimbledon champ Boris Yablonsky failed to impress her. At least she was more supportive of my search for the perfect cup of morning coffee, which gave me purpose for a long while. Even Bella had to admit that she'd enjoyed the rich brew that percolated from the handcrafted coffeemaker from the Netherlands I'd purchased after months of research. At sixteen hundred dollars, it was admittedly a bit of a splurge, and complicated to use (Bella said it looked like a mouse-trap), and after a while it became a chore to have to special-order the filters from Holland, so I was not as upset as I might—or should—have been when the electrical wiring went kaput, possibly the result of having to run it through a converter to transform it to 110 volts. (I was somewhat relieved because by then I had discovered a new Star-bucks in our neighborhood and was drinking my way through every variety of coffee on offer, inventing, in some cases, combinations of shots and flavors, like mixing Blonde Roast with Tazo passion-fruit tea, that the baristas said had never even occurred to them.))))

With a tiny video camera lent to her by the estate agent, Bella had shown me the faucets on the porcelain farmhouse sink of our new home, had ignited the burners on the stove, had even given me a vir-tual tour of the shelf space in the laundry and utility rooms. She'd gone outside and filmed the grounds, such as they were—this was a far more urban environment than we were used to, having lived in suburbia for the last eight years with a pool and putting green in our own backyard. She'd filmed the stone rabbit that stood sentry in front of the house, and, hoping to get a smile out of Elsa, she'd draped her scarf around its neck and done a silly voice-over in a high-pitched, pretend-rabbit voice. Elsa's reaction had been a little frosty, and it's true that the two of us might have cut Bella a little more slack. Lord knows the woman was trying hard!

Bella considers the existence of this silly stone rabbit a sign, although, as an empiricist, she is probably aware that she was in search of a sign, or of anything that would allow her to get the house hunt over with. After all, at some basic level, one charming, ivy-covered recently renovated English Tudor in a fancy upscale North London neighborhood is as good as the next, is it not? And who can blame her? She is under tremendous stress—not that Bella ever really feels stress, since she is one of those wonder women you read about in magazines, the kind who pumped breast milk while writing prize-winning articles on deadline, who managed, once, to get from a conference in Tokyo to Elsa's field-hockey game in some remote Maryland suburb just in time, who shepherded her mother through the end stages of dementia while working full-time.

Settling in London is a step in the direction toward a more consolidated life: at least she won't be commuting five hundred miles most weeks. Still, the job is highly visible, and she is often on television, so the stress must be lodging somewhere, or so it seems to me, although that's to presume that stress is a physical property, like light. Luxum is doing a huge media blitz to highlight the rebranding campaign, and these next few weeks are critical to a successful transition. Or at least that's what she says; even if I understand only about half of what her new job is about (which is more than I'd understood about the equity-derivatives job), she is managing so many moving parts and so much data that her phone keeps freezing up.

On top of this, there's Elsa. She is unsettled by the prospect of the move, and reports from home are confusing at best. Nabila insists everything is fine, but even the most oblivious parent can't help but detect holes in the otherwise chipper reports. Which is all to say that Bella is entitled to take her signs as they come, or as she thinks they come, and a stone rabbit standing sentry at a house that's for sale is as good as any reason to go to contract, even if none of us actually likes rabbits—not even our own. We haven't actually had a conversation about whether our own rabbit, assuming he has not disappeared forever, will come with us to London. It's possible we each privately see this as an opportunity to unload Dominique and to blame his abandonment on the United Kingdom's draconian quarantine laws. Mostly I can get things right in my head. I can sort my issues into tidy piles: my physical injury; my wife's betrayals; the problem of the light. I can even make everything stay put, sometimes for days at a time, but it only takes the smallest trigger to unravel it all, and this attack of sweatiness feels possibly like the beginning of something bad. I once heard a philosopher, or maybe one of the therapists my wife sent me to (or maybe it was a character on a television show?), say that confusion was good, that it would eventually give way to wisdom, but it's been three years, and I wonder how long this transition is meant to last. The mess I am, the full-blown wreck of me, can be really quite embarrassing. I do my best to keep the worst parts hidden, so when Bella asks again whether I'm okay, when she puts her hand on my shoulder and looks me in the eye, this time with genuine concern, I insist, somewhat testily, that I am fine. Maybe I'm not fine, but I am determined to be, and that is half the battle— or so I also read somewhere. It might have been in an article in an in-flight magazine about jet lag and how it's best just to power through it.

SOMETIMES, AS WE have already established, an easy, albeit temporary, fix comes along in the form of an entertaining new kitchen gadget, or a new kind of pill, or, in this case, a Polish contractor named Jorek, who arrives at the house right on time. The minute we shake hands, my symptoms disappear. Don't misunderstand: there is no ambiguity in my sexual orientation (I am, or was, a real ladies' man. One newspaper described me as looking like Liam Neeson, another like Peter Frampton; go figure, since the two men do not have much in common, apart from being, to women, devastatingly attractive), and yet I feel something like love, and an intense magnetic attraction, as soon as Jorek steps through the door. I know he will save me, and I wonder if I have conjured him somehow, especially since he turns out to be the kind of person who is exactly as you might imagine him to be from the sound of his voice on the phone—a pleasant, skinny fellow who speaks very little English, but who understands intuitively the problem with the light.

"Put two there, done deal, have a nice day!" he says as we stand in the living room. He points to the ceiling above the stairway landing and makes a sawing motion with his hands. He is Slavicly emphatic, his Polish accent thick, but I understand him perfectly, and I explain to Bella that he means to carve two skylights into the roof.

"Yes, I get that," she says.

Then Jorek turns to the window, which looks out onto the back garden, and he says, "Too small. We take these out. One very big one from here to here."

I begin to explain this to Bella, and she interrupts me and asks if Jorek has a license.

I try to translate, but Swedish and Polish are not even remotely the same language, and we are not communicating as effectively as we might. English seems better. He pulls from his back pocket some papers.

Bella studies them, scowls, and then says that for all she knows, these could have been made at home on a Word document template. My wife, she is really a computer whiz, so she thinks that just because she might be capable of making a fake license on the computer, everyone else might be.

Jorek begins to say something in Polish, and again I try to translate, and then Bella interrupts.

"It's cloudy today, Lars," she says. "You know that famous London fog they name the raincoats for? It's because there isn't a lot of sunlight to be had here. Could you at least consider the possibility that the light in this house is poor because there is no light outside, and not because the house is lacking in windows?"

"But it *is* lacking in windows," I explain. "Wouldn't you agree, Jorek? It has fewer windows than it should."

"Yes, this is true," says Jorek. "It should not take so much to brighten it up. Skylights is where we begin. That may be enough."

"Please, Bella? A little more light is all I need to be happy here."

"What if we install a chandelier? A big beautiful one with lots of crystal. The glass will even refract the light. Think of that, Lars. It will bounce light all over the place. Triple the bang. And we can fill the place with lamps. That will be a fun outing. You love to shop. You can take the credit card this afternoon and pick out anything you like! Maybe Jorek can go with you."

"It needs to be natural light, Bella. I think you know that. Artificial light offers no nourishment."

Bella looks like she might begin to cry, and I feel awful about this. Please believe me when I say I don't want to make her life more difficult, nor do I mean to insult the house she has purchased for our family. Now that there is an easy fix, now that I have stumbled onto Jorek, I am actually relieved, and I wish I could do a better job of making her understand that we are now on an upswing. I worry sometimes that we are so connected, me and Bella, that I have unintentionally transferred to her my initial grief, that it has transmuted like particles of light (did you know that ν is the Greek letter nu, which stands for the frequency of the light wave?). Maybe with physical contact I can now transfer to her a few nus, and some of my newfound optimism.

I take her in my arms and hold her tight. She sinks into me for a moment, but then her cell phone rings and she frees an arm from our embrace and wrestles the phone from her pocket. She looks at the screen and hits a button, and then she looks back at me. She runs her palm across my stubbly face the way you might if you were staring into your lover's eyes, preparing to lean in for a kiss, except that in this case she quickly retreats.

"Okay, we can do a skylight, but what if we wait until we move in?

I'll ask around at work, get some contractor recommendations. Or"—
she looks at Jorek apologetically—"we can find someone to help . . .
him." Her phone makes a different sound this time, and she pulls it
out and looks at the screen. "Elsa," she says. "Another 'socks' message.
Also, I really need to return that other call."

"I'll help supervise Jorek," I say. "We're here for four more days,
and I have nothing to do. It will get me up and out of bed. We both
know I need a project." I feel a fierce attachment to Jorek, and I'm not
going to let him go.

She looks at Jorek, and then she looks at me, like we are, the two
of us, a logic problem on a standardized test: one possibly unlicensed
Polish contractor + one emotionally damaged husband with absolutely
no manual skills = x. If she stares at us long enough, the solution will
possibly come:

    a. Property Damage
    b. Sunlight
    c. Sparkle Kittens!

(b. Sunlight) (A colleague once told me that the correct answer is
always "b," and this has proved to be one of the more useful bits of
advice I have been given in life.)

"Fine," she says at last. But she doesn't look happy. "I've got to run,
and unfortunately I have a dinner tonight, but I'll call you late afternoon to check in. Okay? Can you keep your phone turned on, and
keep it with you, so I can find you?"

Jorek rubs his fingers together to indicate money.

Bella takes out her wallet and counts five twenty-pound notes into
Jorek's palm.

"Two hundred. Time and materials."

"I'm afraid that's all I have."

"Don't worry, darling," I say. "We'll walk with you to a cash machine."

Bella winces, checks her phone again, and looks at me like she might cry.

It's a bit of a long way back to Hampstead Village, where there is an ATM. We have to maneuver a hilly, winding cobbled road. I'd been light on my feet (a whirling dervish in Tretorns, a sportscaster once quipped), but since my knee troubles began I haven't been in great shape, and I'm winded from our half-mile walk.

Generally, I prefer driving to walking, and am rather attached to my SUV. The bigger the better is how I like my houses, my fast-food meals, and my vehicles, but I can see that will likely prove problematic in this congested little village, with its quaint historic homes, its fey cafés, and these looping narrow roads. Also, I have no friends here, apart from Jorek; not that I have any friends in Maryland, but at least no one there ever requires me to walk. Add to this the damp, dank chill, and the utter lack of light.

Thank God we can do something to repair the latter.

ELSA

After dinner, while I am doing my math homework, I keep thinking about Dominique. I once heard my dad say that he thought Dominique was a sick rabbit. Not sick like he had a sore throat or the flu, but sick in the head. My mom said maybe Dominique should take some of my dad's Praxisis, and my dad said maybe he wouldn't need medication if he didn't have a pretentious French name. They both laughed.

"Nabila, do you think Dominique is okay out there all alone? He's only ever lived indoors."

She turns off the water in the sink, where she is scrubbing the pot she used to make us whole-wheat pasta, and turns to face me. "I'm sure he's fine, darling."

"Do you have rabbits in your country?" Sometimes when I speak to Nabila, I feel dumb. Everything she says sounds smart, especially with her accent. She's also very beautiful, tall and thin like a super-model. She always wears scarfs in her hair and thick silver hoop earrings that I love. My mom says I'm too young to get my ears pierced.

"Of course we have rabbits. They can be a little scrawny, but my mother's a great cook and she can make the best . . ."

"The best what?"

"Never mind."

"Never mind why?"

"I forgot what I was going to say."

"Can we go look for him?"

"I promised your mum you'd do your homework. I'm sure Dominique is fine. And remember how hard we looked for him already? If we couldn't find him during the daytime . . ." I know Nabila is right, but of course she probably doesn't like Dominique, either. He's just a poor rabbit without his rabbit mother or his rabbit father, and he lives with a bunch of people who don't especially care that he's gone.

On the other hand, maybe it's a good thing that Dominique ran away, that he was able to recalibrate when he knew that he was in a bad situation that he couldn't fix. I know about recalibration from my dad. Just before leaving for London, he told me that back when he was a professional tennis player, before he hurt his knees and got fat, the reason he was so successful was that he'd been a master at recalibration. When I asked him to explain what that meant, he said he always had a big-picture plan, even when it had to do with small details. As he reached his arm back into the sweet spot to smash the ball in one of his famous killer serves, for example, he had a specific intent; he knew precisely where he was sending the ball, and he could also anticipate the response, like he could almost get inside the other guy's head. He said that this skill wasn't really all that special, that any professional athlete could think this part through, but what made him a superstar was his ability to recalibrate in a nanosecond if the way the wind was blowing or the way the crowd was cheering made him think that the better idea was to smash it far right instead of to the back left corner. He used the idea of recalibration to talk about

all sorts of annoying things, like me doing my homework or running laps at field-hockey practice or dealing with Diana, who is supposed to be my best friend but is mean to me sometimes, so I didn't
expect him to start crying when I asked why he hadn't been able to
recalibrate when he wrecked his knees and couldn't play tennis anymore. He said it was because he was stuck. And then he said something that made no sense: he said that no matter what, he'd always be
my dad.

Of course he'd always be my dad. Plus, he wasn't stuck. He was
walking around the room while he talked. I didn't understand. He
explained that he wasn't physically stuck, he was stuck in another way
he couldn't really explain to me, since I was too young.

But I did understand two things: My dad was very unhappy. Also,
I was never going to get stuck.

NABILA FINISHES THE dishes and then she says she is going downstairs to put the laundry in the dryer, unless I need any help with my
homework, which I do not.

Then I pick up my phone and send a text to my mom. "Call me
please. Important. Socks!"

I wait awhile, but she doesn't reply, so I send her another message.
This one just says "SOCKS!!!"

I try to call my dad—he doesn't do texts—but there is no answer.
I leave him a voice message that says, *Dominique still hasn't come
home.* I wait a long time, but he doesn't call back, either, which isn't
surprising, because he doesn't really know how to use his cell phone.
Once, he asked me to help him check his voice mail and he had eleven
messages. One of them was from a friend who was visiting from
Sweden and wanted to see him, but when my dad called back he learned
the message had been on his phone for three months, and by then the
friend had already gone back home. My dad is really lame about

computer stuff, too. He's on Facebook, but he never put a picture up, so there's just the outline of a man's head, and he only has about five friends. One of them is me.

Nabila doesn't come back upstairs, and I sit in the kitchen alone for a long time, waiting for someone to reply to my texts, or for her to return. I wonder if she is doing the ironing, or if she's gone into her room, which is in the basement and is the one that is called a half-room in the advertisement about our house, where it says "4.5 bedrooms," which the Realtor says is because her room doesn't have any windows or closets or a bathroom, so maybe it's a bedroom for Nabila, but technically it's not.

After a while, I put my books in my backpack and go up to my room. The American Girl food is still spread on the floor, and the girls are still sitting there with their Key lime pie and soup and the ends of the kebob skewers hanging off their plates. I feel a little sorry for them; they probably thought they were finally finished with this luau and could lie down in their beds, or at least change out of their bathing suits.

I start to pick up the toys, and then I realize no one has fed Molly's dog in at least a year, so I dig through the pile, looking for his food, but I can't find it, so I make Molly say, "Hello, Bennett! Would you like some soup?"

Bennett says, "Arf."

Molly says, "Yummy, yummy soup!"

I start to laugh, and then, I have no idea why, I start to cry. I curl up on my bed, feeling very sorry for the dolls and for my rabbit, but mostly for me, because I don't want to move to London and no one has even asked my opinion about this. I don't like the new school my mom described, where the girls have to wear really ugly plaid uniforms with blue blazers, and I don't like the pictures I saw of the other school, either, even though you can wear anything you like. And I don't like how there is no swimming pool in our new backyard. My mom said, "Elsa, I don't know the last time you even went for a swim, but if you want to swim, we can join a pool!" But who wants to swim in a pool with a zillion other people who will see you in a bathing suit? I don't like how I look in a bathing suit, especially after I heard Nabila's friend Annie say, when she didn't know I was listening, "My, my, that girl is becoming a little chunky."

I don't want to cry anymore, but there are so many things I keep thinking about that make me sad, like how my mom is away because she's just beginning her Important New Job, and my dad is helping to get the new house ready, and no one is answering my texts.

After a while, I stop crying and open my eyes, and the first thing I see is the Stager's bag on the floor. I'm not a snoop, but I go over to the bag, and since it's already open and stuff is spilling out anyway, I look inside. Her wallet is in there, and a little notebook and some pens, four lipsticks that are all basically the same color, tortoiseshell sunglasses, cinnamon Orbit gum, extra-strength Tylenol, peppermint Tic Tacs—stuff like my mom has, except everything in my mom's bag is always very organized. She would never put her glasses in there just floating around with the pens, because they might get scratched or even stained with ink, and then everything you would see out of the lenses would have splotches on it. Glasses need to go in the case! And the lipsticks belong in one of the separate zipper pouches! I decide to organize the Stager's things for her, so I turn the bag upside down and dump everything out, which is not the best idea, since there is so much junk, like crumbs, old dirty pennies, squashed M&M's, and two more French fries.

I'm not sure what to do with the bits of crumpled paper or the tampon that's already ripped open, so I just set them aside and start to organize her wallet, which is in very bad shape. There's so much stuff in there it barely closes. I look at her driver's license, and it says that her name is Eve Brenner, she lives at 22 Hollyhock Lane in Rockville, she has black hair and brown eyes, she's five feet and one inch tall, she weighs 103 pounds, and her birthday is June 24, 1968. And also that she is an organ donor.

I want to call the Stager to tell her that we both have names that begin with the letter *E* and end in a vowel and we both have summer birthdays. I wonder if maybe she has a picture of Moses in there, so I look in all of the little compartments. There aren't any pictures of a dog, but I do see a lot of pictures of a boy, maybe the nephew she mentioned. She has those small school photos of him in there, and on the back they're labeled, so you can tell that there's one for every year since prekindergarten. He looks best in the one where he's about fourteen. His braces have just come off, and he has a big toothy smile, and his hair is long and shaggy. And there's a picture of someone who looks like Eve from a long time ago with another woman who looks almost like my mom, but I can't see her face because she's standing sideways, and also because she's wearing big sunglasses and has a scarf wrapped around her head like an old-fashioned movie star. They're both wearing pretty summer dresses.

I keep staring, but it doesn't make sense, because the woman who looks like Eve is pregnant, and this Eve didn't mention having a child. This is almost as confusing as the story about the lady who might have had a nail gun. But the bigger problem is that these photos are getting all crumpled up in her wallet, and I remember that for my mom's birthday my dad got her a photo album to put in her purse and she never used it, ever. It's in her dresser, in the right-hand drawer, still in the box from Saks. It's beautiful black leather, and even though it has my mom's initials in the corner, they're really small and you wouldn't necessarily notice them, so I run upstairs to borrow it. My mom won't mind. Or maybe what I mean is that she'll never notice.

While I'm organizing the photographs, the bag starts vibrating. I feel around and find a cell phone inside another compartment with a zipper. I pull it out and look. There's a text message from Vince that says, "call me—question about the loft." I wonder who Vince is. And also, what is a loft?

I think about sending the Stager a message to tell her Vince has a question about the loft and also to ask what a loft is and also to tell her about our name and birthday coincidences and that I have just put her pictures in an album, but then I worry she'll think I'm snooping through her stuff, which I'm not—I'm just helping her get organized. Then I laugh at how dumb that is, because obviously I can't send her a text since I have her phone right here! Also, and this is kind of embarrassing, I feel jealous about Vince and the loft, because I want to be the Stager's friend and . . . well, I want her not to have other friends.

I look at my phone again. There are still no replies to my texts. I understand that things are kind of crazy and happening very quickly, and that I should be very happy for my mom, and I am! Everywhere I go, people say, "Wow, Elsa, congratulations to your mom. I just read about her new job!" Or, "I just saw her on TV! You must be so proud!" And I am proud. Obviously. It's really cool to have an important mom. My mom is a role model. That's what they said when she came to Career Day at school. When I grow up, I definitely want to have a job, and be a role model, too. But I want to have a job where I can return text messages when someone says to you "SOCKS!!!" I take the Stager's phone and I send a text message to myself that says "SOCKS!!!" And then, when I receive it, I write back to her, "YUMMY YUMMY EGG!" It makes me feel better, but only for a minute.

Then I get a better idea and I look at the Stager's phone again and see in the contact list a number that says Home. So I hit that button. I'm going to tell her that she has a message from Vince about the loft and that I really want to paint some chairs.

Nabila comes in and says, "Darling, are you going to pick up this mess?" and I say, "I didn't make that mess, the Stager did. Plus, I'm busy on the phone." Nabila stands there with her hands on her hips again, looking at me like this is the wrong answer. "Anyway, you are supposed to help me. Isn't that why my mom hired you to be my friend?"

I can hear a voice saying "Hello?" I try to ignore it, but then the voice says "Hello?" again, and it's very loud, because I've accidentally hit the speakerphone button.

"That's not your phone," Nabila says.

"No. *Duh*. It's the Stager's phone."

The voice in the background is still saying "Hello, hello?" So I turn off the phone and put it back in the bag.

"What are you playing at here, Elsa, darling?" Nabila says in a fake sweet voice. "I talked to your mom, and she said she thought it was creepy that the Stager was playing with you and your dolls, and she said that she was going to call Amanda and ask about this Stager person and that I should keep a close eye on you."

"You talked to my mom?"

"I did."

I couldn't believe my mom had time to talk to Nabila but not to reply to my "socks" message.

"What were you doing with that lady's phone?"

"Telling her she left it here."

"Obviously, she knows her phone is here. She'll get it tomorrow. And if she needs it before then, she knows the way. Now, young lady, you need to pick up this mess and get yourself into the shower and finish your homework and get ready for bed!"

Nabila has never spoken to me like this before. She takes the phone and the lady's bag and tells me to pick up the mess right now.

"Don't you tell me what to do," I say. "I didn't make this mess, and I don't see why I have to pick it up!"

"Now, miss, don't you be talking to me like that. Your mum said . . ."

"My mom isn't here, is she? And you're not the boss of me, so don't tell me what to do."

Nabila takes a deep breath.

"I'm going to go downstairs to finish up some chores, and when I come back up, I expect you to have cleaned up this mess. I'll be back in ten minutes."

She leaves the room, and I sit on my bed, thinking about what to do. My parents are gone, Nabila is being mean to me, the Stager is no longer here, and it seems like, if this was a television show or a book, this would be the time when the kid packs a bag and runs away. I consider it, but it doesn't sound like much fun: Where would I sleep? What would I eat? And also, how much would I miss at school? Still, I have an obligation to my rabbit. Even if no one likes him, he does not deserve to be out there all alone.

I'm tying my shoes and thinking about how I can get out the door without Nabila's noticing when I hear my phone beep. There's a text message from my mom. It says, "Sorry sweetheart, it's really late here. I'll call you tomorrow!" I thought it was earlier in London, but then I realize maybe I'm confusing the time in London with when we went to Mexico over Christmas, where it was earlier. Or was it earlier in Rome, where we went last summer? Or maybe it was earlier on the long weekend we went to California for Presidents' Day. I wonder why they can't just make the whole world the same time, even though I know the answer, of course, which has to do with the sun. Then I hear another beep from my phone, and it's a second message from my mom. It says "SOCKS!!! SOCKS!!! SOCKS!!!"

I notice there are three SOCKS, with three exclamation points each. This seems possibly meaningful, and I want to tell the Stager about it and the Rule of Three, but it will have to wait. I bring Bennett into bed with me, and try to think happy thoughts about Dominique. I hope he's found someplace warm to stay.

LARS

Our Bethesda home is sixty-two hundred square feet. It is so big that there are times when I have trouble locating my family. This is why, when we first moved in, I looked on the Internet and found a company that could install an intercom system. The wiring process became a little fraught, and with hindsight perhaps I should have asked for references. An unexpected glitch required drilling through the just-painted living-room wall, and when that failed to locate the trouble spot, they cut a jagged hole through the drywall. A few minor related installation issues caused a circuit breaker to pop, resulting in a small fire in the garage. These things happen—there are growing pains in home improvement, after all—but in this case it's true that the intercom system never worked very well, or maybe we just never figured out how to use it.

Bella doesn't reference this directly, but I sense the intercom incident looming in the backdrop of our Jorek conversations. But that is not why I mention it here. I mention it here to contrast the size of our Bethesda home to the size of our hotel room in London, where we occupy a mere five hundred square feet and we can hear each other respire.

I don't expect to find Bella back at the hotel when I return after Jorek and I purchase the skylights, but she's stopped in to change into evening attire for her dinner. She is on the phone. (She is always on the phone, my wife.) When she sees me enter the room, she looks a little startled, puts her index finger in the air to signal to me that she'll be back in a minute, and goes into the bathroom and closes the door. Logically, at first, I think that the reason I can still hear her talking, even with the door closed, is our close, really our too-close, proximity in this tiny hotel room. But soon I will come to understand that, thanks to certain peculiar and extraordinary circumstances, I can hear her talking from any place at all. No matter where she is physically located, the transmission is as clear, barring static or other atmospheric disturbance, as if she is standing right beside me. It's like she's inside my head.

On this particular occasion she seems to be talking to my doctor, and what I hear her say is this:

"Maybe his reaction to the new house and this whole light business has to do with his Swedish childhood? They're big on light over there. Summer solstice and all that stuff."

The voice on the other end asks what she means by this. (Full disclosure: I am only guessing at this. I don't know for sure what the other person is saying, since I can only hear Bella.)

"Well, maybe it's just *too British*? What with the chintz curtains and the Aga . . . Oh, it's a fancy English oven, sort of a status symbol here, like a hearth version of a fancy car, kind of hard to explain, I'm not sure I really get it myself. But anyway, my point is that the house he grew up in was right out of Swedish central casting. Honestly, you could use it for an IKEA catalogue photo shoot. You should see it . . . It's a small, sleek, unassuming rambler, the furniture's all spare straight lines, absolutely stark, and now that I think about it, with those sheer white panel curtains in every room, it's like a Nordic winter itself. Last time we visited his mom, there was even a Volvo in the driveway, and nothing but wheat fields as far as the eye could see. His mother still lives there with his thirty-seven-year-old brother, something I obviously should have paid closer attention to when we first met, although I get that I can't blame this entirely on genetics. Well, maybe a little bit."

The doctor then asks more about my brother, I assume.

"I don't know. He never married. I don't know if they ever diagnosed him. Maybe he's just . . . off somehow. I never thought about it too much before, but you're right, it's a little strange."

There is a long silence as the doctor responds, and then Bella, sounding disappointed, says, "I see. So you think maybe just give in . . . that his behavior, this whole light thing, isn't necessarily indicative of some sort of psychosis?"

Bella sounds skeptical, and although I only hear half the exchange, my guess is that the doctor is taking my side. He understands that my reaction to the light is a reasonable response to the new family home. What is happening here is that we are having a petty domestic dispute, and not a mental-health crisis.

"Look, I hear you," Bella says in frustration, "but my concern is that, okay, maybe the house is a little dim, but I honestly don't think this is about the light. My theory—and, please, just hear me out here—is that he's having some kind of adverse reaction to the new medication. Or maybe he's taking everything in the wrong order—would that make a difference, do you think? Or maybe the dosage is off? I'm not saying that would be your fault, of course. Maybe the pharmacy screwed up? . . . What? . . . Oh sure . . . Let's see, he's got about a dozen prescription bottles here. We've got Zuffixor . . . Romulex . . . Luxemprat . . . Zumlexitor . . . Praxisis— and I'm a little worried about that one, the bottle is almost empty and we just refilled it. He eats those like candy . . . Also there's Volemex, Zaxivon—although I'm not sure if he still takes that one— and Amulerex. There's more at home, I think. That's a lot to be taking, isn't it? We had trouble clearing customs. I mean that literally. We were brought into a back office and we had to talk to the police."

She listens for a while longer, then says "okay" and then "uh-huh" and then "okay" a few more times, and then she hangs up the phone.

All this while I've been feigning absorption with my computer. Jorek has sent me the link to a YouTube video on skylight installation. He says that although he has never done one before, he has Googled around and found this demonstration, and it looks so simple he's sure he can do it on his own. We've agreed to each watch this, and then to meet back at the house in the morning to get started.

After Bella gets off the phone with the doctor, I urge her to come watch the video with me. I tell her that Jorek has suggested that installing a skylight is a piece of cake, and that, with my help, we can do it in a day.

"Really, Lars? You're going to help install a skylight?"

My wife is evidently in a bad mood.

"I've never seen you so much as change a lightbulb without causing some catastrophe!" (This is not true, but in a marriage one has to allow for occasional hyperbole of precisely this sort.) Also, I have just popped a Praxisis (she is right about that part—Praxisis is, hands down, my current drug of choice), and I am therefore feeling rather mellow. And one more also, and this is sad to say, but I am used to being treated like this by Bella. I know she cares about me in her way; she treats me with kindness—just not with warmth. She addresses me in a different tone than she does Elsa. With Elsa she is pure sweetness; with me it's just duty.

This is what I think Bella thinks: because she has made this mess of me, she is obliged to take care of me. That's my working theory most days, but, then, I have a few other theories as well. Is it possible, for example, that each individual is allotted only a certain amount of bandwidth? Like, say, perhaps, a person can be super-brilliant, but only a smidgeon warm?

I'd recently asked her, for example, if she still found me attractive, and instead of saying yes, she'd stared at me for a full minute, considering her reply. "When I look at you, beneath the flesh I still see hints of magnificent bone structure. I see a formerly handsome man who has become too round," she said.

I had quipped that she could have just told me I was handsome, and that no one was going to call in *The New Yorker*'s fact-checking department to confirm the accuracy of her reply.

But let's not dwell on the past. That is, I assure you, a black hole, a motherfucking bottomless pit that has, for now, been covered only by leaves. The past is break-your-neck treachery. I gravitate not toward darkness but toward light.

"Of course I can help Jorek with a skylight," I say. "And I wish you wouldn't make such a big deal out of this. It's perfectly normal to want a little more light in one's house."

"Things in our life have been so weird for so long, Lars, that our definition of normal has become frighteningly elastic."

On this point, the fact-checking department would have to agree.

EVEN BY THE least elastic measure of the word, however, the rest of the day is pretty normal. Bella goes off to her dinner. I order room service, watch a movie, and go to sleep. I dream of animals, and there is even a rabbit, but nothing menacing occurs.

One day at a time, as they say. Two normal days in a row is a lot to ask for, even under normal circumstances, which ours, admittedly, are not. Accordingly, the next morning begins with a predawn phone call, which is rarely a good thing unless, perhaps, you are expecting word from the Nobel Prize selection committee or such, which, again (see above re *not normal circumstances*, and apologies in advance for the forthcoming word repetition), admittedly, I am *not*. I confess that I hear my phone ring, but I am emerging from one of those deep sleeps that feel heavy, like the fog of general anesthesia, a sensation that I am unfortunately all too familiar with as a result of the multiple operations on my knees.

It takes me a few moments even to remember where I am, but then the scent of Bella moving over me, her lump of a husband wrapped tightly, inertly, a practically calcified man inside a duvet, helps me locate. She fumbles in the dark for my phone—someone is apparently calling *me!*—but not before knocking over a glass of water and causing our accumulated nightstand debris, our miniature marital still life of Bella's many books that she rarely has time to read yet carts around the world with her, as well as our glasses, watches, and pill bottles, to spill to the floor.

Not that the additional mess is of consequence, given the state of our hotel room. Until Jorek came into my life, I'd been sleeping half the days, explaining to Bella—reasonably, I think—that it made no sense to adjust to U.K. time, since I'd be headed home in a week. I'd put the DO NOT DISTURB sign on the door and drawn the curtains, and turned the maid away whenever she tried to enter our suite. Room-service trays have piled up, the minibar is mostly drained, and all of the towels (really, every last one of them, including the washcloths) lie in a wet heap. I regret this, and the laundry situation as well; even though I've promised Bella I'll take care of it, I've forgotten to organize her dry cleaning, and she is now out of fresh shirts. (Because I have nowhere to go, or at least I hadn't before Jorek materialized, my own laundry situation is less dire.)

My phone is very porous, and I can hear the lilt of Jorek seeping through the tiny speaker as he asks for Mr. Lars. Bella points out that it's not even 7:00 a.m., that I am asleep and, for that matter, so was she. Poor Jorek; I know he is intimidated by Bella, so, whatever this is, it must be pretty important for him to call this early. He asks again to speak to me, and Bella tries to shake me awake, but my instincts— always sharp except when it comes to my enduring fealty to my wife— tell me to continue to feign sleep; besides, my body feels heavy, as if I am doing all of this listening and thinking from under water. Bella takes my arm and pulls it from beneath the warmth of the duvet and feels for my pulse, a gesture that's sweet enough to cause me to continue to play dead just to see her reaction, and, I confess, to solicit more of her touch, even if only in the form of her hand on my wrist. If she feels no beat, will she call the British equivalent of 911, or just pull a sheet over my head, order a room-service breakfast, and get ready for work? I do not learn the answer, because she detects the flicker of a life force in me. She asks Jorek if she can take a message, and promises she'll have me call him back.

"Tell Mr. Lars that I decided three skylights, not two."

Now Bella sits up in bed and turns on the nightstand light. She begins to use what I think of as her "office voice," which will be familiar to you if you've ever seen her on TV, which you likely have. It's a blend of morning news anchor—fake friendly, fake warm—with the not-so-subliminal suggestion that she will slash your throat with the thin tip of her Pilot pen should you make her cross.

"I don't think that's a good idea," Bella says. "Let's put this entire project on hold, Jorek. It's better to do this once we have properly moved in."

"But I already bought another on my way home last night."

"I only gave you money for two."

"So now you pay me more."

"That's not how this works, Jorek."

This is one of those classic chicken-and-egg situations one reads about, by which I do not mean the money (and, frankly, I am a little embarrassed that Bella is giving Jorek a hard time about money, given how well off we are). What I am talking about here is the light. Bella doesn't seem to understand that we can't possibly move in until we create more light; she thinks we should create more light *after* moving in. I'm not entirely sure what Jorek says in response, since by now Bella is out of bed and moving toward the bathroom. After a few more exchanges, she clicks off and returns the phone to my bedside, then undresses and gets in the shower. Once I hear the water running, I call Jorek back and arrange to meet him at the house in a couple of hours.

Now I feign sleep again. Bella emerges from the shower, does her morning ritual of hair and makeup with a practiced efficiency, and then dresses. As she is getting ready to leave, she sits down beside me and says, even though I am fake asleep, "If you are really so light-obsessed, Lars, perhaps you ought to consider opening the curtains." Then, without further ado, she grabs her bag and leaves.

Here she has a point. Not only are the curtains drawn decidedly shut, but I have also employed the special room-darkening blinds. Even at midday, it is deliciously cavelike in this room. This is emotionally tricky territory. I need light in my life, yet prefer darkness in my room. Please don't ask me why. I don't have all the answers.

After I hear the door click, I lie in bed contemplating this riddle, the riddle of me, Lars Jorgenson, until I can motivate myself to emerge from beneath the tangle of bedclothes. Finally, with trepidation, I approach the window. I stand with my fingers clutching the pull rod on the curtain, but find myself frozen—I try to shift it in a rightward direction, but I actually, physically cannot. It's as if I'm having some adverse reaction to the possibility of light, or at least light in this room, and the complete illogic of the situation is paralyzing. I sit on the edge of the bed for a while, staring at the curtains, and then I go into the bathroom and swallow a Praxisis. These can be slow to kick in, so I crawl into the bathtub to wait. And let me tell you, if you have never taken a Praxisis, it's always worth the wait. Although lately it seems the wait does not always deliver, and after an interminably long time, when nothing happens, I swallow a couple more.

After about thirty minutes, I climb out of the tub, walk over to the window, pull the cord on the blinds, and then draw back the heavy flax drapery. It's almost biblical what happens next: the sun streams in so blindingly that I have to shut my eyes and fumble about the room until I locate my sunglasses.

And then—outside! A rich emulsion of pedestrians streaming by, every one of them looking so purposeful, carrying coffee and newspapers, computer bags slung over shoulders; a young woman, her hair still wet from the shower, or maybe from the pool, clutching a bouquet of wildflowers, which makes me wonder if she's having a dinner party, or if it's someone's birthday. Some refrain from a book Bella often refers to pops into my head. Something to do with flowers and dinners and glorious days in June. I feel myself begin to soar. Maybe this is why she likes books so much; the poetry is its own high. I wish I liked books. But for now, I find Praxisis to be a good facsimile of the intellectual stimulation I am lacking in my life.

Across the street is a patch of greenery, and I wonder if perhaps we're situated across from one of those famous London parks. Bella had said something about our hotel being in a posh section of town, within walking distance to many popular attractions (a bit of travelogue, dropped frequently, and not very subtly, into random conversations, surely meant to plant the seed of my going out), but this failed to entice me before now. I'd chosen to see the entire city as cold and aloof, although maybe it was just all that steely wrought iron, the beeping horns, the ever-present chill in the air. Still, I have the sense I could live here for the next ten years and never really belong, or even comprehend what's going on. But then I see a bunch of schoolkids in uniforms emerging from the park, and that's an easy thing to understand, no matter where you are. From the D.C. suburbs to an upscale London neighborhood to, perhaps, Jorek's Poland, your compass points in a certain direction when you see a group of kids. This seems possibly profound, or at least it does for a second or two, while I search for a pen and a pad of paper on which to write it down, but all I manage is "kids" and "compass," by which point I can't really remember what it is I wanted to say, and whatever it is was probably trivial and clichéd, or at least no longer an observation that might hold the key to my repair. I sit there for the longest time, staring out the window, pen still in hand, but can't think of anything else to write down.

ELSA

At school, I'm so busy I almost forget about Dominique and the Stager and the Rule of Three. I take my math quiz, and I know even before the teacher grades it that I got everything right. Also, I know all the answers in French class and raise my hand seven times, although Mademoiselle Shapiro only calls on me once. But Diana is being weird. We always sit together at lunch, and we almost always eat pizza and French fries (although sometimes we eat macaroni and cheese and chicken nuggets), but today she's brought a turkey sandwich from home, and when I ask her why, she says she's decided to stop eating unhealthy food. I explain that pizza and French fries aren't *necessarily* unhealthy, that it depends on how they're cooked, but she says I'm wrong; they're always fatty and greasy. French fries are potatoes, I say, refusing to give up. And since potatoes are organic and locally grown and from Whole Foods, they're good for you. Ditto for the pizza, which has both calcium and vitamin C.

I don't know if any of this is true, but sometimes facts are the enemy of truth. Or maybe it's the other way around. I'm not entirely sure what that means, but I once heard my mom say this on television when she was talking about problems at the bank where she works.

"To each his own," Diana says. Then she picks up her tray and goes to sit with Zahara and leaves me alone with an entire sausage pizza, which at first seems like a good thing, but after I take a bite I feel the grease ooze down my throat and realize that Diana has ruined it for me. Then, even worse, after school, Diana acts like she actually *enjoys* running laps at field-hockey practice. Usually we run together, although we don't really run, we walk until the coach notices we aren't running and he yells at us. Then we run a little bit until he looks away again. But there she goes, up ahead with Zahara, who is the fastest runner in our class, and that makes me move even more slowly. After a while, I just stop. The coach yells at me and says if I don't try harder I won't be eligible for the team when we get to middle school next year, and I say big deal, I'm moving to London anyway.

I sit down in the middle of the track.

The coach comes over and asks if I'm okay, and even though I am, I know I'm about to get in trouble, so I say I'm having difficulty breathing and that I need to go back to the main school building to get my inhaler. When I get there, I open my locker, find my inhaler, and take a fake puff. By then it's almost time for Nabila to pick me up, so, rather than go back to the field, I stand in front of the school to wait.

NABILA THINKS IT'S important that we talk each day. On the way home she asks me the usual annoying questions about school: what did I learn, what did I have for lunch, did I have a lot of homework? Fortunately, she doesn't ask me about field-hockey practice, because I know she won't be sympathetic. She always talks about how exercise is good, and sometimes after school she even proposes we go for a bicycle ride or a walk. I don't want to have that conversation.

When we arrive at the driveway, I see the Stager painting the front door. I roll down the window and shout to her: "Hey, what are you doing?"

"She's painting the door," Nabila says, as we pull into the garage.

"Yes, I know that, but why is she painting it white? It looked good black."

Nabila shuts the garage door behind us, using the automatic opener. "You need to let the lady do her job," she says. "The lady has a lot of work to do to get the house ready to sell."

"I know that, but . . ."

"I spoke to your mum again, and then I spoke to the lady, and everyone agrees it's a good idea for you to just let her do her job."

"Yes, I get it. But I *am* letting her do her job! I just want to know why she's painting the door white!"

"The first open house is in four days. The lady does not have time to be your babysitter."

"God, Nabila, you are being so mean! The lady has a name. It's the Stager. Well actually, it's also Eve Brenner. And I know she isn't my babysitter. Anyway, she's the one who wanted to play yesterday, not me."

"Okay. Let's change the subject and go have a snack, and you can think about what you'd like for dinner. Oh, also, your mum said to tell you she's going to be on the television tonight. And she's wearing your favorite dress. She said she already taped the show and she blew you a secret kiss, so you should watch very closely and you'll catch it."

"Big deal. She's on television all the time, and if she means the green dress with the stripes, it's not my favorite anymore. I get embarrassed when she leans forward and I can see her bra and so can everyone else who's watching TV. What about my dad?"

"What about your dad?"

"Did you talk to him?"

"No, sweetie."

Nabila is digging around in her gigantic bag, trying to find her house key. Her purse is always a mess, like the Stager's. I once counted and it took her nearly a whole minute to find the key, which is not a good safety practice, especially since the garage light automatically goes off after a minute. I once told Nabila she should wear her key around her neck, so she could find it quickly in case a criminal was hiding in the bushes or, in this case, inside the garage, but she didn't listen, and now I'm thinking maybe I can do Nabila a favor and organize her purse for her, too. I wonder if the Stager has even noticed what I've done for *her* purse, but she might not have had any reason to look inside or use her wallet if she's been at the house doing her staging all day.

"I won't bother her, but I just want to know why she's painting the door white, and also what rooms she staged today."

"I'm not sure. Until I left to pick you up, she was mostly in the front hallway and the living room and the kitchen."

"Is the smell gone yet?"

"Funny you should ask. It *was* gone. I thought the Stager fixed that horrible garbage smell, but now either it's back or there's another smell. I hadn't noticed it until today."

"Is it the same smell?"

"It's the same but different."

"Better or worse?"

"I don't know if you can quantify how bad a very bad smell is. Sometimes I smell it and sometimes I don't, so maybe I'm imagining the smell. Who knows, maybe I'm losing my mind."

I hope Nabila isn't going crazy, too.

"Well, maybe it's good that our house smells bad, because I don't want anyone to buy it. I don't want people knocking my wall down and painting my room some other color, and I don't want to move to London. Will you come to London?"

"We already talked about this, remember? I'm going to university here, so I can't go with you. But you'll find a new friend in London. And maybe I can visit you sometime."

"I want you to come."

"I know, honey."

"I don't want to move."

"I know. I understand. Moving is very hard, even for grown-ups. I had to leave my country to come here, and I miss my own mum and dad every day. But look, at least you aren't going to leave your family."

"Maybe I could just stay here with you and we could keep the house."

"I like that idea, but unfortunately life doesn't work like that."

"I have to leave my room, and my friends, and you, and Dominique is probably dead and I'll never see him again."

"Don't be morose. He's probably fine. I'm sure he's found a lot of rabbit friends by now. Maybe he's hopped back to his own family!"

"No, he came from a farm in Frederick, don't you remember? Or maybe you weren't here yet. Maybe that was Adriana. Or Fatima. Or wait, maybe it was before her . . . the girl from Romania. Anyway, Frederick is, like, an hour away, so I don't know how he could have gotten that far."

"You never know. Rabbits are good hoppers."

"Not Dominique. He's not that good a hopper, plus I'll bet he just bites all the other rabbits anyway."

Nabila laughs, but I'm not trying to be funny.

She finally finds her key and is about to stick it in the door when the light switches off, and we just stand there for a moment in the dark.

ALREADY THE HOUSE looks different. The painting that we bought in Barcelona, the one that hangs above the table where my parents always put their keys when they walk in the door, is gone. My dad is going to have a meltdown. Not only does he love that painting, but it cost a lot of money.

I keep staring at the space, trying to figure out what else is wrong, and then I see the green table is gone, too. There's a different table there that looks familiar, but I can't say why. Then I realize it's the table from the living room. Now there's a mirror over the table instead of the painting. And the mirror is from . . . I don't know. I've seen that mirror before, though. Maybe it was in my parents' room once, and then it got put in the attic?

And the pig that I love is gone! The naked starving person/pregnant lady/African statue, too! The bowl of tulips is still there, but it's alone, so now there is no cluster of three. For almost my entire life, there has been the green table and the pig and a vase of flowers (but not always tulips), the naked starving person, and then, since last year, the famous yellow painting, and now it's all gone.

Also, the kitchen is all wrong. Everything has disappeared. All of the pictures on the refrigerator—me at the beach with my cousins from Sweden, and the schedule that tells me when I have field-hockey practice, and my last report card. I look at the counter and can see that my dad's coffeemakers are all gone, too. Even the toaster has disappeared. Suddenly I love and miss my toaster and I want to have a Pop-Tart for my after-school snack, but how can I do that without a toaster? I think I'm going to cry again, which is really ridiculous, so I decide that instead of crying I will just fix this situation. I open the cabinet and find the toaster, which has the cord wrapped around it neatly. I put it back on the counter, unwind the cord, and plug it in. Then I open all of the cabinets until I find the coffeemakers, and I put those back out, too. Once everything is where it belongs, I climb onto the counter and stand up so I can reach the higher shelves. I begin to look for Pop-Tarts, but everything is in the wrong place now—all the cereal boxes are on their sides instead of standing straight up, and the cans of tuna are stacked one on top of another—and I can't find anything.

I hear someone enter the kitchen and turn to see the Stager passing through on her way to the basement. She has the can of paint in one hand, and holds the brush over it, to catch the drips.

"Hi, Elsa," she says, but she doesn't stop to talk to me, or ask how my day's been. She doesn't even comment about me standing on the counter with my muddy field-hockey cleats on, or about the coffee-makers and the toaster being back out again.

"Hey, why are you painting the door white?" I yell to her as she walks down the stairs. "And why are you going downstairs?"

"I'm painting the door red," she says.

"But it's white!"

"That's the primer. You have to put a coat of primer on to get it ready for the new paint. Also, it will help cover up the black."

"Oh." I don't really understand why you'd put white on black before putting on red, or why you'd even put red on in the first place when the black looked perfectly good.

"After it dries, I'll start layering on the red. I'm just going downstairs to wash the brush in the laundry-room sink."

"But why?"

"Because it's full of paint."

"No, I mean why red?"

"Oh, it's just another staging thing. Mostly because it's a cheerful color. It's eye-catching, it has curb appeal. But there's some symbolism, from what I've read. In some cultures—maybe Ireland?—it actually means the mortgage has been paid and the house is owned free and clear. And in feng shui it means stability and fortunate rest inside."

She's halfway down the stairs now, and I want to keep her from disappearing into the basement.

"What's feng shui?"

"Oh, just some Eastern-religion design thing."

"Do you know if we have any Pop-Tarts?"

"I don't know, darling. Ask Nabila. I'm sorry, but I really need to get back to work. There's a lot left to do, plus I have another appointment later today, so I'm in a bit of a rush."

I wonder if her other appointment has to do with Vince and the loft. I wonder, too, if it involves another girl, maybe one who

likes to run laps at field-hockey practice or who has a better collection of American Girl dolls. I ask her who Vince is, but she doesn't
answer, so I shout another question. "Hey, what did you do with the
pig and the naked starving person?" But she's already all the way
downstairs, and I can hear the water running in the sink in the utility
room.

I KNOW WE have Pop-Tarts, somewhere, so I take everything out of
the cabinet to see if they're way in the back. The counter is getting
crowded with food, and a box of crackers falls to the floor. Looking at
all this food is making me hungry. I think maybe I should stop trying
to find the Pop-Tarts and just eat the crackers, or maybe have a bowl
of Froot Loops, but I've already taken the toaster out and feel weirdly
like I need to use it, so I keep looking. There's a lot of ramen soup, like
almost a hundred packages, but I don't particularly like ramen soup.
None of us really do, but my mom says she keeps it for emergencies.

Maybe the Pop-Tarts are on the very top shelf? Even standing on
my tiptoes on the kitchen counter, I can't see what's all the way up
there, but I can reach it with my hand, so I just start pulling stuff down,
and some of it's heavy, like the bag of flour that falls, almost knocking
me down. It splits open, and there's flour everywhere. Still no Pop-
Tarts.

Nabila comes into the room and stares at me.

"What in the world are you doing?" she asks.

"I'm looking for a Pop-Tart."

"A what?"

"You know, a thing you put in the toaster and eat for a snack. Or
for breakfast, maybe. They have different kinds, like chocolate, or
strawberry, or ones with sprinkles . . . I know we have some. I know
we used to . . ."

"My God, Elsa. What are we going to do with you?" She opens
the freezer door and pulls out a box of Hot Pockets.

"No, silly!" I find this hilarious, confusing Pop-Tarts and Hot Pockets, and I start to laugh, but now Nabila is clearly furious, and I feel bad, since where she comes from not only do they have scrawny rabbits, but they apparently don't have Pop-Tarts, either. I realize that I don't even know what country she's from, but this doesn't seem like the best time to ask.

"Look at this mess you've made!"

"It's not my fault," I say, even though it is, sort of, although if someone had put the Pop-Tarts where they belonged and closed the bag of flour properly this wouldn't have happened. There's white powder pretty much everywhere.

"What's gotten into you, girl?" Nabila asks. "I've been with you for almost a year now and I've never seen you behave like this."

"I'm not behaving like anything. I just want a Pop-Tart. Why is everyone being so mean to me?"

"Okay, I get it. Your mum and dad are away, and that's tough. I understand that myself. I haven't seen my own mum in two years. Also, this moving stuff is very hard. Maybe you're upset because the lady is changing everything around here. Your mum explained this to me."

"What about your dad?"

"What about my dad?"

"Why don't you miss your dad?"

"Well, I do, darling, but he's been gone six years."

"Gone where?"

"Gone. Gone."

"Did he have cancer?"

"No. The warlord came to our village and . . ."

Now I burst into tears.

"Oh no, darling. I understand, I really do. On top of everything going on, your mom said you might be getting a little moody, be-tween the move and your body growing so fast."

"I am *not* moody!" But maybe I'm a little moody. And it makes me even moodier to think of my mother and Nabila talking about my body. But really what makes me cry is the word "warlord."

"Oh no, Elsa, please don't cry. You're such a big girl. Your mum will be home at the end of the week, and probably she'll bring you a present. And she said the new house is so nice, you'll have a lovely big room all to yourself, and a pretty garden . . ."

"I already saw a picture of my new room and I don't like it. And I already have a lovely big room all to myself, here. And we won't have a pool. And there's a stupid stone rabbit in front of the house that's going to make me think of Dominique every time I see it. And I don't miss my mom, so I don't know why you're talking about her. I'm crying because . . ."

"Elsa." She comes over and puts her arms around me, but I push her away. She looks startled, like she might cry herself. "I don't even know what to say to you anymore, Elsa."

"Don't worry, Nabila, it's not your problem. I'm going to clean this up and do my homework. I'm just going to go downstairs to get the vacuum." But I'm not really going downstairs to get the vacuum. I'm going downstairs to find the Stager, even though it occurs to me that it wouldn't be the worst thing in the world to try to make Nabila happy, to just go get the vacuum and clean up the mess.

On my way to the utility room, I pass by Nabila's room. She's left the light on, and when I look inside I remember how small and dark it is in here. She doesn't even have a closet, so her clothes are either piled neatly in stacks on the floor, or hanging from a rack. We have two empty bedrooms upstairs, and I wonder why she doesn't just move into one of those.

Her bed is unmade, a wet towel is lying on the floor, and her jeans are crumpled on the chair. I decide to do something nice for her to make up for being so mean, so I clean up a bit. First I make her bed, then I pick up the wet towel and put it on the hook behind her door, and then I pick up the jeans, which are perfect; they're just the right color of faded denim. They're so long that when I hold them up they're almost as tall as me. When I begin to fold them, something falls out of the pocket.

It looks like a baggie full of smashed-up leaves, or maybe even tea, which is what I think it is at first, until the word "marijuana" pops into my head from the unit we did at school on "harmful narcotics," which was right after the unit on "stranger danger." It seems pretty unlikely to me that Nabila would do any harmful narcotics, since she's always talking about being healthy and eating fruits and vegetables. She's become friends with the guy who works across the street, at the farmstand in front of Unfurlings, and she's even convinced my mom that it's better to buy the vegetables there than in the grocery store because they don't use pesticides. I open the baggie and smell the leaves, but I don't know what marijuana is supposed to smell like, so this doesn't help.

Someone knocks on the back door. I hear the Stager open it, and she starts talking to a man. Then I hear another voice, and then another, and then Nabila comes downstairs to see what's going on, and all of a sudden there are three men in the basement, carrying equipment. I don't know who they are, but one of them has a video camera that says "HGTV" on the side, and he's standing outside Nabila's door, talking into a microphone.

"And now we journey to the leafy suburb of Bethesda, Maryland, located just outside Washington, D.C. *Forbes* magazine has named Bethesda one of the most affluent and highly educated communities in the country. CNNMoney has listed it first on top-earning American towns, and, most intriguingly, *Total Beauty* has ranked it *first*—and, yes, I did say *first*, ladies and gentlemen—on its list of the country's Top Ten Hottest Guy Cities . . . This is of course a nice segue into the home of a celebrity couple who wish to remain anonymous, which is why they have chosen to live in relative obscurity in a tony enclave of million-dollar-plus homes known as The Flanders . . ."

The camera is pointed at me, and I cling to the baggie, terrified that I've just been caught on camera snooping *and* holding drugs.

I stuff the bag of leaves in my pocket and squeeze past the HGTV people into the main part of the basement, where the door leads out to the pool. A blur of white races across the garden and squeezes under the fence. The next thing I know, I'm outside, where it's raining, with a bag of smashed-up leaves in my pocket, chasing after a rabbit that might or might not be Dominique.

LARS

Bella is in the middle of another important dinner when she learns that Elsa is missing.

We had originally planned to make this our big London date night, to dine at some five-star fusion restaurant in Soho she'd heard about from a colleague, but then she remembered that she had a work-related "thing." This is not atypical Bella behavior. Sometimes when we have plans, her memory is jogged at the last minute by a chirp of the calendar function on her phone, other times by a flip through her pocket diary. Another method involves smacking herself on the side of the head as she recalls suddenly that she has another obligation. Last night it was dinner with Luxum's CEO; the night before, drinks with the outside counsel in from Frankfurt. Tonight is the marquee event, an expensively catered welcome-to-London-I'm-the-face-of-Transparency-at-Luxum-International dinner with various dignitaries, celebrities, and big-time investors. How one forgets about this until an hour prior to the event is something that eludes me.

And there she is, seated between the visiting prime minister of

Kazakhstan—or maybe Kyrgyzstan (I am reasonably well traveled, but my experience is confined to places where I have either lived, played tennis, or vacationed)—and the boozed-up American ambassador, who seems to be hitting on her.

Bella can see on her phone, which she pulls discreetly from her jacket pocket a couple of times as it vibrates, that she's missed several calls from home. (This is where I begin to understand what I was beginning to understand back in the hotel room when I could hear her talking on the phone even though maybe I could not. I have a working theory about why this is possible, but I'd like to string it out a few paragraphs longer to be certain it is true.)

Bella is beginning to worry, but not overtly. Right now it's just a low-grade worry, the equivalent of a dull toothache. She tells herself that it's probably just Elsa calling with more field-hockey shenanigans; the coach has already e-mailed us to say that we need to meet to discuss the problem of our daughter when we return. Or maybe there's simply a homework-related question, or the violin teacher needs her check, which Bella now realizes she has forgotten to write, or perhaps there's some update on the Dominique situation. Then Bella's assistant comes in, a stunning young woman of South Asian descent. (Might I note, perhaps irrelevantly, that Bella's assistants are always lovely? If I had to speculate, I'd say this is her way of demonstrating that she is confident enough in her own skin to surround herself with beauty.) She taps my wife on the shoulder to tell her that her estate agent from the States is on the phone, and that, unable to reach Bella by cell, she's called the office directly to report a real-estate emergency.

Bella's train of thought goes something like this (and please note, this is not a verbatim transcript, because her thought process is interrupted by the hullaballoo in the background, the ambient sounds of people who want a minute of her time as she struggles toward the exit, of clanking silverware and dishes being collected by waiters, as well as overheard snippets of conversation, which I have edited out for the sake of brevity): *A real-estate emergency? This Realtor is one high-maintenance piece of work, what with her constant phone calls and her demand that I fork over thousands of dollars to have the house professionally staged.*

Nevertheless, Bella is relieved to have a reason to leave the table, even if it means forfeiting the yellowish puréed vegetable soup that looks, and smells, pretty good.

I'm dozing intermittently, while watching some silly British sitcom, when I realize with alarm that something is wrong with this scene. It was one thing to sort of be inside Bella's head when she was a few feet away and I could hear snippets of her telephone conversation with the doctor, but now she is all the way across town and I am in bed in our increasingly fetid hotel room, wearing only my boxers.

I bolt upright: this point of view is not meant to be! I wonder if this condition might have something to do with the light. Up on the roof, helping Jorek earlier that day, perhaps I absorbed too much sun.

Praxisis. The answer is always Praxisis, even when it isn't answer "b." I conjure an image of the lovely vial, slim and cylindrical, the perfect repository for my treasured pill, and try to remember when I popped the last one—was it this morning, before I'd gone off to meet Jorek, or have I taken one since? Truly, I cannot recall.

I anticipate the bliss, the battle forged as the molecules dissolve in my bloodstream, their tiny swords slaying the enemy. If only, like infatuation, there was a way to make this last forever! I know too well that it does not, that the Catch-22 is the massive anxiety caused by thinking about the ephemeral nature of the bliss. That, plus the fact that I will soon run out, and I am under the impression that Praxisis is not attainable in the U.K. It is counterproductive to overthink this situation, and it's clearly sometimes best to throw caution to the wind, to travel without a map, to avoid the limitations of too much left-brain planning. Accordingly, I make my way to the bathroom, wrestle with the child-safety lock, triumph after a few false starts, and swallow a handful of pills, mixing in a couple of Zuffixors for good measure. I can no longer remember what they are meant to do. Then I return to bed and wait to be enveloped in Praxisisity.

It is even slower than usual to arrive, however: an emerging problem is that I am building up a tolerance, and the Praxisis, even in higher doses, is taking longer and longer to kick in. Unsurprisingly, this situation is generating its own vicious anxiety cycle. What if it eventually stops working? Is it really too much, God, to ask for a drug that works the way it is supposed to, without endlessly sprouting newfangled complications?

Slowly, slowly, I feel it working, but now with a new Praxisis twist: when I turn my dial back to the dinner party, this time I am not just inside Bella's head, but I am inside the heads of everyone she can see from *her* point of view. Interesting, perhaps, yet the cacophony of these disparate, random voices is almost deafening.

A hefty, balding man in a gray suit seated at the left corner of Bella's table summons the waiter and asks him to refill his glass with wine, even though he knows that he's already had too much to drink. He's desperate to sneak out for a smoke, notwithstanding the fact that he's quit, or sort of quit, or at least promised his wife he's quit. But he has problems—liquidity, a delinquent kid, an aloof wife—and who can blame him for needing a little nicotine crutch? At the far end of the table, the actor who's currently performing as Hamlet in a much-acclaimed West End production is worrying about his weight, although he understands, rationally, that this is ridiculous. Still, he shreds the bread on his plate and rolls a small bit between his forefinger and thumb, then drops it in his mouth, takes a sip of water, and feels the yeasty glob inflate. Bread is healthier this way, he tells himself, and more nutritious, because it is both food and beverage at once. Besides, he's an edgier performer when at his most stick-thin.

I can hear, or feel, or sense, the waiter sneer as he clears Hamlet's untouched soup. He has his own problems, this waiter. Would it be insensitive of me to say the waiter's problems are of the usual waiter sort? He is, indeed, a frustrated actor himself, and he thinks he's a better actor than this anorexic Hamlet, whom he considers something of a hack.

Why, for the love of God, am I privy to all of this private chatter? Does such knowledge require me to care? But, more to the point, what am I meant to do with the painful realization that Bella has not invited me to this dinner? Yes, of course, she has dinners most nights, and I rarely attend, and that's fine by me; these dinners can be dreadful, especially when people ask me what I *do*. Since I feel obliged to come up with an answer more substantive than that I am lately engaged in ordering high-end gadgetry on line, I tell them I used to be Lars Jorgenson, Wimbledon semifinalist, a whirling dervish in Tretorns, and then they light up, and then they take a good look at me and go dim.

But now that I am inside her head, I can see that this event is not so run-of-the-mill. This is Bella's official welcome dinner, and though I don't claim to know the etiquette, it seems to me this ought to have been a spousal affair. The insult sort of fells me; it's a physical reaction that causes me to draw the curtains again, even though, now that it is nighttime, there is no light.

IF I AM to attempt to deconstruct the strangeness, I need to back up to a point earlier in the day when I'd been helping Jorek on the roof. I am able to isolate in that scene a moment of pure joy. It had to do with my sense of purpose, I suppose: I loved being useful, helping Jorek with his tasks, hauling his equipment up the ladder, fetching his tools, popping over to the store to get an extension cord, going to the deli to buy us both lunch. I am in awe of Jorek, and strangely attracted to him, although let me again emphasize that this is entirely nonsexual in nature, and even if it was otherwise, skinny old Jorek, with his belt drawn tight to hold up his too-big jeans, and his very crooked teeth, is not someone I would find particularly physically compelling.

Maybe it's simply that he lavishes me with attention, he's the friend I don't have. Or maybe it's more elemental, and simply has to do with an admiration of his prowess with power tools.

Up on the roof, I pleaded with him to let me have a go with the chainsaw, which he finally did. It was harder than it looked, holding steady this heavy, vibrating, thrumming instrument, forcing its blade into the tar of a shingle. The sun was beating down and was far more potent than it looked. Despite my insistence to the contrary about the lack of light, etc., I'll admit, without prejudice, that I should have worn a hat.

Somehow, and perhaps because of what was beginning to feel like possible sunstroke, I lost my balance and accidentally bore down with the blade in the wrong spot, creating an unfortunate gash just beside the gutter. Don't laugh! It is harder than it looks; trying to keep the blade steady is, I imagine, not unlike wrestling an alligator or riding a wild bull. I teetered inches from the edge and could see, below, daffodils in blooms, and that stupid stone rabbit, and I imagined myself falling, falling, falling, and I wondered where I'd land and what I'd break and whether anyone would take care of me if I wound up in traction, or would miss me if I died. But just as I was about to plunge, there he was, his surprisingly strong hands around my waist, wrenching me back to the land of the living.

Jorek, my savior.

Later, he told me that I'd fainted, and that he was in the process of calling an ambulance when I'd finally come to, but I think he might have been embellishing this part of the narrative a bit, perhaps to make himself seem more heroic.

We hadn't entirely finished for the day when Jorek's wife called and urged him to hurry home. She was roasting a chicken and baking a pie, and some cousins were coming for dinner. I asked a variety of questions about the meal and about his family, pining for an invitation, but none was forthcoming. I wondered if Jorek had even told his wife about me, or if, as for Bella, I was some shameful secret.

And now I wonder if I can conjure Jorek at *his* dinner. I think hard on Jorek, on his family and the chicken and the pie. I meditate on the smell of a broiling onion and some potatoes basting in the juice of the bird, to no avail. Just the thought of a home-cooked meal, even if I can't get a whiff, makes me hungry, so I return to Bella's dinner, hoping that perhaps my new superpowers might enable me to co-digest.

They do not. Instead, I am back in the static of her head. She is engaged in a very boring struggle to remember correctly the name of her own assistant. Is she Priyavishnu, or Vishnupriya? By now she has arrived at her office, one floor below the banquet room full of dinner guests, and she is preparing to take Amanda's call. She wants to thank her assistant by name, but she hesitates. Names, there are too many names! She's having trouble keeping in her head the names of several of the men at the dinner as well, and has devised a strategy at least to differentiate them, based on the patterns of their ties. Yale stripes is the visiting CEO of a Korean media company for which Luxum manages funds; leaping fish is an important solicitor at a large London firm; deep blue matches the eyes of Luxum's head of human resources based in New York, who just happens to be in London on holiday with his family. (Bella entertains the fleeting thought that he's attractive.) There are other important people in the room she ought to be fêting more aggressively, but they sport mostly a variety of tactful, unremarkable stripes, and hence she can't remember their names or their roles. To get her attention right now requires something fairly astonishing, as I know from my own experience. Animals with bows and arrows, or disconnected body parts. I try to tell her this, to make a joke, but it seems our mind-meld extends only one way. Bella and everyone around her have become transparent. But transparent only to me.

I am then seized by a sudden, distressing thought. Perhaps Praxisis is not my friend, but my enemy. Not the solution, but the problem itself. Perhaps Bella is actually onto something after all, with her relentless harping on side effects. Making my way to the bathroom, I gather my collection of pills and then dump the lot on the bed. I study the label on each vial and then plug the data into Google, first individually and then in various combinations. Praxisis + Zuffixor + Romulex + Luxemprat = dizziness and nausea, insomnia and diarrhea, and frequent but unsustainable erections. In some cases, where the dosage of Praxisis exceeds five hundred milligrams and is taken in conjunction with Texicor and Ciraxes, strokes may occur. Zuffixor + Volemex = mostly the same as the above, with the addition of migraines and a sense of desolation and despair. Zaxivon + Amulerex = weight gain, strange food yearnings, miscarriages, and a burst of euphoria frequently followed by suicidal thoughts. Nothing unexpected or out of the ordinary there.

I continue to play with the combinations, varying the dosages to see what comes up, and finally I stumble onto the website of *The German Journal of Medical Metaphysics*, and it speaks to my condition, which is a huge relief, since, for a moment there, I was thinking I am possibly losing my mind.

Apparently, when a certain dosage of Luxemprat + Zumlexitor is followed by a thousand milligrams of Praxisis, "in some rare cases, the combination of these particular serotonins, painkillers, and anti-anxiety medications containing a surplus of the letters z and x have been known to result in the development of a limited but omniscient point of view."

I'm not entirely sure what this means, but it doesn't sound good.

I consider calling Bella, since she is one of those people who always rally in a crisis, but she's already on the phone and I'm already inside her head, where she's reflecting on something she once overheard on a train, a stray fragment of dialogue that has stuck with her for many years. A man, a dull bureaucrat type, unmemorable but for this interesting snippet, had quipped to his seatmate that he'd never experienced pain, that he'd never had so much as a headache. This seemed to Bella frankly unbelievable, but later, when she reflected on it, her own version of being superhuman was that she'd never, before now, felt real stress. Things arose, problems needed solving, complications sometimes became extreme. But there was always a solution, and the trick, Bella thought, was to see life as an ocean, to stay atop the waves. There would always be another Davos on our anniversary, another Aspen on Elsa's birthday. She did the best she could, and avoided getting caught in sentimental traps. She forgave herself her shortcomings and mistakes. Even when the mistakes were not forgivable.

It's interesting to know this suddenly about my wife, but it also feels mildly invasive. Although not quite as invasive as reading her e-mails, which is something I once did, for a brief interval, and what I learned nearly made me blind. As much as I abhor the darkness, there is definitely such a thing as too much light.

BELLA PICKS UP the phone. "Amanda, greetings!" she says cheerfully, while at the same time bracing for bad news, like maybe the house has just failed a termite inspection, or crumbling Chinese drywall has been discovered, or a sump pump has stopped working, leading to a flooded basement, which happened a few years ago, destroying three of my exercise bicycles and a new flat-screen television that had just been delivered and was still in the box.

"I've been trying to reach you for an hour. I tried calling your hotel, your husband, your nanny, and your cell . . . I hate to disturb you at work—your assistant said you were in the middle of some important dinner, and I'm so sorry—but I'm a little worried."

This is what the Realtor says. Or what I think she says. My point of view is *omniscient but limited.* My knowledge of the conversation is being strained through Bella's brain, and it's possible that bits of information, like lemon seeds, are getting stuck in the mesh.

"Worried about what?"

"Both the front door and back door were open when I got here, and there's no sign of anyone home except for the camera crew."

"What camera crew?" Bella feels a small jolt of terror. Or I think she does. Maybe I feel a small jolt of terror and am projecting this back onto her. (Now that I am inside her brain, I'm having trouble telling which part is her and which part is me, although, in truth, even before these powers emerged, my inability to separate myself from Bella has always been a problem.)

"I'm sure I told you—a friend of a friend is a producer for a cable station that does reality shows about real estate. They're doing a piece on Unfurlings. How the foreclosure has impacted real-estate prices throughout the surrounding region. And then, when they realized this was *your* house—well, not just you, but you and Lars—well, you know, the whole celebrity angle, not that you are actually celebrity celebrity, but in Washington, well, even the Salahis are celebrities."

"Okay, thanks, Amanda. I'm not sure I have any idea where to begin deconstructing the string of insults there, but the headline is that we never had a conversation about a camera crew coming into the house, and I would never, not in a million years, have been okay with that. I want them out of the house immediately. Do you hear me? Let me talk to Nabila right now!"

"I'm sorry you don't remember that conversation, Bella. I have it here in my notes."

"In your notes? Just because you made notes doesn't mean we had a conversation."

"Actually, it does. I'm a very organized person."

"So am I. Let me speak to Nabila."

"Well, if we can back up a minute, that's why I called. I don't know where Nabila is."

"Where's Elsa?"

"No idea. That's why I called. The doors are open and no one is here."

"Is anything gone? I mean, does it look like someone broke in? Where's that Stager person I keep hearing about?"

"Gone. No one's here. Just the camera crew, as I already explained. I don't think anyone broke in, although in the kitchen—well, it's odd, there's food all over the floor, and it's a complete mess. And then, I'm not sure if this is related, but your garden is sort of a mess, too, like some animal dug up a bunch of the tulips and daffodils. Probably it's just those rabbits again, but it almost looks like the garden was vandalized. Some of the flowers look . . . beheaded. Do you think someone might have done this deliberately? Do you have any problems with your neighbors, or is there some grievance with someone at work? Or, forgive me for asking, but there are a lot of angry Luxum investors out there; do any of them know where you live? The open house is Sunday, and I'm going to have to get a landscaper over here ASAP. I mean, I'm not even sure if I can get someone in on time. It's Wednesday afternoon already, for God's sake. It's going to be expensive. Also, and I hate to tell you this, the smell, which I thought we'd resolved, well, it's back. It's different but it's back. It kind of comes and goes. It's hard to figure."

"I thought that Stager woman had fixed this."

"Well, she had. As I said, it's hard to figure. We can't seem to isolate where it's coming from, and sometimes it's there, sometimes it's not. We're working on it."

"Okay, more to the point, I can't tell from your report whether we should be worried about Elsa. It sounds like they might have all just gone off somewhere, right? Or does this seem suspicious somehow? How long have they been gone? Should we call the police?"

"Definitely not. It's bad karma to call the police before an open house. It'll get people talking—they'll think there's a curse on the house. Remember that house in Rockville where they found a dead body in the garage during an open house? Come to think of it, there was a bad smell in that house, too."

"For the love of God, Amanda, why would you say that?"

Bella sort of shrieks that last part, and her beleaguered assistant,

Vishnupriya or Priyavishnu, who is being forced to work late to oversee this dinner, still droning on upstairs, comes running into the office. "Everything okay, ma'am?"

Bella nods to VP/PV, but the assistant remains frozen at her door.

Then, suddenly, I can hear Elsa and Nabila in the background, and then the disconnection of the phone. Bella redials repeatedly, to no avail. She texts a "SOCKS!!!" message, takes the elevator back to the twenty-fifth floor, and returns to the table just in time for the second course, which looks, and smells, like overcooked fish.

ELSA

Nabila makes me write a list of the things I did wrong.

1. I went into a stranger's house (even though she was very nice and was only trying to help me).
2. I ate her food (even though I was very hungry because we had no Pop-Tarts, and she was baking these delicious little cupcakes called fairy cakes).

Nabila isn't happy with this list. I'm supposed to work on it more, add other things, like running off without telling anyone where I was going, and messing up the kitchen and spilling the flour, and not cleaning up the doll stuff, and refusing to run laps at school. Probably I should add that I still have Nabila's bag of mashed-up leaves in my pocket, but she hasn't noticed it's missing yet, and I definitely don't want to bring it up.

Just like in that movie *Groundhog Day*, where the same thing happens over and over and over, I'm walking through the basement on my way to get the vacuum, since part of my punishment is to clean up the kitchen floor, when something catches my eye, a white blur racing through the garden, and I'm pretty sure, again, that it's Dominique. I have my hand on the latch and I'm about to open the door, but then I hesitate—I'm not supposed to leave the house, not even to go into the garden.

Still, I think about it and decide that if I get in trouble again for trying to catch Dominique, which is actually the right and even *morally correct* thing to do, I'll just recalibrate and go back to Unfurlings. I met a wonderful family there, a lady named Marta, who has seven-year-old twins, a boy and a girl, and she told me to come back anytime. I wonder if I could just move in with them and stay forever. Then I wouldn't have to go to London.

I'm still staring out the window, my hand on the latch, trying to decide what to do, when I see *another* rabbit squeeze under the fence and into the neighbor's yard, and I'm not sure if *that's* Dominique, and, as if that's not enough, out of the corner of my eye I see a third rabbit, except that one is in the swimming pool, floating belly-up.

I scream one long, loud, continuous scream. Nabila hears me and she comes running from the kitchen and down the stairs, and she says, "Easy, easy, calm down, Elsa." Then she says, "You have sure been doing a lot of emoting lately."

I point toward the pool. Nabila looks, squints, moves toward the door, looks again, and starts screaming, too. Then she steps back, spins me away from the glass at the door, and puts her hand over my eyes, which is ridiculous, because I've already seen the possibly, probably, dead rabbit. She leads me upstairs to the kitchen and sticks a brownie and glass of milk in front of me. Then she runs up to the second floor and comes back down with the Stager.

"Stay here," Nabila says, "and don't look out the window."

As if I am not going to look out the window! How can I not look out the window, even if a rabbit isn't floating in the pool with its feet sticking up? The entire wall of the kitchen is glass! Beyond the pool and the rest of the yard, now with flowers all ripped up, is the eighth hole of the golf course. You can even see the little flag on the green when you sit in the chair at the head of the table. Sometimes balls fly into our backyard, and more than one has landed in our pool. I take a bite of the brownie, but it isn't that great, at least not compared with the fairy cakes, which I can't stop thinking about. They had blue-and-pink frosting, with sprinkles shaped like stars. I wonder if maybe they had some magical properties, like the Turkish Delight in *The Lion, the Witch and the Wardrobe.*

The Stager and Nabila are talking by the side of the pool. I'm trying not to cry, and I'm also trying not to laugh, which I suppose means I'm trying not to *emote.* I already had to try not to emote in school today, when everyone else in my class got to work on their schedules for electives for next year. They told me I didn't need to bother, since I'm moving, and even though I was upset, I pretended I didn't care. I didn't even cry when I was asked to go to the office to bring the attendance sheets to the secretary and Ben Simpson, who was waiting for his mom to pick him up because his stomach hurt, threw up and it splattered on my shoe.

I watch Nabila go to the shed. She comes back to the pool with the long pole that has a net on the end that my dad uses to scoop up leaves and dead bugs, except this time she's going to use it to grab the rabbit. It looks pretty dead. Even from the distance of the kitchen window, it looks dead, as stiff as an animal in a diorama at the Museum of Natural History. Nabila starts to pull the pole back, but then the automatic pool cleaner—which is a little robot that floats around the pool, clinging to the walls and sucking up debris—rises to the surface and squirts a stream of water from its spout, splashing Nabila. She screams and loses her grip on the pole, and then *she* starts to cry. Now the pole is floating in the middle of the pool with the rabbit in the net, and it drifts out of reach.

The Stager rubs Nabila on the back, and they briefly hug. There is some conversation I can't hear, and then Nabila goes to the shed and gets another long pole, and they take turns using this one to nudge the other pole, with the rabbit in it, toward the side of the pool. Finally, it's close enough, and the Stager gets on her knees and lies down on the side of the pool and reaches into the water and pulls that pole up onto the concrete patio, and then the pool cleaner surfaces again, like a whale rising to the top of the ocean, and it squirts water at the Stager, and this time *she* screams. Nabila and the Stager both laugh, and then the Stager stands up and they hug each other again. Then there's a little more conversation, and Nabila goes back to the shed. She returns with my *Beauty and the Beast* beach towel and puts it over the rabbit like it's dead, and then, unbelievably, they *both* start to cry.

By the time they come into the kitchen, I'm onto my third brownie, even though they're really dry, and I'm feeling a little sick. They look at me with grim faces, and Nabila says, "That was terrible, darling, and I'm so sorry if you witnessed any of that, but the good news is that I don't think that's necessarily Dominique. He's been gone a long time, and we both know—especially after what happened yesterday, with you chasing rabbits all over the neighborhood—that all of these rabbits look alike."

"That's kind of a racist thing to say, Nabila! Dominique was very distinctive-looking. He had a brown splotch on his stomach. Did that rabbit have a brown splotch?"

"I guess you're right. I didn't look, but I don't recall Dominique having any brown splotch. Do you?" Nabila asks the Stager.

I haven't noticed until now how disheveled the Stager is, with her mascara smeared from all the crying and laughing, her garish lipstick faded, her shirt untucked, and her trousers and shoes all wet from being splashed. "Dominique and I didn't have much time to get to know each other, which I now regret, of course, and I definitely didn't get a good look, really any look at all, at his stomach. I only knew Dominique for a few minutes before he hopped away. I found him in the laundry room the day I was trying to figure out the source of that awful smell—well, the first awful smell—remember?"

As if we could have forgotten, two days ago. Although I *had*, until she'd just reminded me, almost managed to forget this was all the Stager's fault. To be honest, I couldn't really remember if it was true that Dominique had a brown splotch, and I wasn't entirely sure why I'd just said that. Did he have a brown splotch? Or had I just made that up? Apart from the possibility of a brown splotch which he may or may not have had, I couldn't make the case that he was all that distinctive-looking. He was sort of white, but also sort of the color of heather, and everything else about him was pretty standard rabbit stuff: a puffy white cotton-ball rabbit tail and pointy rabbit ears and very sharp teeth. Even if he was mean, you couldn't look at him without wanting to hug him and snuggle up. But that didn't make him very distinctive, and I realized that there might be a little bit of truth in what Nabila was saying.

That's not to say I didn't spend time with him. After school, just about every day, we'd lie on the carpet in the television room and watch reruns of a Bravo show about people getting makeovers, which he seemed to enjoy as much as I did. We'd stare at the TV in shared amazement that a person could look transformed just because she'd had her hair cut, and every once in a while someone would burst into tears when she saw her new look. (People emote all the time, I might point out, even when they aren't moving to London and their parents haven't left them alone for ten days and their rabbits haven't possibly drowned.) Dominique and I would always share an after-school snack while we watched television. The vet had given us a list of forbidden items, but most of them seemed dumb—like, Dominique wasn't supposed to eat iceberg lettuce, even though it didn't have any calories, because maybe he'd get so full chomping on stuff that was essentially nothing but crunchy water and air that he wouldn't eat his regular rabbit food. Then, in theory, he'd wind up not having enough protein, and he'd be malnourished, which was ridiculous, because Dominique never got full. He would just eat and eat and eat until you ran out of food, and then sometimes he'd throw up, even though the vet said that was impossible, that rabbits technically can't regurgitate food. I told

this to my mom, but since there was, in fact, rabbit vomit on the carpet, I'm not sure she got my point.

"Everything in moderation" was one of my mother's favorite things
to say.

So we tried that, me and Dominique, a little bit of everything in
moderation in our little after-school snack club. Apples were allowed but were boring, so we spiced them up with peanut butter
and honey. He liked the peanut butter so much that he licked it
off my hand and didn't even bite me, so I went the next logical step
and began to bring him Reese's Peanut Butter Cups. He liked
those, too.

"I want to look more closely and see if that's really Dominique,"
I say.

"I don't think that's a good idea," the Stager says. "It's not a pretty
sight. Better to just remember Dominique as he was."

I remember Dominique as he was, my best friend, the only pet I'd
ever had, and I worry I'm going to start crying or laughing or screaming again, so I get up from the table and leave my current half-eaten
brownie sitting there, then I run out into the backyard quickly, before
anyone can stop me, and I pull the towel off the rabbit. It's horrible to
see something dead up close, especially something matted, bloated,
wide-eyed, and reeking of chlorine.

This may be difficult to believe, but I swear, at that very moment
another rabbit that looks just like Dominique hops by, looks me in the
eye, and squeezes under the very same hole in the very same fence
that the rabbit had squeezed under yesterday.

I can't help it. Now I'm *certain* this new rabbit is Dominique, and
I go running after it.

"YOU KNOW, ELSA, you're becoming something of an unreliable
narrator," my mother says later that night, after Nabila and the Stager

find me at Unfurlings and send me, like the tragic child who has been kidnapped in some fairy tale, to my room without supper.

I sit on my bed, holding the phone, staring at the easel. I'm trying to paint a chair. I think maybe if I get it started, the Stager will see it and she won't be able to resist coming into my room to help me make it better.

"What's an unreliable narrator?"

"It means your version of events might not be believable. Your story keeps changing. You're making poor Nabila miserable, and you're not letting the Stager do her job. I don't know what to believe anymore. You run off, you don't tell anyone where you're going, and you frighten everyone half to death. I'm also starting to get the feeling that maybe *you're* the one who dug up all the flowers yesterday—did you know that I had to leave a pretty important dinner to take that call? I nearly had a heart attack—I thought something really awful had happened to you. Do you think you might illuminate me?"

"I don't understand the question."

"What don't you understand? It's pretty straightforward, I'd say. Did you dig up all the flowers?"

"No."

"Okay, who did it, then?"

"A rabbit."

"You know this how?"

"I just do."

"You didn't touch any of the flowers? Like maybe what I was thinking was that you were trying to make a bouquet for me. I thought that was sweet. A welcome-home gift?"

"You're coming home?"

"Well, in a couple of days."

"Yes. That's it. A welcome-home bouquet."

"Great, thanks. So you did pull up the flowers, then?"

I now see this is a trick question. I had not pulled up the flowers, but I want her to think I made a bouquet. Also, this is starting to make me sad about moving again. "Remember how we'd plant bulbs every fall? How we'd go to the garden center to pick out a pumpkin and we'd always buy daffodil bulbs and also some tulip ones with crazy names? Remember the Hillary Clinton tulips?"

"Of course I remember, Elsa. We did that every year since you were old enough to hold a spade."

"Yeah, and you always said, 'Someday, Elsa, we'll have the most beautiful garden in the whole world!'"

"And we do!" I walk over to the easel and use a black marker to draw a rabbit in the half-finished chair. I put my mom on speakerphone while I draw the outline. Or try to draw the outline. I'm not a very good artist. It looks sort of like a rabbit, but one ear is longer than the other. The rabbit looks less like Dominique than like a villain rabbit in a Batman movie.

"We do. It's a beautiful garden, and now we have to leave it for someone else."

"Of course. Okay, that makes sense. I get it, Elsa; this is really hard stuff, and I'm so sorry about Dominique, and . . ."

"Don't worry, Mom. That wasn't Dominique. There was no brown splotch on the stomach. I know he's okay, because I saw him today. He squeezed under the fence, just like yesterday. That's why I ran after him again. I'm just trying to bring him home, where he belongs."

"Okay, well, we're going to talk about this more when I get back. I've got some books we can read about moving. And maybe about pets passing, too. You've got a whole lot going on, and I feel awful that I'm away right now, but I'll be back very soon. In fact, your dad is on his way back right now. His flight gets in late tonight. I could tell you needed one of us home. In the meantime, please remember that when we get to the new house we can plant a *new* garden, and it will be just as beautiful. We can even talk about getting a new rabbit."

"I don't want a rabbit. I'd like a dog, remember?"

"Okay, I get it, Elsa. I understand. But just tell me one more thing. Why did you run away? Did anything bad happen with the people with the cameras?"

I'm not sure how to answer this. Maybe something bad did happen. Maybe they caught me stealing Nabila's bag of leaves that are maybe tea and maybe marijuana. I am definitely not going to be the one to bring this up, however.

"No, Mom, I told you, I saw Dominique, and I followed him. But he squeezed under the fence, so I went around into the Shays' garden and he was there, but he was just getting ready to squeeze under *their* fence into the Mehtas' house, so I walked around into *their* yard, and then, when I got there, he went under the *back* fence, which was really a problem."

"What do you mean?"

"Well, because I had to walk all the way around the block."

"Elsa, I don't understand why you didn't try to get Nabila. You know you aren't supposed to go wandering around the neighborhood by yourself."

I have reached the point where my own lies are so confusing I don't know how to keep them going.

"I did try. Remember? I got locked out. I was in the basement, looking for the vacuum, and I saw the bag with leaves in Nabila's room, and then these strangers showed up with cameras, and then I saw Dominique, and . . ."

"What bag with leaves?"

Have I mentioned the bag with leaves? I truly didn't mean to. I am terrified that I'll get Nabila in trouble. I remember the cleaning lady who disappeared after the stirrup broke on the American Girl horse. I don't want Nabila to have to leave, too, and I especially don't want her to have to go back to the country with the warlords and scrawny rabbits. So I just say, "What?"

"What bag with leaves are you talking about?"

"I don't know. What bag with leaves? What are *you* talking about?"

"Okay, never mind. This whole conversation is getting a little loopy, Elsa, but just go on, tell me what happened next."

"Well, I walked all the way around the block, but by then I couldn't really figure out where Dominique had gone, and then I saw a whole bunch of rabbits in the other direction. Why are there so many rabbits, Mom?"

"It's spring. Breeding season, I guess. You know, think about the whole Easter thing, with the chocolate rabbits and stuff."

I think about Easter bunnies, and I look at the Dominique I've just drawn and think he couldn't look any less like an Easter bunny unless I put a cigarette in his mouth or drew him a mustache.

"Anyway, there was a fence, and there was a hole in the fence, and all of a sudden I was someplace else."

"You wound up in Unfurlings. And you know very well you aren't supposed to cross the road."

"I didn't! I'm telling you, I just squeezed under the fence and I was there. Maybe the back of the Unfurlings place backs up to The Flanders."

"Maybe," says my mom. "Although I don't quite see how that would work, given that it's across the street."

"Well, maybe there's a secret passageway."

"Sure, Elsa. Why not toss in a little magical realism? I mean, really, with everything else going on, why not?!"

"What do you mean, Mom?"

"Nothing, Elsa. Go on."

"Well, actually, now that you mention it, it *was* like some magical place. There was all this land, and so much green, and it wasn't even a golf course! And there were patches with giant vegetables, and I saw a llama!"

"Well, that sure sounds like Unfurlings. Maybe you were back in the service area or something."

"What does that mean?"

"I just mean maybe there's a parcel of the land that extends farther than I thought."

"Unfurlings is a dumb name."

"Not as dumb as The Flanders!"

"I know, right?" I start laughing. "The Flanders" really is such a stupid name. It always makes me think of Ned Flanders on *The Simpsons*, even though my mom has explained that where we live is about a different Flanders, in Belgium, where the houses look sort of like our house, but actually not really, since our houses are all twice as big.

My mom starts laughing, too, and we stay on the phone laughing for a while, and I think maybe we're done with this conversation and I'm not going to have to talk about it anymore, but I'm wrong.

"So then, Elsa, what happened next? Tell me about this so-called fairy-cake house."

"It's not a fairy-cake house, Mom. It's a house where they were baking fairy cakes. Can we do that sometime? Marta—that's the mom of the kids who live there, who are twins—said she'll give me the recipe."

"Sure, but really, Elsa, this is so astonishing. Don't you remember all the conversations we've had about not going into strangers' houses? And then you just go waltzing right in there, and you eat their food, and Nabila doesn't even know where you are?"

"I know, Mom, but you also said sometimes you have to follow your gut. Like how you bought the new house because of the stone rabbit."

"I know what you're saying, sweetheart, but, still, don't you see why this is different?"

"Not really. You would have gone inside, too, Mom. They're really nice! The twins are only seven. A boy and a girl. They go to that school on River Road and they can walk there. Why don't I go to that school? Why do I go to a school where I have to drive half an hour?"

"That's an excellent question. One more way for your mom and dad to watch their money bleed away so you can learn to play field hockey and eat with a salad fork."

"What does that mean?"

"Nothing. That was a dumb thing to say. In London, you can walk to your new school."

"I don't want to walk to my school. I want to take a bus. I've never taken a bus before." I keep staring at the painting, and then I have the idea that maybe I can fix the crooked ears with red paint, the same color that door is going to be. I go over to the easel and pick up the pot of paint, but the lid isn't screwed on properly and it winds up spilling on the floor. Now there's red paint on the white carpet, and I wonder how much more trouble I can possibly get in. I walk to the bathroom to get a towel.

"Elsa, promise me you are going to stay away from this place!"

"They drank milk out of wineglasses, Mom. Can we do that? There aren't any real dishes, just the pretend ones on the table that is always set, and makes it look like whoever lives there is about to eat dinner. And they have a television but no cable, so it's just for show, so that other people, when they visit the house, will see that that's the place where the TV would be if they lived there. Except that now no one is even trying to live there, so Marta said, Why let a perfectly good house go to waste?"

The towels are gone in the bathroom that is attached to my room, and all I can find is a bag from Target with new towels in it. I wonder if it's worse to use new towels to wipe up the paint, or to just leave it there. Probably best to just leave it there.

"So this lady, this Marta person, is squatting with her kids in the model home at Unfurlings?"

"It's a real house with beds and everything, it's just that it doesn't have a lot of regular stuff in it."

I turn from the bathroom back toward my room and realize that I have accidentally stepped in the paint, and now it's all over the carpet, and you can see where I walked from the easel to the bathroom and back. Little red footsteps, like Hansel and Gretel but with paint instead of breadcrumbs.

"I've got to go, Mom. We can talk more when you come home."

"Elsa, wait. I want to tell you something else."

"Gotta go do my homework, and Nabila is calling me for dinner. Bye!"

"Wait, Elsa! A couple more things. I'm going to be on television at seven p.m., that's seven p.m. *your* time—and you'd better watch, because I blew you a secret kiss."

"Okay. Great."

She starts to say something else, but I push the button to end the call.

LARS

f you've ever been on an airplane, then I don't need to sell you on the light. It's of a different quality up here: purer, brighter, practically symphonic in its brilliance. Also, you can see the clouds from inside out. Although I can't actually feel the light to assess its texture, I bask in the warmth through the Plexiglas window.

A somewhat dour steward offers me something from his clanking cart, and even though I no longer drink (not because I've ever had a problem with alcohol, but because several of my prescriptions come with surely overblown warnings about not consuming alcohol, as well as not driving or operating heavy machinery), I ask for one of those tiny bottles of gin. Why not? The light is making me giddy, and I feel like celebrating. A toast to our new life in London! It's time to be positive, and now that we have three spanking-new skylights, I am turning the corner, leaning into optimism. A toast to Jorek, my savior, my new best friend! A toast to Dominique, and a mournful moment of silence, may he rest in peace!

The first two bottles go down nice and neat, and I feel a surge of something like euphoria. (Funny that they don't mention *this* as a possible side effect, instead of dwelling on the negatives.) I push the call button to summon the steward; given how much there is to celebrate, why not one or two or three more tiny bottles of gin?

Outside the window, I imagine below some cows and sheep and rolling dales, even though in reality we are probably over the ocean. The strangest part of this is that even though I am nicely insulated inside this metal tube, and actively trying *not* to think about my wife, the Bella transmission becomes increasingly clear, and even intrusive. No matter what I do to try to blot her out, she is right inside me, crystal clear.

I study the label to see if it might offer insight, but all it says is that it's been distilled in the U.K.; that it contains 47% alcohol and is 94 proof. The more I drink, the worse it gets. I see Bella in the taxi, even though it's pouring and the windows are clotted with rain. She is tapping in frustration at her phone. I see the chip in her red nail polish on the fourth finger of her left hand, beneath which is the wedding band she's twisting in circles, a tic that doesn't require a psychotherapist to deconstruct. I know that she is about to ask the taxi to pull over and drop her a few feet away, which seems to me a bad idea, given that she has only an already battered fold-up umbrella that will be useless in this sort of blustery, sideways-slashing rain. Also, she is wearing heels. She looks at her watch, fishes from her bag a twenty-pound note, and tells the driver to keep the change.

DID I TELL you that Bella and I first met on an airplane?

We met in business class, which, with hindsight, is a pretty soulless place to meet, and arguably all the detail that you need about Bella and me. I'd been on the circuit that summer, en route from the Hamburg Masters to a match in Cincinnati, which included in the itinerary a nonstop flight from Frankfurt to New York. Bella had been connecting home circuitously from Florence, where she'd gone on holiday to visit the family she'd lived with ten years earlier, during her junior year abroad. That's the wrong place to meet, at thirty thousand feet, sipping port and sampling runny French cheeses on someone else's dime. We both feigned sophistication, pretending to be the sort of discriminating travelers who could tell a Pont l'Évêque from a Brillat-Savarin, when in fact we were people who were privately content with Kraft cheese and cheap Pinot Grigio.

I wish I could say that a feigned enthusiasm, and then the eventual need for luxury items like five-star boutique hotels with high-thread-count sheets and Patek Philippe watches, is what led to our undoing, but it was much more complicated—or, really, maybe much more simple—than that. In fact, once I had been corrupted, the embrace of high-end consumer goods actually became a helpful balm.

Bella had been bumped up to business class the day we met (although it wouldn't be long before she was a regular on first-class manifests), and, me, I was deep into my fifteen minutes of fame, and had I only realized how short-lived they'd be, and how swift my descent, I would have doubled my consumption of port and smelly cheese that day.

It's hard to fathom, looking at me now, but as I may have mentioned, back then I turned heads. I had that celebrity rock-star glow. *Le Monde* had said of me just that week, "If the Romans were to name a God of Tennis, they would likely have named him Lars Jorgenson."

I was not the sort of obnoxious celebrity who wore mirrored aviator sunglasses indoors, but I admit that my habit of wearing an Adidas headband, even when I was in a suit, was its own version of swaggering. I was so giddy back in those days that I couldn't even say who was footing my bill. I had an agent who took care of those sorts of things, and I just speed-dialed him whenever any scheduling snags arose or some financial reckoning needed to be done.

Bella had had one of those enlightened but slightly dull, solidly middle-class childhoods somewhere in a San Francisco suburb famous for its staunch embrace of mid-century functionalist housing, a style she grew to hate. Now the place has been overrun by the newly rich, and the last time Bella and her sister went to visit and worked up the nerve to knock on the front door of their childhood home, they learned it had been purchased by a twenty-five-year-old who had designed an interactive beer-bong app. Bella's parents had both been academics, and from what she'd described, it was not the sort of hot-blooded household where hideous things were ever said, or dishes were flung; to the contrary, emotions were as repressed as the architecture, and it sometimes felt like she was living in a PBS series, or some reality show about whether a family could set out to raise two children in a community resembling some Scandinavian-inspired ideal. The most traumatic incident she ever reported was her sister falling off a swing and breaking her arm. Bella had been a model child—good grades, no miscreant teenaged behavior. Her only act of rebellion was to move back east to attend Barnard, even though her parents had pleaded with her to stay on the West Coast.

From every exam she took to every fellowship she applied for, Bella's trajectory was a steady upward arc. She got every job she wanted, as well as every man. Nothing got in her way until the day, two years into our marriage, that she met Raymond Branch.

What a difference those two years made! The Bella I met that day was humble, so giddy at her luck of being bumped up to business class, of being seated next to me (might I remind you that I was, back then, a handsome, famous tennis player?), that you might have supposed, as she settled into her seat, sorting out her belongings (laptop, newspapers, a novel called *Independence Day*), that coach was the only deprivation this woman had ever known.

So there we were, as fate would have it, sitting next to one another in 4A and 4B, in one of those subpar business-class situations lacking in the proper degree of privacy, which in our case turned out to be a plus. Before the plane became aloft, we had already discovered one another, and wasted no time in acknowledging our fierce attraction, clinking glasses of champagne, toasting—what?—we weren't quite sure—the few dazzling moments we sensed we'd experience in the forthcoming months, tinged with the slight foreboding that they would quickly turn ruinous? (The career-ending knee injury, the weight gain, the depression, the scum of the affairs, the child, the rabbit . . .) If there is a moral to the story, it is perhaps only this: people who are going to commit themselves to spending their lives together ought to be grounded at the moment of inception. I say this with no pun intended. A neighborhood barbecue, a college classroom, the aisle of a bookstore, or some sort of cute meet, like the accidental bumping of carts in a grocery store, dogs colliding in a Frisbee chase at the park, a mix-up of orders at the doughnut shop—those are good ways to meet, ways that might provide some sweet shared memory to lean into when things get rough. Of course, it's possible that the fissure already present at our inception might have had less to do with the empty trappings of United business class than with the fact that at least one of us was engaged.

Oh, it was real, all right. I fell in love with Bella, and, for the record, I am still in love with my wife.

I went back to Stockholm and called off the marriage to my childhood sweetheart. That these things happen every day does not diminish the heartbreak, and all these years later, I am not sure that my own mother has forgiven me. My family and friends all gossiped that I had been hijacked by my ego, and they may well have had a point. Such is the price of fame. Bella and I married shortly thereafter. It was a big, blingy wedding and I think we were happy for a time. We bought a new house in an exclusive suburban enclave. Although it was a bastardized Tudor, it was close enough to the sort of phony colony I dreamed about as a child who'd been raised on a diet of beamed-in American television. And though it has now become fashionable to disparage this style of living—to suggest that a place like The Flanders is the embodiment of excess and sprawl, and that this, combined with my own gas-guzzling Lincoln Navigator, is contributing to the breakdown of American society in general—that misses the point. What could possibly be wrong with living in a house one has earned, particularly when one is an upstanding citizen who pays his taxes and minds his own business and just wants to live a quiet life on a little patch of land? That this is how we live these days in the wealthier suburbs of Washington, D.C.—some of us, anyway— well, I can only say that this way of living was not my own very bad idea.

Digging into and embracing this life was my version of making the best of things once I could no longer do what I love after blowing out my knee in a practice tournament. I had three surgeries, first to reconstruct the cartilage, then two more to attempt to isolate the infection. Then the other knee collapsed in solidarity. I couldn't walk for months. I put on thirty pounds in less than a year, and once you put on thirty pounds, the next thirty practically puts itself on you, and ditto for the next, and then, before you know it, you are, by definition, clinically obese. So I think I deserve a little credit for trying to be happy with the things that money can buy: titanium golf clubs and a fourteen-cup Cuisinart Elite Food Processor, among my latest spoils.

I'm a wreck, man, but I think I might have rebounded with a little more support. But there you have it, yet another of those classic chicken-and-egg situations (like improving the lighting of the London house and whether to do it before or after we move in). Would Bella have fallen in love with Raymond Branch had I not gone down the tubes? Or was it because Bella fell in love with Raymond Branch that I was ruined?

IT DOESN'T OCCUR to me, or obviously to Bella until after she's stumbled along four blocks of uneven cobblestone in the rain, her heel twice getting caught in the grout, that she doesn't have the keys to the new house. I have one set of keys up here, tucked in my trouser pocket, and Jorek has another. The third is in our kitchen drawer, back home.

At least, by the time she arrives at East Heath Road, the weather

has begun to lift. She takes a scarf from her bag (the same one she
used a few days earlier to mop my sweat, I note tenderly) and dries as
best she can the stone bench outside the house, then sits down and
contemplates what to do. She looks at her phone, puts it in her pocket,
and stares up at the sky (perhaps looking for me?). After a moment,
she stands up and walks around to the back of the house and peers in
the window. She looks stricken. There's water on the living room floor.
An inch or so has seeped in through the roof, either from the poorly
fitted skylights or from the gash I made while having my euphoric
turn with the power tool. She feels that thing called stress again, then
silently curses Jorek. She pulls out her phone, intending to call him,
but realizes she doesn't have his number. She considers calling me,
then remembers I am up in the air, so she has no one with whom to
share the news that there seems to be massive water damage to our
new house.

She moves toward the ladder that Jorek has left leaning against
the brick, but has the good sense not to climb to the roof to inspect or
attempt any DIY repair. Instead, she makes a loop around the house,
inspecting each of the ground-floor windows, running her finger
along the brick like she's marking her territory with a trace of her
perfume. She then goes back to the bench again and pulls out her
phone. She stares at it contemplatively before dialing Elsa.

Her call goes to voice mail: "It's Elsa, yo, leave me a message and
I'll get back to ya!" Bella winces at the sound of the word "yo," and
also at the word "ya," and waits for the beep. "Hi, Elsa. It's Mom. Just
saying hi. Listen, when Dad gets home tonight, can you do me a favor
and have him call me right away? I know it will be very late, so, if you
are going to bed, maybe just leave him a note, okay? I'd leave him a
message or send an e-mail, but you know your dad. Tell him there's a
problem at the house. The new house. Well, not a problem, nothing
you need to worry about, just some water seepage. Tell him I need
Jorek's phone number. Okay, that's all. I miss you, Elsa. No more running off. Okay, darling? Hugs and kisses and socks!"

Bella sits for the longest time, and I think the look on her face, and the stuff churning through her head, might best be described as *wistful*. She is trying to visualize us here, a new beginning, light streaming in through the new double-glazed skylights, the water in the living room gone. She's thinking hopeful thoughts, imagining me stabilized, possibly even with a job or a constructive hobby that does not involve home repair. She sees Elsa bounding out of the house in the tartan skirt and blue blazer that are her new school uniform, safely on the other side of whatever phase she's currently transitioning through. Whatever it is, it's probably documentable: "At age ten and nine months, girls become somewhat moody and recalcitrant and are apt to record subtly snarky voice-mail messages with the subconscious goal of unnerving their mothers." Of course, Bella understands that Elsa is managing a lot right now. On top of the normal bodily changes, there's the indisputable fact that moving is hard. Bella feels awful uprooting her, but this is one aspect of things, possibly the only one, that she can't beat herself up about. Families move. This is a reality. Life goes on. In this world, Elsa is lucky to have a roof overhead, even one in which the rain is seeping through.

WITHIN MOMENTS, BELLA'S phone vibrates with a text from Elsa. It says, simply: "Socks!!!"

My wife smiles and texts back: "Socks!"

She puts the phone away, still smiling, but it vibrates a second later, and when she looks at the screen, it says: "You need 3 !!!s. Things shld come in 3s. Like the 3 blind mice."

Bella types: "!!! xxx"

"Or like, the pig, the naked starving person, and the bowl of tulips."

"?"

"You mean ???"

"???"

"But the pig is gone. So there's a new set of 3."

"Elsa what r u talking about?"

"I can't find the pig. When I get home I'm going to ask the Stager."

"Nabila said it would be better to let the Stager just do her job."

"She's nice Mom. U would really like her. She has purple nail polish like mine."

"Nice."

"Remember u said purple nail polish with sparkles was not for grownups?"

"No."

"You said it was tacky."

"I did not say it was tacky."

"Yes you did."

Bella remembers that each of these international texts is costing one dollar. "I think you misunderstood me," she writes. Although maybe she hasn't. Now Bella seems to have some dim memory of Elsa wanting to paint Bella's nails purple just before she left for a conference in Brussels, and she'd been in both a rush and a bad mood.

"Ok Elsa. I'm glad u like her but she has a lot of work to do."

"Ok. Wait. Mademoiselle Shapiro wants me to put the phone away."

"Oh my goodness, yes, put it away! I didn't realize u were in class."

"It's ok. I told her it's u. She knows u r very important and so she said it's ok."

"No. It's not ok. We'll talk later."

"Ok. Also I am going to leave the Stager alone but first she said we could paint the chair and fix the rabbit that has crooked ears."

"What are you talking about?"

"I painted a chair like the Stager. She likes to paint chairs. Ok bye Mom! Socks!!!"

"?"

Elsa doesn't reply, so Bella tries again: "Does she like to paint chairs, or pictures of chairs?"

Still no answer. Bella has been uneasy about having a stranger in her house, mucking around with her things, particularly while we're both away, but Amanda has insisted that the house needs staging in order to sell, and Bella figures this is probably true. After the house sat idle for three months the first time it was listed, she's in no position to argue. Disturbingly, Elsa seems to be weirdly fixated on this woman, the Stager, whoever she is. And this thing with chairs—does she paint the chairs themselves, like a furniture restorer, or does she paint pictures of chairs? It is a possibly important distinction.

Bella sends another text. "Did you hear my voice mail?"

After a moment, she writes again: "Don't forget your dad is on his way home. Remember to give him the msg."

I am, indeed, on my way home, and I order another tiny bottle of gin to celebrate this fact.

NOT SEEING RAYMOND was part of the promise Bella made when I learned of the affair. She said we were going to have complete transparency in our marriage, from that moment forth. "Transparency" became her favorite word. She used it in reference to her interactions with Raymond, to our finances, to her work and travel plans. I began to feel strangely proprietary about transparency, like it was *our* word, the key to *our* repair, and I bristled when I heard it used in other contexts (see transparent Belgian lace curtains, transparent data encryption, transparent fish, etc.). Then, when Bella was named Luxum's Vice-President for Transparency, I began to wonder if my life was someone's practical joke.

Even back in the pre-omniscient days, I knew more than she knew I knew, which is to say I knew not only about Raymond, but also the salient details of the sordid liaison with Guillermo Peña and the resultant mess. Guillermo she hadn't seen in ten years, although that had less to do with self-restraint than with the fact that he'd essentially disappeared off the face of the earth. Bella was under the impression that after his brief if celebrated three-year stint as the Yankees' first baseman, he'd gone back to El Salvador, although she could no longer recall where she might have heard this. Possibly from one of our housecleaners, who claimed—unreliably, I think—to be his distant cousin. Bella had tried to look him up, but there'd been no mention of him in cyberspace since his contract had failed to be renewed, which was only a few months after his name had surfaced in reference to performance-enhancing drugs. She wasn't really looking for him, but if she happened to run into him in a dark alley someday, she'd tell him not to worry—Elsa wasn't his, she didn't want anything from him, and, so far as she was concerned, it was for the best that he'd disappeared. She had no lingering interest in Guillermo. To be honest, she'd never had any real interest at all.

Raymond and Bella had both been huge Yankees fans, and they'd even once managed to attend a game together, which was something of a coup, since there were few opportunities for them to appear together in public. But back in the flush days of print journalism, the newspaper had leased a corporate box, and it was sometimes possible for employees, and even for summer interns such as Bella was at the time, to finagle a free ticket or two. Finagling was one of Bella's specialties, one of many sidebar talents, which is why she became such a successful banker. "Finagle" was not necessarily a word in Raymond's vocabulary: he got everything in life he wanted, and free baseball tickets was the least of it.

Hot dogs and beer, the national anthem sung by a troop of Boy Scouts from Staten Island, the whiff of Raymond with his fabulously exotic cologne, the name of which he refused (pretentiously) to disclose but which had traces of sandalwood and Scotch, his difficult-to-isolate accent, part British, part Irish, part New York. Bella had pulled out her phone and sent her friend a message: "I am love." (Not to be confused with the Italian movie of the same name, starring Tilda Swinton, which appeared several years later.)

Her friend had gotten stuck on the typo, which turned into a jokey exchange about whether Bella was in love, or whether she was love itself. They decided on the latter. Then the friend said that *being love* was fine, but being *in love* with Raymond was a train wreck.

Bella knew this already. It wasn't simply that they were both married, or that he had young children—that was the normal sort of train wreck that happens every day, whether of the sordid tabloid variety or the more refined opera-libretto version, in which the protagonists, because they are successful or highly educated, think their tryst of literary or cosmic significance. From the moment Bella laid eyes on Raymond, she knew it was going to be bad. Bad with the precision of a Swiss watch; you only had to read his poetry, steely and unsentimental and harsh, to get that he would add Bella to the list of people he'd eventually undo. He was not just a known philanderer; he was coldness personified, which might explain his need to so compulsively find women with whom to warm himself in bed. Even his rare pastoral sonnets (ears of corn, grazing sheep, farmhands with craggy faces, etc., etc.) had in their cadence a nuclear chill.

In a *New York Times* review of his most recent collection, *Black Monday*, the critic remarked that Raymond Branch's sonnets were defined by the same cold concision that made his name, back when he'd worked in finance, synonymous with Ivan Boesky. Did I mention that the thumb on his right hand was missing? Or that he leaned on a cane? Or that he was more than ten years older than Bella? I'm not sure what makes the man attractive to my wife; perhaps it is simply that he is not me.

That night, at the baseball game, after dating Bella for about six months (the use of the word "dating" was theirs, which added a quaint air of innocence, I suppose), Raymond tried to break it off. He delivered this information during the bottom of the sixth inning, with no prelude, at a particularly inelegant moment, when Bella had a hot dog stuffed in her mouth and a bit of mustard dribbling down her chin. She'd actually been thinking the very opposite sort of thought, had been in the midst of some sentimental or maybe just hormonal surge that had her fantasizing about leaving me, easing his wife out of the picture, and creating a future with Raymond, hanging curtains in the beautiful New York penthouse they used as a pied-à-terre. (Bella had been there a few times—Raymond was apparently not hampered by pedestrian sentiments about bringing other women into the marital bed.)

She figured he was bluffing about the breakup, even though Raymond had spent half the baseball game on his phone and at one point he told whoever was on the other end that he loved her; from what Bella could tell, he hadn't been speaking to Seema, his wife. She texted some of this to her friend, who replied sharply, "I told you he's an asshole."

Peña was on fire that night. He'd batted two home runs and had tagged Hernandez at first base. During one spectacular maneuver, Peña leaped into the air, twisting like he was about to do an acrobatic flip, glove extended, and fell flat on his back without dropping the ball, ending the inning with runners on each base. Raymond, who had missed the play since he'd been in the middle of sending a text, slipped his phone back into his pocket, clapped distractedly, and then gave Bella's knee a little squeeze. She leaned into him and whispered, as a joke, that if he ever really let her go, she'd get Guillermo Peña to take his place. He was the man of the moment, Guillermo, landing on the covers of the *New York Post* and the *Daily News* about once a week, celebrated for both his athletic prowess and his celebrity dalliances: he'd been spotted variously with an eighteen-year-old rapper who had just won a Grammy, and with the forty-seven-year-old philanthropist wife of a billionaire hedge-fund manager. One had at least to applaud his range. Raymond had laughed, and told her to go for it. Bella couldn't tell if he thought this was simply amusing in its audacity, or if he was mocking her. It hadn't really occurred to her at the time that Raymond didn't particularly care what she did.

What she didn't know, which might have saved her a little heartbreak, was that Raymond always cycled back to where he began. His life was one repetitive and multi-pronged adulterous loop, from which someone with a sharp eye and a dark sense of humor might have crafted a successful reality show.

All this occurred back before I was the beneficiary of omniscience, so I was getting my information the old-fashioned way, by reading her communications with eb@hotmail.com. I stopped reading Bella's e-mail long ago, and have simply taken her at her word when she volunteered that she hasn't had any contact with Raymond for more than ten years. We have tried not to talk about it, but his name has come up from time to time, most recently, in fact, when we saw his latest collection in a bookstore at Heathrow. When I inquired as to whether Raymond was currently in London, and whether that had anything to do with our relocation, the VP for Transparency implied that I was crazy and paranoid. And since I was, by this point, crazy and paranoid, she sort of had the upper hand.

And yet here I am, watching her navigate the labyrinthine streets of Hampstead Village like an old pro. Without consulting her map or her phone, she seems to know exactly where she's going, and it turns out to be only ten blocks from our new home. She takes a left turn and steps into a leafy cul-de-sac of stately multimillion-dollar Victorians, her eye drifting, on its own accord, to the largest address of them all. Tall and thin and severely vertical, with stone masonry and the kind of triangular arch on top that looks like it might impale a wayward bird, the house weirdly resembles Raymond himself. To say that is, of course, to ignore that on display in front of the house is the nourishing detritus of family life: Rollerblades on the doormat, a bicycle leaning casually against the tree, a shaggy dog with its head peeking out the downstairs window, gardening shears and gloves and a pair of women's clogs on the stoop.

No one understands what goes on inside the Branch home, but there are theories that have made their way even to someone as oblivious as me. Some speculate that Seema medicates herself into acceptance; more appealing is the possibility that she is one of those wonder women who are so above it all that they can absorb and forgive and simply not care. But the more salient theory, almost impossible to fathom, is that she simply doesn't know.

THE PILOT ANNOUNCES that we should buckle up; we're about to head into a bad patch of turbulence, and even before he finishes speaking, we hit a bump and the steward loses his balance and bits of cutlery go flying. In one gulp, I swallow what is left of my gin as a precaution against its spilling, and for a few minutes there, I lose my feed of Bella, which is now suddenly cutting in and out and is full of intermittent static. I try to order another gin to help refocus my point of view. I hit the call button, wait another couple of minutes, and then shout, but now the steward has been knocked to the floor by the turbulence and is being helped to his feet by a burly fellow passenger who shoots me an angry look. I fumble through my various pockets, trying to locate the Praxisis, but realize I must have put it in my bag in the overhead compartment, and when I try to get up, I'm quickly scolded about the seat-belt sign being on.

Even if my transmission is still a little fuzzy, I can see Raymond coming out of his house with a newspaper tucked under his arm. He turns a key in the top bolt of his door, checks his phone, then smiles and waves and goes to Bella. They begin to walk together in a way that suggests familiarity, fluidity, like they are figure-skating partners who know each other's moves. They walk several blocks toward the Heath, cross the busy road, and find a bench. It is only then that they kiss.

I refuse to believe this is happening, and am fairly desperate for it to end. I try several approaches, from putting on eyeshades and earplugs to turning on a movie, but nothing stops the transmission; to the terrifying contrary, the harder I try not to see, the clearer the picture becomes.

Since I cannot make this scene go away, I turn my focus to some children playing near where Bella and Raymond sit. Rosy-cheeked with white-blond hair, they appear to be twins. They're engaged in some sort of hunting game that seems incongruous with their earthy appearance. Across the way, a toddler kicks a ball; his rusty aim barely misses a pair of girls who sit cross-legged in the grass playing one of those games that involves wiggling fingers and a loop of string. It's all a bit much, these wholesome children at play, juxtaposed to my adulterous wife, and I am somewhat heartened by the sight of a couple of possibly delinquent teens sitting on a bench, smoking cigarettes and generally looking like they're up to no good; though I can't say exactly why this comes as a relief, it's helpful, I suppose, to be reminded that the world is a generally murky place full of people and their problems.

I'm in shock, and yet I'm not surprised. I've figured out a thing or two in my years-long decline, and I've had plenty of time to philosophize. I haven't quite honed my central thesis, but it's along the lines of this: Clichés, character types, archetypes—all true. We each have our place in the world, and I, Lars Jorgenson, was apparently put on this earth to play the role of sap.

Yet there are purpose and dignity in my degradation. I am a vessel. I absorb and contain the fallout of other people's sins. I wake with my animal nightmares so that others can sleep tight.

ELSA

abila and her friend Annie, the one who had said I was "a little chunky," are standing by the stove. Annie is stirring something in a large saucepan, and Nabila has just taken a dish out of the oven. She removes her mitt and curses when she accidentally grazes the side of the rack with her bare hand.

"We made you your favorite dinner," says Nabila. "Macaroni and cheese and French fries."

"I had that for lunch."

"Oh, bummer. Well, for dessert, we also got you every flavor Pop-Tart that Annie could find at Safeway."

"I don't want a Pop-Tart anymore. That was yesterday. What I want today is a fairy cake. Can I have a glass of milk, please?"

"What's a fairy cake?" asks Annie.

"Enough already with the fairy cakes," says Nabila as she goes to the refrigerator to get the milk.

"In a wineglass, please," I add. "The big one that you are supposed to use for Chardonnay, not the smaller one that's for one of the other kinds, like the red wines."

Nabila stares at me for a long time before she goes to the cabinet to get a wineglass. She holds it by the stem and sets it in front of me. "Here you go, mademoiselle."

"Listen, Elsa," she says, "I want to ask you something private. Well, private between you and me and Annie."

"Sure."

"Something is missing from my room, and I wonder if you know anything about it."

"The bag of leaves, you mean?"

Nabila and Annie exchange worried looks.

"What were you doing, snooping around in my stuff?"

"I wasn't snooping around, I was cleaning up your room for you. You shouldn't leave wet towels on the floor. And you should hang up your clothes so they don't get all wrinkled."

"Pretty rich for *you* to tell *me* to clean up my room!" I'm not sure I've ever seen Nabila this mad. "I'd like the bag back. And I'd like for this to remain private. I can do something for you in return."

"Like what?"

"What would you like?"

This is intriguing, but I can't think of what I want in return, other than not to move to London, or for Diana to be nice to me, or maybe not to have to run laps at field-hockey practice.

"Why, what's in the bag? Is it drugs?"

"No. I don't know what's in the bag. The guy at the farmstand in front of Unfurlings gave it to me and he said it was tea. But, honestly, I don't really know what it is. Annie and I tried to drink it, but it doesn't really taste like tea. It could be something else, and we don't want to get in any trouble."

"Did you try to smoke it? Or maybe chop it up and snort it up your nose? But wait, if it's marijuana, I think you are supposed to roll it up in paper, like a cigarette. You only snort it if it's cocaine. But also now you can chop up your parents' prescription drugs and snort those. We learned this in the DARE class at school. The police officer showed us. I can probably help. Do you have any rolling paper?"

"Elsa! Please don't even say stuff like that. We don't want to upset your mum. You know how hard she's working. She has a lot on her mind, and I want her to think I'm taking good care of you. Lord knows I'm trying."

"But we're moving to London, and you're staying here to go to college anyway, so why do you care?"

"Well, for one thing, because, believe it or not, I care about you and your family. But also because I need a reference, darling. And your mum has agreed to sponsor me for a green card."

I don't know what a green card is. But I do know this: this is an opportunity. "I won't ever tell my mom, but you have to let me play with the Stager."

"What is your obsession with this woman? We need to let her do her job. She spent an hour helping me find you the other day, and another hour yesterday helping me deal with that dead rabbit. Plus, your mom wants you to stay away from that woman. She said something about how this doesn't sit right."

"My mom isn't here, is she? And she's never even met the Stager. And I'm not obsessed with her! We just had some fun playing with the dolls, and I like her nail polish, and she paints chairs, and we need to finish the painting I started yesterday of Dominique in a chair, and also I never even asked her if she likes her wallet."

"Her wallet?"

"I can't tell you. It's private."

"Good grief, girl. What's gotten into you these last few days? Oh, look! It's seven-oh-three already. I'm so silly, I almost forgot. Let's turn on the television."

She hits the remote, and there's my mom right away, sitting across a table from another lady. My mom is wearing her green dress, as promised, and when she leans forward, I can see the lacy part of her bra. I want to yell to her, "Mom, sit up straight, we can see your bra!" but I know she won't hear me, not just because I totally get that the show is prerecorded, plus she's in London in a television studio and I'm sitting in a kitchen in Maryland with a plate full of macaroni and cheese and French fries, but also because my mom is busy speaking. "No, Maria, I understand what you're saying, but there are some who might suggest that argument is faulty. Luxum's problems are completely in the past. From now on, we're all about the Sunshine Act. Look at our new CEO, he's . . ."

I grab the remote from Nabila's hand and turn off the television. Then I bring my plate to the trash and scrape all the uneaten macaroni and cheese and French fries into the bin. "I'm going upstairs to find the Stager," I say.

Nabila stares at me, incredulous, which is a word that means skeptical, unbelieving. Then the Stager appears at the kitchen entrance. She's putting her sweater on, getting ready to go home. She gives me a pat on the head like I'm a dog and says, "Good night, Elsa. Sweet dreams."

"But we didn't get to paint!"

"Maybe tomorrow."

"I don't want to paint tomorrow. I want to paint now."

"Now, now, Elsa, you know you're a big girl and you're not supposed to behave this way. Your mother wouldn't be very happy about this, would she?" says Nabila.

"My mother isn't here, is she?"

Annie makes a tsk-tsk noise with her tongue.

"Well, she was a minute ago, until you shut off the television!" says Nabila.

"Is that supposed to be a joke? She's in London, and it's, like, already midnight there. Don't you know that? The television isn't real!" I know I should be nicer to Nabila, because where she comes from maybe they don't have television, so she might not know you can tape things in advance and air them hours, or even days or weeks, later.

"I'm ready to go home now anyway, I just need to get my stuff from upstairs before I leave, so what if we paint tomorrow, Elsa?" the Stager asks.

"But yesterday you promised we'd finish painting today!" I'm aware that I'm being obnoxious.

"I'm going to call your mother and tell her how you're behaving if you don't stop this right now, Elsa," says Nabila.

"No, you're not!"

Nabila looks at me, doubly incredulous, and goes into the kitchen, gets the phone, brings it into the hallway, and starts to punch the buttons. "I'm going to put the Stager on the phone, too, so she can explain how you are not letting this nice lady do her job. Boy oh boy, is your mum going to be angry with you, Elsa!"

"Hang up the phone or I'll tell my mom about your bag of leaves."

"Elsa!"

"Let's all calm down," says the Stager. "Don't call Bella. Look, here's a good compromise. What if we work on the painting for just a few minutes? Ten minutes or so? Whatever we do, we'll need to let it dry overnight, right? Then, in the morning, we can paint on top of what we do now. And you do whatever it is Nabila tells you, okay? Is that okay with you, Nabila?"

Nabila looks at Annie and shakes her head in disbelief. But on our way up the stairs, I remember the red paint on the floor. I'm in enough trouble as it is, so I recalibrate and try to divert the Stager into a different room.

"Wait! I have a better idea," I say. "I don't want to paint anymore. Let's read a story."

"Sure. Let's pick a book from your shelf."

"No, let's go to my mom and dad's room and you can make up a story."

"Why would we do that? I'm not so good at making up stories. Let's go to your room and read a Max book."

"I don't want to read a Max book."

"Um, okay. You have lots of other books to choose from."

"We're going to my parents' room," I say, running up the stairs. There's a small table on the landing outside my room, next to the bathroom, and I see the Stager's bag. I grab it and run up the next flight.

"Now you *have* to come read to me upstairs!" I call, leaning over the banister. "I have your keys, so you can't go anywhere until you come up here!"

Nabila is standing at the bottom of the staircase, looking up at me. She says something in her native language that I can't understand, but it doesn't sound good.

I HAVEN'T BEEN to the top floor, where my parents' bedroom is, for about two days. When I get there, things are different, especially in the bathroom in the hallway. Even though this bathroom is up a flight of stairs, it's the one I like to use, since the one that connects to my room is too pink. My mom said we could repaint to make it more appropriate for a girl my age, but that was before she got the Important New Job and announced that we had to move to London. Obviously the Stager doesn't know this, because in the green bathroom she's put everything away like she did in the kitchen, except, instead of hiding the toaster, in here she's hidden my toothbrush and toothpaste, and also there's no shampoo in the shower, so I don't know how I'm going to wash my hair. Another thing that's different is, the towels are folded like in a hotel and the bath mat is gone. I'd really liked that bath mat, and had even picked it out from a catalogue; it was very shaggy, and it reminded me of a Labradoodle . . . well, actually more of a goldendoodle, because of its color. Another bag from Target sits on the counter, and I open it. Inside is a new bath mat, but this one has flat hair, like a sheep that's just been shorn, which I know about because Diana had a birthday party at her weekend farm in Middleburg, where we got to ride horses and look at the animals—but only look. We couldn't pet them, because we might get *E. coli* germs.

Things in the hallway are different, too. I don't understand why at first, but then I realize the Stager has taken down all of the framed family photographs; on the wall right in between the green bathroom and the extra bedroom, where my grandma used to stay before she died, there was one of those big frames that have room for lots of pictures inside of it, and there were, like, twenty pictures of us from a bunch of summers at the beach, and also some of the drawings I made when I was really young, like one of a cow that says, "When I am a cow I will moo!," which is a ridiculous and embarrassing thing to have drawn, but my mom had said, "Don't be silly, Elsa, it's very cute!" There's one of me and my dad playing mini-golf, and there is one of me and my cousins eating ice cream, and there's one of me and my mom that is my favorite, where we're lying in beach chairs with sunglasses, reading books, and we both look up and smile for the camera at the same time. I like this picture because everyone says me and my mom look exactly the same in it. And we do. Except that was before I started eating more than I should, and now I'm not sure I look like her anymore.

"What sort of story would you like, Elsa?" the Stager asks as she comes up the stairs behind me. She looks, and sounds, worn down. I feel bad. I'm not sure how to make it better—I've done so many things wrong these last few days.

"Something funny about Moses."

"I already told you my funny Moses story. Remember, about Moose?"

"Yeah. Well, if you really don't have another story about her, tell me about the boy in your wallet."

"The boy in my wallet?" She looks confused, and then alarmed. "When were you in my wallet?"

"You didn't see?"

"See what?"

"I straightened it all up for you. I organized everything."

"Wow, is it possible that I've been so busy the last couple of days that I haven't even opened my wallet? Let me think . . . Did I get gas, or groceries, or cash . . . ? How crazy is that? It's like I'm in some liminal space in this house."

"What does that mean?"

"Just that time seems to have stopped. Like I'm in some other world. Some parallel universe."

I look at her, confused.

"Don't listen to me. I'm just rambling."

"Well, come in here and tell me a story."

"Okay, but can I have my wallet? You have me a little concerned."

"You'll have to come get it." I'm hugging her bag tight to my chest as I step back into my parents' room.

"Don't worry. It's all fine. I didn't take anything."

"I believe you, but still, I should check. I mean, I have a lot of important things in there. My license, my credit cards."

"It's all there, I promise. Just come in." I take her hand and try to pull her inside, but even though she's tiny, she's still stronger than me, and I can't get her to budge.

"Elsa . . ."

"What's the big problem? We're going to my parents' room. You're supposed to stage that room, aren't you, Mrs. Stager? Oh, sorry! I mean *Ms.* Stager."

"I was already in here and decided it doesn't need staging."

"What about all of the pictures on the dresser? Like the wedding pictures and stuff. I thought you have to *depersonalize* everything!"

"Well, I do, it's true."

"So come on!" I give up trying to pull her in, and instead I run inside and flop onto my parents' bed. I love this bed. The mattress is soft and the duvet is beautiful, blue and yellow with lotus flowers. My mom got it in India, which is where the bed is from, and whenever

I see it I want to jump on it, even though I'm not supposed to any-more, on account of being too old (or maybe just too *chunky*) to jump on a bed. But I do anyway. A few feathers escape from one of the pillows when I land, and they fly up in the air; then one floats onto the sleeve of my shirt.

"Be careful, Elsa," the Stager says. She's still standing in the doorway.

"What's the big deal? You look like you're afraid!"

"Okay, I have an idea. Instead of reading a story, maybe you can help me. Why don't you take those pictures off the dresser and very carefully put them away."

"Okay. I can be the stager helper!"

"Exactly. In fact, take everything off the dresser and, very, very carefully, put it all . . . how about right there?" she says, pointing to the big carved chest.

"The maharajah cabinet?"

"Whatever . . . the one right there."

"Yeah, that's the maharajah cabinet," I explain. "We call it that because, look, you can see the maharajah painted there. He's playing polo! My mom had this shipped back when she went to India for work."

"Yes, fine, put the pictures in there. But be very careful," she says. She's still standing in the doorway.

"She got the bed in India, too, when she went there to have a meeting. She got it on the same trip when she got the maharajah cabinet. We had to wait, like, three months for it to be shipped."

"The bed? No, she got it in Jakarta."

"That's in . . ."

"Indonesia."

"Why are you saying that?"

"That Jakarta is in Indonesia?"

"No, silly! That she got the bed in Indonesia!"

"Oh . . . I don't really know that. I'm just saying it looks Indonesian."

"Have you been there?"

"I have."

"Why? Do you get to travel all over the world like my mom and go on television?"

"No, sweetheart, I don't. But once I went to Indonesia with a friend."

"That's funny. My mom went to Indonesia with a friend, and she told me she almost bought a bed there but something bad happened and so she didn't. That's why, when she saw this bed in India and it looked almost the same, she said she had to buy it. I want to go to Indonesia with a friend someday. Maybe with Diana."

"Be careful what you wish for," the Stager says.

"What do you mean?"

"Nothing. Never mind. I'm just talking too much. Here, do me another favor," she says, "as long as we're here and you are being so helpful." She goes into the green bathroom and comes back with a cloth and tells me to wipe the top of my mom's dresser. Then she tells me to go to my dad's dresser and also to take everything off the top and put it in the maharajah cabinet, too. Then she tells me to wipe *that* with the cloth, like I don't have anything better to do, like clean my own room, or do my homework.

"Why don't you just come in here and do this yourself?" I ask.

"You are doing such a great job, I don't have to," she says.

"Do you want me to put my dad's medicines away, too?"

"His medicines?"

"Yes. Here, on the dresser, he has this little tray. But I guess he took most of the bottles to London. I think this one is empty, so maybe I should throw it away."

"No, you shouldn't throw it away. Look, just put it in the medicine cabinet in the bathroom, okay?"

I remember what my mother has said about privacy, and feel a wave of shame. Even though she says that things to do with fathers staying in their rooms and taking pills for depression are all "totally normal," they are also not meant to be "publicly broadcast." Those were the words my mom used when she spoke to me about keeping things private after my teacher called her to say I'd been talking about my dad at school. I get it, but I also know what "publicly broadcast" means, and it's not as if I actually went on television and talked to millions of people about it. And if I did, at least I wouldn't have the lace of my bra showing.

"Fine. I'll put it in the medicine cabinet. But aren't you going to come in here and stage the bathroom?"

"Yes, I will. Maybe tomorrow. I'm a little tired right now."

"If you're tired, you should come lie down. You should rest, so we can paint again. I have an idea. Instead of painting just one rabbit in a chair, we paint, like, a hundred tiny rabbits in a hundred tiny chairs. I was thinking we could make a grid, like a wall calendar, but instead of dates, each one would have a different rabbit in a different chair."

"That's very creative, Elsa."

"It could be a tribute to Dominique. Maybe we could even make a Dominique wall calendar."

"Great idea. But it sounds like a lot of work. Maybe we should wait until we have more time and energy."

"Well, if you come in here and have a rest, you'll have energy! I'm telling you, this is the best bed in the world. Sometimes when my mom and dad are away I like to sleep in it."

"I can't lie in your parents' bed, Elsa. That's just not very . . . professional."

Her phone starts ringing, but she just stands there. I take it out of her bag and hold it up in the air. "Come in and get it!" I say.

"It's okay. Just let it go to voice mail."

I look at the display. "It's Amanda."

"Okay, thanks, Elsa. I'll call her back."

"Do you want me to tell her that?"

"No, Elsa, I want you to put the phone back in my bag and to sit down, and even though it's not my job to discipline you, I want you to behave. You are giving poor Nabila a lot of grief, and now look what you're doing to me."

The phone stops ringing, and then, a few seconds later, there's a text from Amanda that says "c u at oldchester." I report this news.

"Great. Thanks. I actually have to go, so can you give me my bag?"

"What's oldchester?"

"It's the name of the street where I'm staging a house."

"You're staging another house?"

"Yes. That's my job, remember?"

"Is it nice? Is it nicer than our house?"

"It's nice, but it's very modern, very different from your house. Listen, I really do have to go," she says. "I'm going to be late as it is."

"You can't go, because I have your bag."

"I'm aware of that, you scoundrel. Can I have it back, please?" She's switching strategies, trying to sweeten me up.

"Not until you come in here and see how comfortable the bed is. And you said you'd tell me a story!"

"If I come in there, I'm going to tickle you!"

"So tickle me!"

"Elsa, this is really ridiculous. We've just wasted all the time I had for storytelling. We'll do it tomorrow. I promise. And we'll paint, and we'll work on your calendar idea, but right now I really must go."

I reach into her bag and start to dig through it. "Let me just show you the wallet . . . Where is it? Boy, this is a huge bag, and you have so much stuff in here!"

"Elsa, it's really not polite to rifle through someone else's personal belongings."

"Yeah, just a sec . . . What's this?" I feel something hard and cold and round with two sharp points. It takes me a second to realize what it is, and when I do, I scream even louder than when I'd found the dead rabbit in the pool.

"Elsa!" the Stager says. "Good grief. Calm down!"

I take a deep breath and scream again.

Nabila comes running up the stairs, and she, too, says "Elsa, calm down!"

Suddenly I can't breathe. I'm making loud wheezing noises. The Stager comes into the room and pulls me down into a sitting position and rubs my back while Nabila runs to my room and gets my inhaler. I need two puffs before I can breathe freely again. Then I exclaim: "The Stager is a thief!"

The Stager looks at me, her eyes wide. "Elsa! That's a horrible thing to say. Apologize!"

"You *are* a thief! Look, Nabila. She has the pig!" I pull it out of the bag and hold it up in the air. "The Stager stole the pig."

We all stare at the little pig, its ears sticking straight up, the crooked, jaunty smile on its face. I give it a shake. We hear the rattle, like it has bits of sand inside.

PART II

DIFFERENT
CHAIRS

EVE

t's true that in my friendship with Bella there was always a slight unease, a micro-seed of discord that might have remained dormant but for the dramatic circumstances of our demise. The first time I laid eyes on her, my body tensed and my system went on full alert, as if with some primal knowledge of this friendship, of its capacity to nurture and transform me, and then inflict a devastating wound.

My response that first night was weirdly physical, although, in retrospect, that likely had to do with her smell. A gentle breeze, a harbinger of the thunderstorm that would soon send us all rushing indoors, hectic with the thrill of impending catastrophe that only an innocent weather event can bring, delivered to the pillar against which I was leaning the distinctive whiff of Bella: Jo Malone gardenia lotion, and Tide laundry detergent, as I would soon come to learn.

There were twelve of us summer interns, and about twenty editors and assorted VIP guests gathered at our boss's P Street mansion that evening. We were ushered out back for pre-dinner mingling, into a garden so stiffly manicured that even the rosebushes looked starched. A glimpse of the swimming pool glistening in the middle distance of the sprawling grounds made me begin to perspire, and I tried to be discreet in using the tiny cloth cocktail napkin to mop the beads of sweat that pooled at my neck. Uniformed waiters proffered drinks and a variety of ethnically incongruent finger foods: kebobs, sushi, and samosas had been staples of the rotation so far. It was hard to look professional while ripping chicken off a skewer with one's teeth, and nearly impossible not to dribble the accompanying peanut dipping sauce, but this seemed preferable to giving the impression of being too nervous, or weight-conscious, to eat.

Bella, a few feet away and in a white dress, seemed to be suffering no such qualms about etiquette. I watched her pop a California roll in her mouth and then, while chewing, take a sip of wine, accidentally dribble a bit on her white linen dress, and dab at the spot with a napkin, all while carrying on a conversation with the deputy political editor. Personally, I would have been embarrassed if I'd spotted my dress with wine, or worried I might have rice stuck in my teeth, but I got the impression that Bella didn't care, and such absolute self-confidence was the quality I would come to admire most over the course of our complicated, and ultimately devastating, friendship.

Bella and I hadn't had much previous contact at work, although I'd noticed her in the newsroom, looking like the sort of girl reporter only a fashion editor could dream up—as if any of us, apart from Bella anyway, really wore pencil skirts, tailored blouses, and pumps with just the right amount of heel to work. She was an intern on the business desk, and she unabashedly explained to anyone who asked that she was essentially just doing time at the paper, expanding her own knowledge base before moving on to banking, and that she had no real aspirations of becoming a journalist. This didn't mean she wouldn't excel, of course. Bella excelled at everything she did.

I was doing time myself, although without the direction or focus of my future best friend. For me this was a complete lark. As with everything in my life, I had sort of drifted into this place. I was an artist, a floater, an oddity. I was apparently the only applicant in the history of the intern program to have specified the Home and Design section as her first-choice assignment.

Despite our different interests and professional metabolisms, Bella and I became fast friends. There was an easy, if unlikely, camaraderie between us, as well as what would quickly develop into deep affection, but the thing that threw us together initially was (and this is embarrassing in its simplicity and its clichéd, girlfriendy nature) our shared love of books. Not just any books, but, well, clichéd, girlfriendy books, the sort that serve as a code for people who think, or think they think, the same way—*Breakfast at Tiffany's* cropped up in our first conversation, and I would come to wonder, with the subsequent high drama that seemed to fuel Bella's life, if she had simply read too many books. Maybe she couldn't settle into normalcy because she saw herself as some tragic femme, some postmodern Holly Golightly who happened to be saddled with dull middle-class concerns like a husband and a mortgage. That was one way to look at it. Another was that she was a narcissistic woman who made a series of bad choices that resulted in your garden-variety mess.

We were both several years older than the others in our group, most of whom had just finished graduate school, and a few of whom were just out of college. Also, perhaps more compellingly, we were among the very few interns who were already married, and, meaningfully or not, we quickly discovered that both of our marriages were showing early warning signs of trouble.

I was late to journalism, having spent most of the first post-college decade painting, reading voraciously, and picking up occasional freelance work in the art department of the local newspaper, where my husband, whom I had married the same year I graduated from college, worked. I had applied to this intern program on a whim, or maybe on an unspoken dare. My chances of landing a coveted slot were about the same, I figured, as those of buying a winning Powerball ticket. I'd put in an application only because of Vince. Vince, who had been a part of my life for so long, since junior high school in fact, that he simply *was*, like the watch you strap around your wrist each morning, or maybe like the wrist itself. That we had come to take each other for granted was actually more the strength of our marriage than the problem. The problem, which I hadn't yet fully come to appreciate, was on evidence here, at this garden party, where I leaned against the pillar of a gazebo, and where he did not.

Vince had a graduate degree in journalism and two years' experience on the small but edgy alternative paper in Minneapolis, where we had lived until moving to D.C. a month earlier. I'd always been the first pair of eyes on everything he wrote; accordingly, I'd been coaching him on the internship application. At some point along the way, I began to fantasize about my own answers to the questions, and I wondered how one embarked on a career as a writer, or maybe even as a professional illustrator, in the field of home design. I found this idea so intriguing that I would have been happy to be just the person who brought the writer or professional illustrator his or her lunch. I tossed out the idea of putting in my own application, and Vince was encouraging, if condescendingly so. He assumed that I didn't stand a chance; intern slots at the premier newspaper in Washington, D.C., were usually awarded either to hot-shot kids just out of the Ivy League, or to young reporters, such as my husband, with already promising if fledgling careers, but almost certainly not to thirty-year-old women who had spent about a decade illustrating pictures of settees and chairs for furniture catalogues. I can only assume my application caught the eye of some similarly aimless soul on the selection committee who was impressed by my half-baked essay about the intersection of art and journalism and the benefits of not getting caught in a rut, or, perhaps more inspiringly, someone had actually believed in what I was proposing to do, and thought some of my whimsical suggestions for improving the newspaper's anemic Home and Design section were worth exploring. Whatever the explanation, I was hired into the intern class of the summer of 2000, and Vince was not. Nevertheless, it seemed a good moment for change, so we loaded a U-Haul and moved.

Bella was in her early thirties, although in her own career path nothing had been left to chance, even if her trajectory didn't follow the typical straight line. She had a fierce ambition, and had set out to collect as much varied work experience as possible to add to her already impressive résumé, which included a stint teaching English in China, a year interning at an investment bank in Hong Kong, an M.B.A. from Wharton, and now this prestigious internship.

It was the kind of hellishly humid evening that caused me to recall that Washington was once considered a hardship post for foreign diplomats; I self-consciously slipped into garden-party small talk about this with two of my fellow interns who happened to work on the Metro desk. With the summer air so thick you could almost hold it in your fist, along with a malarial mosquito or two, incentives were needed to lure people here. For most of the ascendant young professionals—the men in khakis and preppy striped ties, the women in floral summer dresses, everyone looking like slightly poorer, shabbier versions of the senior editors they hoped one day to be—the promise indicated by an invitation to a party such as this was surely all the incentive that was required. Besides, anything was possible on an evening like this. The editor-in-chief's wife, for example, had been a somewhat mousy brunette from the class of 1990; rumor had it that she'd apparently had too much to drink the evening of her own intern party and had dived naked into this very same swimming pool. Her wild streak, not to mention her presumed promiscuity, was the talk of the newsroom for a while, but a month or so later, a monster rock showed up on her ring finger, and she proclaimed herself the fiancée of our boss, at which point the rumor mill froze; as if in a game of verbal tag, no one wanted to be remembered as having said the last, wrong thing. Once his divorce was finalized, she became the fourth Mrs. Roth, and had held that spot for seven long years, which was, apparently, a record. This was what I'd heard, anyway, as prelude to the pool in the lunchroom that day regarding whether it was time for a fifth Mrs. Roth, and if so, who from our intern class was most likely to take the literal plunge. Bella's name topped the list, notwithstanding that she was already married.

WHAT I FOUND most inspiring about Bella Sorkin wasn't her beauty—although she was striking in an unconventional way, a newsroom Modigliani with her crooked nose and hazel eyes that didn't quite match, everything just slightly, perfectly, askew—it was that she looked like she belonged. Not just there, at that garden party, but wherever she happened to be. She didn't look like me—a recent transplant from the Midwest with a thin résumé and a marriage that was beginning to show its first cracks—in fact, I think part of my attraction had to do with the impression she gave of being so blessedly unfettered. At least, that's what I thought as I studied her from a few feet away, while feeling a pang of guilt over having left Vince at home. Discussions about whether he would come with me this evening had been fraught. I was of the school that this was not a big deal unless he allowed it to be, that the thing to do was simply to shrug off the surely random rejection by the selection committee and accompany me to the intern party and move on, look for a job, maybe even make a connection or two at this event. He was extremely talented, and it was easy enough to imagine the scenario that had him in a position of power at this or some other newspaper just a few years down the line, laughing about that moment when his wife got the job and he did not, the way an actress might boast about the number of auditions endured before the big break. Perhaps it was easy for me to say I would have happily accompanied him had the shoe been on the other foot. Nevertheless, he had said he'd come with me that evening but then pleaded the sudden onset of a summer flu.

I stood inside the gazebo, watching Bella while half engaged in a conversation with my colleagues about the capture two days earlier of a local serial arsonist who had been making headlines for a couple of months. It had been the predominant story in the region all summer, and most everyone was giddy, having been up for nearly forty-eight hours, getting the newspaper through two cycles of breaking news. I felt slightly guilty, or at least like I wasn't pulling my weight, having been sequestered over in the Home and Design section, working on a story about the best places in the Mid-Atlantic region to view the forthcoming fall foliage. I listened to Ahmed, a twenty-two-year-old whiz kid who had been the editor of his college newspaper, explain that he'd been instructed to call victims for reaction quotes, and how embarrassed he was to have to interview people who'd just lost their homes, their pets, and in some cases even their families, and ask such stupid and invasive questions.

I made a quip about how, if there was going to be a spate of serial arson, it wasn't surprising it should have happened this summer, what with the record-breaking heat. I should have stopped there, but in a short, boastful monologue that would later make me cringe, I heard myself go on about how it had been so hot the entire month of August that meek little wives would fondle the edges of their carving knives and study their husbands' necks.

I drew perplexed stares, and felt suddenly old. I turned my gaze toward Bella, a few feet away, and watched her throw her head back and laugh at some thread of conversation I strained unsuccessfully to hear. No sign of nervousness, no darting of the eyes as she mingled with her superiors, no sign of concern as she bit into another piece of sushi that she might have just said something profoundly dumb, or that she felt self-conscious about her age. I sensed I was observing a woman who did not appear to have spent the better part of the week fretting about what to wear to this party, or what she should, or should not, say, to any number of the important people in this room, including the newly elected mayor of D.C., or the famous financier turned poet, Raymond Branch, who had roomed with our boss, Norman

Roth, when they'd both spent a year at the London School of Economics back in the 1980s. They had remained close friends.

Bella must have noticed me staring, and she looked at me and smiled. She then came over to where I stood, and we all shook hands and made the usual round of introductions.

"Eve sounds a little unhinged. She was just going on about wives and carving knives and husbands' necks. Ought I call and warn someone?" Ahmed asked.

"Oh, I love Raymond Chandler!" said Bella.

I felt like throwing my arms around her, and I confess I nearly did. Quickly the conversation moved on to other books we loved. Joan Didion essays punctuated by dust motes, gauzy curtains, and certain slants of light. I had never before encountered anyone with a specific memory of the description of, yes, of all things, a chair, from *Breakfast at Tiffany's*. More specifically, one sofa and chairs, plural: "fat chairs upholstered in that itchy, particular red velvet that one associates with hot days on a train."

Was this enough of a foundation upon which to build a friendship? A mere convergence of taste in books? Well, it's not nothing, not something to be shrugged away. But with hindsight, to have thrown myself at Bella as if I had just found true love, to have assumed we spoke the same language, that we would make the same well-considered choices, that we would never betray a husband or a friend? That's a different story, as it happens. I can only say that, just like that, Bella Sorkin was my new best friend.

This may sound like a stretch, and yet it's true that, at some basic level, everything you need to know about me and about Bella Sorkin, the entire DNA of our friendship, is contained in the moment of our meeting. Though there's a painful and salacious narrative that bookends the then and the now of me and Bella Sorkin, it's also true that you can isolate that moment at the party and map the entire me-and-Bella story, the arc of my conflicting, jealous emotions so easily tamed by her attention. Of the wrenching outcome when things went bad.

It's mind-boggling to consider that there at the party was Raymond Branch. He seemed to me a bit of a cad, what with his slicked, thinning hair, the smart linen suit with a silk handkerchief protruding from the breast pocket, the polished wingtips—who dressed that way for a casual summer garden party, in Washington, in August? But he was so handsome in that worldly way of an older man that his vanity was forgiven, at least by some. One other distinctive thing about Raymond that added to his supposed allure (please know that he did nothing for me personally): while he was spending that year at LSE, he rode in a subway car that got blown up by the IRA. His leg was mangled when the aluminum ceiling collapsed, pinning him for hours, and he also lost a thumb. Oh, he was a catch, all right, but I'd suggest that, had he been anything other than a gazillionaire with two celebrated collections of published poetry—had he been employed as, say, a Target cashier—a girl might not necessarily have swooned to see him wobble through the crowd, his four fingers clutching the stem of a glass from which wine sloshed over the rim.

At some point while Bella and I were talking, I noticed the two of them connect. He walked over to us, and small talk ensued. The weather provided a natural opening, since we were clearly moments from the eruption of a violent summer storm. Quickly the subject drifted to baseball—there was a game of some import that night, and they were concerned it would be rained out. Bella and Raymond discovered they were both Yankees fans, which, too, would prove farcically, tragically significant. Then a woman who was presumably Raymond's wife came over, and he put an arm around her waist and introduced her as Seema. Raymond's wife was Indian, or so I presumed from her coloring and jewelry, and the textured shawl draped artfully around her shoulders. Bella and Seema began to chat. Bella complimented her on her shawl, and Seema unwound it from her shoulders so both women could inspect the cloth, and then Bella tried it on. Moments later, pictures of the three Branch children were produced from Seema's small jeweled bag. Bella made a fuss, asking their names and ages, then cooing loudly about the adorableness of each one.

Did I sense, all at once, something bad in the air? By this I mean something more than the obvious rumbles of thunder. I don't mean to suggest that I'm prophetic; if I were able to see the future, then I'd have no excuses for my own bad choices, including the one I made that night to attach myself to Bella. I could tell, or I thought I could tell, that Bella had her sights set on Raymond, which made me uneasy. I politely excused myself, aware that I had become extraneous to this conversation.

Inside the house, alone in the dining room, I watched the catering staff tend to some final arrangements. A woman roughly my age, dark eyeliner unsuccessfully masking too many late nights working parties such as this, gave me a weary smile as she lit the votive candles scattered throughout the room. Another waiter appeared and poured ice into the tubs behind the bartender's station, while a third made final adjustments to the arrangement of the food platters, in one case replacing the plate of poached salmon with the cold sliced meats, only to have the woman with the eyeliner swap it back. I felt more comfortable around the catering staff than around my new colleagues, even if I could more or less hold my own. After my parents split, my mother waited tables for years. We were hardly destitute—my father was not a monster, and he wrote his monthly checks—but she had no professional skills, and she said this occupation at least gave her purpose. I spent a lot of time as a kid waiting for her in the back of a variety of diners, and in college I followed in her footsteps, waitressing myself through school. Which is only to say that I am not averse to hard work. I take each job as it comes. I have no chip on my shoulder about what some might consider menial labor.

I watched these quiet, familiarly soothing machinations while inhaling the cool indoor air and studying the sumptuous surroundings. Above me hung an enormous crystal chandelier, the set of Louis XVI dining-room chairs pushed against the wall to provide better access to the imposing table upon which the buffet was spread. I studied the frightening mythical creatures carved into the table's knees, observing the way they then tapered into fluted shins and sharp-clawed paws. I pulled out my notebook and did a quick sketch.

Through the window I watched a bolt of lightning strike just beyond the swimming pool. An intern from the sports desk dropped her wineglass, which shattered on the flagstone. She looked around, terrified, as if she might be instantly relieved of her position, but no one seemed to notice in the chaos as everyone rushed inside. Alone by the pool, she knelt to begin picking up the shards.

———

- Statistically, staged homes sell faster and for more money.
- Ninety-four percent of staged homes sell in one month or less.
- Homes that were staged spent 80 percent less time on the market.
- Staging increases perceived value.
- Staging is cheaper than a price reduction.
- Today's sellers must do more than ever to compete.
- A staged vacant house sells faster than an empty property.
- Home staging can average 340 percent return on the investment.
- Most buyers take three to six minutes to decide if they like your home.
- Seventy-nine percent of sellers are willing to invest up to five thousand dollars on staging.
- Sixty-three percent of buyers will pay more for a house that is move-in ready.

I am not the sort of home stager you see on those popular television shows—the ones who flit about in heels and perch fetchingly on ladders, pink cocktails in hand. I don't use words like "sizzle" and "pop," and I avoid the trends; you will never hear me advise a client to purge his books, or remove their jackets and then color-coordinate the spines. I go about my work quietly, intuitively, certainly, like a fussy old aunt who comes into your room and tells you to clean things up.

It seems I have a knack, which may not be anything to boast about—being able to strip away the personality of a house requires, in itself, a certain personality, or maybe what it requires is just the lack of one. Whatever the explanation, it would appear I was a smashing success, even though I stumbled into this career, if we can call it that, by accident.

I had some general knowledge of the subject, of course, having worked for six years as managing editor of the monthly glossy magazine *MidAtlantic Home*, a job I was offered after two years at the newspaper. At the magazine, we had a regular rotation of stories on home staging, and we'd usually weave in some incarnation of the above-referenced bullet points, tucked discreetly—or maybe not so discreetly—into an editorial package declaring some quirky shade of color to be the new "off-white." Think "Sea Glass," for example. Aquamarine by a different name. Hold on to your hats and prepare for a brief run on Duron DCR077.

You were meant to be seduced, too, by the complicated balloon shades we suggested you could easily make at home "for less than $100 in under three hours" (sure, if you kidnapped three seamstresses and locked them in your attic), or by the exquisite Ushak rug, a nice replica of which was available at Home Depot, which happened to be one of our best advertisers. Back when there were advertisers, which is to say, back before I lost my job.

Even though I had some basic intellectual understanding of home staging, and I had read *Staging Homes to Sell in This Still Volatile Market!*, to know all of this, and actually to make it so, to get down literally on my hands and knees and bring a house to move-in-ready condition, is a very different thing from editing stories about how someone else might do it. Just because a person loves to read cookbooks doesn't mean she can actually cook.

I committed my first act of home staging on the day of an ice storm. My doorbell rang, and there stood my neighbor in an arresting ensemble, a bracing slash of red wool coat against the white winter landscape. When I saw her, I instinctively prepared for some sort of complaint: we'd lived side by side for nearly nine years, but our relations had always been chilly, mostly because, since Vince moved out and stopped caring for the garden, pretty much every bit of vegetation on my property has emigrated to her yard.

Her complaints were frequent and vociferous: my bamboo had crept under the fence and was now interfering with three separate flower beds; my bindweed (as if I owned bindweed; as if I even knew what bindweed was) was choking her roses; and we'd recently had a rather unpleasant exchange about the fact that my cherry tree was dripping fruit onto her patio, staining her pavement red. This seemed to me a nonstarter. Cherry trees dripped fruit. So be it. I refused to cut it down. She thought otherwise, and after weeks of fraught exchanges, we finally agreed to split the cost of hacking the limbs that splayed into her yard. There'd been a few more incidents, too, mostly to do with my dog, who was also partial to her yard; no matter what I did, Moses continued to tunnel her way next door. My most recent solution was to embed two feet of chicken wire in the dirt below the fence line. This had done the trick, at least so far, and now that the ground was frozen, I couldn't imagine what reason Amanda might have to be ringing my doorbell, especially in the midst of a storm.

Amanda was one of the most successful independent Realtors in the Washington, D.C., metropolitan region, and she had come to me that morning with a favor to ask: her car battery was dead, AAA advertised a three-hour wait, her husband was out of town, and the local taxi monopoly wasn't even answering the phone. She had to meet some buyers, in from Germany, at a house they were about to take to contract, and she wondered if I could give her a ride.

As much as I dreaded prolonged interaction with her, I was intoxicated by the business of Amanda that day: the briefcase bursting with paperwork, the stylish coat cinched at the waist with a thick leather belt, the mention of wealthy Germans, their pockets bulging with euros, or maybe even with gold. I told her to come in and to give me a minute to change out of my sweatpants and grab my keys.

That day I began a new career as a home stager. And, as if I were the protagonist in some Shakespearean drama, or, perhaps more accurately, in some farce, I would soon find myself thrust center stage back into Bella's life.

AMANDA AND I drove the three miles to the property without incident that day. When we arrived, however, there was no sign of the clients. We waited in the car for nearly an hour, with the engine running for heat. I will abbreviate the ridiculous saga of Amanda's inability to reach the buyers by phone, which involved her slow, dim realization that she did not have international dialing enabled on her wireless plan, and her equally belated understanding, already quite obvious to me, that she was being stood up.

I will shorten, too, the narrative of how, once we finally went inside, I won over in friendship the eighty-five-year-old widow who owned the decrepit rambler, and made a suggestion or two about sprucing up her house. (I know this may seem full of irrelevant detail, but it helps explain how I came to stumble—innocently!—into Bella's home.)

Perhaps I was simply relieved to be out of my lonely, boring purgatory that day, but I set about, unasked, manically plugging the holes in the widow's walls, making the foyer look twenty years younger by repurposing a mirror from the attic and a table from the corner of the living room.

I also crafted my first staging tip that day: foyers are far more critical than people realize. Although it ought to be obvious that foyers set the tone, most people give their entryways little thought, even though these are pretty easy to design. All you really need is a mirror so people can check for food in their teeth on the way out the door, and a small table on which to toss mail and keys. A dim, lousy foyer, or one without functionality, is like a flaccid run of words in the lede of the story, and just as you lose your reader, you've already doomed the sale.

Here was another small, related epiphany, the realization that being a home stager was a quite logical next step after being a magazine editor. Home staging and editing share a process; both are about taking what you have and making it flow from the top down. After the lede paragraph of the foyer, you need a nut graph in the living room. This is where you take the key elements and put them in the most prominent spot, and then, from there, you work with what remains. Occasionally you might need to bring in something that was missing from the start—have the reporter contact a new source or find a more coherent quote, or swap in a new armchair or lamp. Bad sentences, bad household décor—both are about untangling things and finding the hidden gem. There is always something to work with, even if it's mostly crap.

I looked around this sad old house and felt myself begin to burn; the certainty of my ability and my intensity of desire were somewhat embarrassing. To fix this place up felt not like work or play, but like some sort of inherent need. I wondered if it was possible that I was put on this earth, was hardwired, to repair the world through interior design.

Amanda and I had a cup of tea with the homeowner and looked (Amanda impatiently and not very graciously) at photographs of her children and grandchildren. I noted how well tended the house had once been, and gushed to her about the potential to renew: with a little elbow grease, some pruning of the bushes that were eclipsing access to the front door, a few replaced lightbulbs, the opening of windows, and a fresh coat of paint, a person might be able to make the future visible here, as opposed to merely past decay.

This was step one of what I would come to think of as staging therapy, because, not surprisingly, there's a lot of emotional volatility involved in selling, never mind staging, a house, and homeowners have been known to burst into tears and/or verbally abuse the stager. My techniques have proved largely effective. In this case, the woman began to speak enthusiastically about having me restore the place to its rightful mid-century grandeur, and this is how I found myself in Amanda's occasional, less-lucrative-than-it-should-be, cash-under-the-table employ. I worked magic on that old rambler, and it sold within a week for $15K over the asking price.

THE EUPHORIA I found in my new role, particularly at my age, might be interpreted as a positive thing if you are the sort who thinks it good to find happiness in being poorly compensated for creative work, or pathetic if you consider that I had, until recently, been making a six-figure salary in publishing. There is a silver lining, however: it is apparently possible to hit rock bottom and bounce back if a person limits her expectations, and as it happens, severely lowered expectations are themselves the silver lining of finally hitting rock bottom, which is where Amanda had found me that day: unemployed, not quite divorced, in the same clothes I'd slept in, defrosting hot-dog buns to use as toast in an effort to avoid having to get properly dressed to go to the grocery store.

Cash-flow problems aside, I was slowly coming to terms with, if not quite at peace with, my circumstances. I never wanted to be the kind of woman whose telling detail was that she couldn't get beyond something, and by this I mean either some small if jarring crisis of normal life, or some cataclysmic event of the sort that would, and should, leave scars. My radar was finely tuned to such stories, because I was beginning to realize I had, despite my protestations, become the protagonist of one myself. Nevertheless, if office gossip was to be believed, there were a lot of damaged people in this world, or at least there had been in the employ of *MidAtlantic Home*. Rumor had it that one of our assistant editors, for example, had been jilted by her fiancé twenty years earlier and that she *never got over it*, and this came to define her, even though she seemed to be one of the happiest people I knew and she was now married, with a dog and three kids. My former in-laws, with whom I'm still in touch, had sold their stock at the exact wrong moment, losing about half of their nest egg, only to see its value recover within weeks. Five years later, their financial catastrophe still inserts itself into nearly every conversation; even a compliment about dinner will incite a monologue from my father-in-law about how they bought the meat on sale at Costco, how they now have to drive forty minutes to shop in bulk because of that goddamned Microsoft stock.

A small quake resulting in four deaths and one miscarriage. The dissolution of a marriage. The betrayal by a best friend—all for the sake of one poet/financier/cad. These are the sorts of things that a person might never get over. But you don't hear me going on about this night and day.

"BELLA" MEANS "BEAUTIFUL," yes, but there's another meaning. Belladonna is a herbaceous plant native to Europe, North Africa, and Western Asia. The foliage and berries are extremely toxic and cause hallucinations that are said to be unpleasant. It was used as a poison by Macbeth, before he became king of Scotland, to decommission opposing troops.

It can lead to severe confusion.

Vince once suggested that I was obsessed with Bella. This might have been, in other circumstances, shrugged off as a casual remark, like noting that a person is obsessed with sudoku, or with getting a perfect tan. Or it might have been an accusation, which in this case it was. But Vince was wrong, or he simply didn't understand the bonds of female friendship, or maybe he was just jealous of my having any outside relationships at all.

I might suggest that *he* was the one obsessed with Bella, or at least he was obsessed with the idea that I was obsessed with her. He blamed her, or, rather, my supposed obsession with her, for all manner of things both extreme and unrelated, and held Bella responsible for what he always referred to derisively as my *ambition*. I mostly ignored this, and figured he was just jealous that I had a friend. That trip on which I accompanied Bella to Indonesia, for example, he once referred to as the beginning of our end, and, eerily, that was even before circumstances conspired to make this so.

In those early years at the newspaper, and even as I'd transitioned to my new role at *MidAtlantic Home*, I thought that if Vince had had something productive going on in his own life he might have let up on me, and given me the space I needed at the time. He was always at home, anxious and brooding and complaining and morose, and I'd wished he'd find something to distract him—a hobby, or even a woman. Not that I really wished for that, but I don't think I would have been shocked; so many of our colleagues at the newspaper had been sleeping around that keeping track of the latest entanglements had become something of a sport.

The subject had become sort of boring to me, these people who couldn't control their libidos (although I think it was really their egos they couldn't keep in check), who couldn't see a step ahead to the wrecks they were about to make of their lives. So I didn't find Bella's having an affair so surprising—although sneaking around with Raymond Branch was of course a bit ballsy, and then the bit with the Yankees first baseman was too shocking for words. Rather, that a snake like him could derail someone as assured and accomplished as Bella was so puzzling to me, such a mystery of the universe, that I soaked up every detail in an effort to understand, and I even began to take notes.

IT BEGAN THE day after the garden party. Lunch led straight to the hotel where Raymond was staying, Seema already en route back to the children in London. Bella told me everything, from what kind of soap they used at the Georgetown Ritz-Carlton to the labels inside of

Raymond's shirts. She provided so many intimate details that I wondered if there was some other level of pathology involved, if the physical and emotional pleasures of the affair were possibly secondary to the electric charge of telling me. I learned what they ordered from room service, the contents of Raymond's toiletry kit, his preferred methods of coupling, and, as the months ticked by, even the terms of endearment used in the e-mails he would send. I feigned indifference, but I suppose I was absorbing the details vicariously in my own, possibly perverse way.

Bella once described how, in the middle of one of their trysts—this one in Vienna—he'd taken a call from his daughter, who had just come home from her first day of kindergarten (they called it "reception class" in England, I learned) and was having trouble manipulating scissors. Raymond had gotten out of bed and put on the hotel terry-cloth robe, then sat in a chair, crossed his gimpy leg over the other, and patiently addressed the situation. He'd had trouble using scissors, too! This was surely nothing to be concerned about! As soon as he got home, they'd do some cutting, together! Bella was impressed that he was such a good dad. And that he was so patient and attentive. He was such a good husband, too, she said. He bought his wife gifts, and always interrupted whatever he and Bella were doing to take her calls. He was such a good man!

What was going on in Bella's head was difficult to imagine, although I did know she was trying to get pregnant at the time, that she and Lars were about to embark on a round of expensive fertility treatments (and, yes, our shared fertility problems were another source of our intense bond), so perhaps she was simply impressed by Raymond's apparent ability to reproduce. Privately, wickedly, I entertained the image of Raymond teaching his daughter to cut, wondering whether he was left- or right-handed and, accordingly, how one could use scissors without a thumb.

––––––

I CONFESS THAT I've struggled, from time to time, with how best to organize my notes, how to structure the scenes from her affair most logically.

By category, perhaps? There are, for example, all the grand hotels of Europe from which Bella brought me details: interior-design motifs, brands of lotions and shampoos, specialties of the room-service menus, descriptions of the pools and gyms.

There are the private details, the things I should not know about Raymond and Seema's marriage, the headline of which was actually that things were very good. He never spoke badly of his wife, but there was pillow talk all the same, some of which made its way to me. Though I hung on every word, I felt tainted possessing certain intimate knowledge of Seema, like that she'd once had a lump removed from her left breast, and that she waxed, instead of shaved, her legs. The disclosure of these small, meaningless details seemed possibly more violating than the fact of extramarital sex.

And then, in my notebook, are the scenes from the unraveling. This is the part with the most gaps, perhaps because I was beginning to unravel myself. My bullet points include snippets from their electronic paper trail, which was sometimes forwarded to me by Bella (astonishing that she was conducting this private, explosive correspondence on her newspaper account).

Some of my notes are merely anecdotal. Bella told me, for example, that sometimes when Raymond went AWOL for a few days, especially toward the end of the affair, she'd call him at his house. If Seema answered, Bella would deliberately wait a few beats, and then hang up. When that failed to produce any movement toward the dissolution of their marriage, Bella began to slip little trinkets—her nail file or her lipstick, for example—deliberately into his Italian leather travel kit, still without any apparent result.

I told Bella she was doing the emotional equivalent of slamming her head against the wall. Raymond was never going to leave Seema.

But my advice did nothing to dissuade my friend from showing up on my doorstep frequently, and at all hours.

She leaned into me so hard, toward the end, that I think our friendship was the only thing fusing her together.

Vince may have had a point: perhaps I allowed Bella to occupy me more than I should have. But I am offended by the suggestion that I was—or am—obsessed with her.

IT IS USUALLY the case that what you see is what you get, both with people and with homes. I may appear, these days, to be a nervous, tiny, sparrow-boned woman, so jangled much of the time that you might want to slap me, or send me out back with a cigarette and a martini, or even force-feed me steak. But this is not really me.

Once, not long ago, I was confident and self-possessed. When I first landed at the newspaper, unlike most of my colleagues, I did not set my sights on becoming the next Bob Woodward, or on climbing the ladder to a managerial slot and an office with a door. Some might have regarded my embrace of one of the "soft" sections of the newsroom as demonstrative of some intellectual, possibly even moral, failing, as if I had exposed myself as the sort of woman who might choose Disneyland over Paris, or Harry Potter over Proust. But Bella didn't look down her nose at me, even after she quickly earned a slot as an official business reporter and was put on a highly visible beat following a trail of post-9/11 money through a couple of high-profile banks in Europe, Asia, and the Middle East. Once, she even said that she admired and respected me; admittedly, that compliment had been solicited, extracted with a whiff of desperation, as if I was asking whether I still looked good in my too-tight jeans.

I had my insecurities, it's true, yet in my heart I knew I was fortunate to be doing exactly the work I wanted to do. Ought I to be ashamed to admit to a more genuine curiosity as to how the afternoon sunlight would look when filtered through a linen Roman shade than as to, say, who the next Senate majority leader would be? Yes. But I was at least being honest in acknowledging where my talent lay. And I *did* have talent, as evidenced by my rapid ascension to becoming the editor of the Home section within a year and then, a short time later, to being poached by *MidAtlantic Home.*

But all of this was blessedly beside the point with me and Bella. Newsroom politics and gossip blended into the fabric of our conversations, of course, but we typically spoke of other, real-life concerns, as well as about books, movies, television, shopping, and occasionally our troubled marriages. But mostly, for three long years, we talked about Raymond Branch. Even during the height of the sniper attacks in Washington, which occurred two months after we'd met, we went out to a deserted shopping mall in Bethesda so that Bella could buy lingerie, because Raymond was in town and she wanted to surprise him. We laughed as we zigzagged across the parking lot and into the supposed safety of Nordstrom, aware that someone had been shot just a few miles from there that morning, and that no aspect of this was remotely funny.

My own professional climb synchronized neatly, and most likely not coincidentally, with Vince's descent. He had begun to struggle, although whether under the weight of his own limitations or as the result of my success wasn't clear. Two months after our arrival, he found a job at a newspaper on Capitol Hill, but he was miserable covering energy policy, and within a year he quit. He wasn't a Washington type, he said, and this was true. He wasn't a jacket-and-tie kind of guy, nor was he suited, temperamentally, to the drudgery of regulatory meetings. At the alternative paper in Minneapolis, his wrinkled, sloppy self was acceptably grunge, and his hours largely self-defined, which had worked well enough while he was investigating police-union fraud and occasionally writing music reviews, but did not translate to getting to Rockville by 8:00 a.m. to sit in on briefings at the Nuclear Regulatory Commission about acceptance criteria for emergency core-cooling systems for light-water nuclear power reactors, and such.

Anyone who'd known Vince a few years earlier would have said he was on his way to something big, and that things never really clicked for him in Washington was surprising. After he quit the congressional paper, he found bits and pieces of freelance work, but it was becoming increasingly difficult to ignore the fact of his drinking. I'd watch him pour half a bottle of bourbon down his gut each evening and wonder what it was he was quietly trying to exorcise, and whether it was me. Vince wasn't a sloppy drinker; he never actually got drunk, just more and more morose; he was becoming erratic in ways that were hard to isolate or connect up. He decided somewhat randomly, for example, that he had a passion for gardening. I had known him by then for some sixteen years and was pretty sure he couldn't tell a pansy from a peony, but I helped him pay for classes in landscape design while he worked at a local garden center. Within a year or so, he became less interested in suburban gardens than in land use and organic farming, which I encouraged, although it was a little eerie, given that my father had been an urban planner, or, more accurately, a designer of strip malls—those convenient if much-maligned blights of the landscape, an integral part of *the way we live now*, although maybe, already, an anachronism, since many of them are already being razed to make way for more public-transportation-friendly lifestyles. And then it seemed that, remarkably, thrillingly, in one of those rare convergences of things meant to be, Vince's interests were finally about to collide to productive result.

With a manic burst of energy, he put together a hundred-page proposal and scored a lucrative book contract with a major New York publisher to write a biography of a guru architect he'd become familiar with in one of his classes, who, again very coincidentally, had been cited as the inspiration for a new upscale, environmentally friendly development that was at the time first being constructed, amidst county-wide, really statewide controversy: *Unfurlings*.

Anyone who lived in the area knew about Unfurlings. New housing developments spread through the suburbs like acne, but this one was particularly vexing and occasionally erupted onto the front page on account of its footprint on what was literally the last patch of farmland left in Montgomery County, or the last lung, as they say in eco-speak. Then the farmer died (that there had actually been a farmer on the farm, one who wore overalls and rode a tractor and was still milking cows until he died in his sleep at the age of eighty-six, took most people by surprise), and his family put the land up for sale.

The fourteen hundred acres were purchased by a team that included a developer from New York, dubbed locally "the Gordon Gekko of Sprawl," and his partner, a department-store heir with a penchant for buying expensive toys, such as amusement parks and NHL teams. The developers countered the criticism by pointing out that the venture wasn't destroying green space so much as repurposing it as high-concept living, an experiment that would change the way we live and would attract attention and investors from around the world. There would be mixed-use housing, enclaves that sorted people into small communities according to whether they were most interested in art, literature, music, cooking, or foreign policy. There would be organic restaurants and a five-star hotel open to the public. And there would be culture and community: a three-thousand-seat concert hall and a block of art galleries, as well as a solar-heated Olympic-sized swimming pool and the promise of free yoga on Sunday mornings, open to all county residents. Also, there would be animals: horses and llamas and chickens and goats, with other species welcome. It sounded more than a little hocus-pocus to me; privately, I stopped thinking of the place as Unfurlings, and instead dubbed it The Village, since it reminded me of the sort of community M. Night Shyamalan might create were he an urban planner and not a maker of creepy art films.

The opposition was fierce. There were arguments about land use, a conviction that the place would flop, and fear of traffic congestion in the unlikely event it succeeded. There was also a fair amount of cynicism about the idea of utopian living in the guise of multimillion-dollar homes. For months, protesters gathered at the front gates, and when construction began, a young woman threw herself in front of a bulldozer and was killed, in an episode that seemed more Gaza than suburban Maryland. Then her family filed suit, generating a whole new round of headlines.

The Gordon Gekko of Sprawl, who was, in fact, named Gordon Stern, countered that his mission was being misconstrued. Unfurlings was his way to give something back to the community he'd grown up in and loved, which was being aesthetically destroyed by big-box stores and cheap, uniform town houses. It was hard to argue with this, regardless of which camp you were in.

While the neighborhood associations held their meetings and collected names on the petitions, the developers quietly developed, and within six years, before they had even managed to get a second meeting with the county commissioner, Unfurlings had become operational. The flagship five-star restaurant, Unfurlings I, which had famously poached a name-brand chef from a celebrated restaurant in Napa, had opened to rave reviews, as had the adjacent folksy breakfast place called The Farms, which was situated in the original farmhouse. The restaurants were flourishing, even though only twelve families had moved into the community. Within a year, Unfurlings was in foreclosure. Twenty-three would-be homeowners were suing to recover their deposits, and the half-paved roads and houses still in their Tyvek house wrap made Unfurlings look like it had ground to a halt mid-apocalypse, or maybe more like all the would-be dwellers had been felled by plague. That might have been the better analogy, given how quickly the fallout spread throughout the region, depleting the value of all neighborhood homes—one of which I was being asked to stage.

Around the time Unfurlings went into foreclosure, Vince's book met a similar fate. He worked on it for a year, or he said he did. Mostly all I saw were the bottles that accumulated in our recycling bin. At one point he was spending close to a hundred dollars a week at the liquor store, and I'd say this was the least of our problems except that it wasn't: I sensed we were going to have to give back the advance he'd been paid for the book, which was already spent, and that was one time I would have gladly been proved wrong.

Fast-forward two years past the official death of his book and the debt incurred, five years beyond the end of our marriage, three months after I lost my job at *MidAtlantic Home*. I was deep into hibernation, digging in my freezer trying to excavate a Hunan stir-fry from its shroud of ice. The local news droned in the background as I read the directions and programmed the microwave. Then I heard this Gordon Gekko character say something that got my attention: it had been his lifelong dream to build a self-sustaining community based on the tenets of the visionary architect who'd been his guru in graduate school, Sherman Rushlander, author of a series of architecture books that were so popular they had inspired a movie, a series of graphic novels, and a board game. Although I knew that Rushlander had been the subject of Vince's aborted book project and I knew he was the man behind Unfurlings, sometimes it can take a while for the mind to make the most obvious connections. I suppose I'd only been paying peripheral attention to the Unfurlings debacle, the way one sometimes does, with no small degree of guilt, to news that does not affect one directly, like famine in Africa or revolution in the Middle East.

I'd called Vince immediately with an idea: that the unemployed might help the foreclosed-upon seemed great synergy—or at least it would get Vince out of his mother's depressing basement apartment—and my instincts on this proved sound. Vince wound up unexpectedly consulting for Gekko, trying to find a way to make the land generate income while the properties sat idle. He designed farming preserves and helped Gekko think through how to harvest, in mass quantities that would then be packaged and sold to farm stands and small grocers, compost tea.

Vince was offered the possibility of a low-interest loan and a substantial reduction in price on a small house at Unfurlings. He'd called me a few times to discuss this, and we slipped, as we always did, into a perfectly normal conversation about the pros and cons, as well as the finances, as if we hadn't been estranged for years—or, more to the point, as if Vince had the resources to put down a deposit. I sometimes mused that perhaps we weren't technically estranged, that our marriage had simply evolved from childhood friendship to cohabitation to separate domiciles and nightly conversations on the phone, and maybe this was a more enlightened and desirable way to be married than anyone understood, or was willing to acknowledge. Nevertheless, despite my own pinched resources, I was, these days, the deep pocket in this relationship, or at least the one with health insurance.

I ADMIT THAT I did something during this long and lonely Bella-free, Vince-less era that I regret. This was a bad phase of my life. I will not dwell on it, apart from saying there were a number of stark, lonely interludes, the sort from which has sprung many a midlife-crisis memoir, a genre I began to read voraciously. I had thought myself inoculated against life blows of this particular nature, as if the reward for having struggled through events in Indonesia, followed by the wrenching disintegration of my marriage and the simultaneous end of my friendship with Bella, were vaccinations against self-pity. As if planning a feature for *MidAtlantic Home*, I began to chart the domestic geography of author unravelings to see if there were any patterns to be detected. Some of the more popular memoirists, ones who had won prizes or sat for long stretches on the bestseller lists, were partial to weeping in bathrooms, and suggested that epiphanies about God, abstinence, and divorce tended to emerge while one was hunched over a toilet or sprawled on a cold tile floor. Laundry rooms featured prominently as well, as did kitchens and back patios, so it was impossible to draw definitive conclusions about which rooms were most likely to yield wisdom. I therefore set about sobbing my way through every room, like Goldilocks looking for the best fit.

The options were depressingly plentiful; there were reminders of happier times everywhere I turned, and I second-guessed my decision to stay in the house after I finally asked Vince to leave. Each stick of furniture sent me back to the moment of its acquisition. There, in the cushions of our aged sofa, was the memory of the coffee we'd had at Starbucks one snowy winter afternoon, just before heading into the mall to buy the couch. How naïve to have considered the possibility that we might have lasted as long as a sturdy stick of furniture! In fact, with its Scotchgarded fabric, it now seemed, cockroach-like, destined to outlive us all.

On top of this, I'd thrown myself so fully into work that, with hindsight, I could see I'd taken for granted the casual friendship of my colleagues and allowed this to substitute for a social life. They politely answered my calls and e-mails, but I could tell that, unlike me, they had other things to do. Once my sister and her family moved to Seattle, I realized how isolated I had become. Previously, I'd seen my nephew, Zed, every couple of weeks, and I'd sometimes babysat for him when my sister traveled. Now, although we still spoke and e-mailed almost daily, it wasn't the same as having her a mile away. But the real problem was that I simply had too much time on my hands, especially after the magazine folded, and it proved harder to find another publishing job than I ever might have thought. I sent out hundreds of résumés and called former newspaper colleagues, to no avail. The only offers that came my way were freelance jobs for little and sometimes no pay, and though I took these on, I found it demoralizing to be back where I'd begun, writing eight-hundred-word features about giving your foyer a lift for spring.

It's sad to say that I didn't even have a love interest, not even any minor flirtation I could turn into some sort of diverting Facebook activity. I confess to occasionally looking at Bella's profile, but her privacy controls were such that I couldn't get more than a superficial glimpse. But there was Lars, access unrestricted, no picture, five friends. Although I'd never met Lars, I'd always felt connected to him, weirdly fascinated by the very idea of him. A strange sense of intimacy occurs when you know details about a person you don't actually know, and I knew a lot, as Bella was pretty loose-lipped with me. Me and Lars, we shared a bond: we were both losers in this life, both emotional victims of his wife. I'd always wondered, as I'd heard Bella talk about his downward spiral, if it was true that Lars was a priori damaged goods, or if Bella had made him damaged goods by not loving him, or by not loving him enough. Perhaps it's better not to love someone at all than to love him halfway. Maybe she would love him fully if he only lost a little weight? If he read more substantive books? If he was a nattier dresser? The questions can destroy the person, who is left wondering what he lacks.

Lars's empty Facebook page did little to illuminate me. I thought about friending him, but I knew that would be crossing some line. Parents fret about their children's online behavior when it is really their own arrested development that ought to be of concern. I visited Lars's page on several occasions without incident. But one dark night, after a couple of glasses of wine, a Facebook event occurred. A message was sent. A wave of anxiety took hold that to this day has not entirely passed. I convinced myself, in that split second before hitting "send," that I was doing the morally correct thing. Lars needed to know the truth about Elsa's paternity. In all likelihood, he was not the biological father. Perhaps I had done this not for Lars but for me. The secret was burning a hole inside me.

I never heard back. I had no way of assessing the damage. I might have given Lars the most devastating news of his life, or, alternatively, he might not have logged onto Facebook in the past five years.

A FEW WEEKS into my new career as a home stager, I found myself staring, for the first time in nearly a decade, at Belladonna Sorkin. She appeared on my television screen midday, on an afternoon segment on CNN—my go-to station for folding laundry. I had the sound off, but I learned from the caption that she was a vice-president at Luxum International. I located the remote and turned up the volume. I might have misheard, but it sounded as though she was in the middle of saying something about a goat.

Random intrusions by Bella were henceforth going to become a regular feature of my life. I'd be going about my business, innocently ironing or sorting whites from darks; then I'd flip on the television, and there she'd be. Each time, I'd brace myself for some emotional reaction, something tender or something violent, but all I felt was a dull curiosity. What had become of her and Lars, of Elsa and Raymond, of Raymond and the woman I'd locked eyes with on that fateful day in Indonesia?

Also puzzling: How did Bella still manage to look so good? Of course she'd aged, but not dramatically so; she clearly had at her disposal every beauty resource available—the fancy hundred-dollars-an-ounce moisturizing creams, the newfangled wrinkle-freezing injections—so if crow's-feet might have formed at the corners of her eyes, or if there was some slackening of the skin, it was not readily apparent, or at least not on my clunky old pre-high-definition television.

Would you think I was obsessed with the subject of Raymond and Bella if I pointed out that her hair was the only thing that was notably different, and that the new, darker color, and the way it hung in stiffened, lacquered layers, made it look a bit like Seema's? Though I had to say, grudgingly, that she looked terrific, her dress was not what I would have recommended for television—a fussy print that made it hard to focus on what she was saying, with a complicated neckline that plunged too low. Then, almost unbelievably, only five days later, there she was again, being interviewed on a *60 Minutes* segment about the rebranding of Luxum International, *wearing the very same dress*. Oh, Bella! This is the sort of thing that happens when you disown your best friend; there's no one around to advise you honestly on wardrobe choices and the like. I felt a surge of affection, as well as an unexpected nostalgia for the more mindless aspects of our friendship—the shopping and the gossipy lunches, the manicures, the sort of stuff that was so easy and lacking in substance that it would prove, counterintuitively, surprisingly difficult to replicate.

MORNINGS, IN THE intervening weeks, began not infrequently with calls from Amanda announcing real-estate emergencies. Few of these qualified as such. So far, in the four houses I had successfully staged, only one really rose to the level worthy of Amanda's histrionics—a new-construction home in McLean where the Sub-Zero refrigerator had proved too heavy for the floorboards and crashed through to the den below, which we were in the process of staging with rented furniture. The plasma television and glass coffee table were among the casualties, and a painter doing some touch-up in the living room fell off his ladder and broke an arm; mercifully, no one was killed.

Even though the market in most of the region remained depressed, with foreclosure signs still as much a feature of the landscape as the quaint farm stands that dotted the roads, there were also pockets where real-estate prices had gone *up*. Whether owners were hoping to minimize their losses, or quickly cash out while the going was still good, Amanda Hoffstead remained the region's number one Realtor. She worked hard, reading the obituaries and pouncing on homes, talking up and befriending strangers in the grocery-store line, and handing out cards. She did her homework, paying close attention to houses that were languishing on the market, and then swooping in for the relist. No one seemed to like her much, from what I could tell, but apparently having fuzzy relations with the person who stood to make a 6 percent commission from the sale of your house was not the point, and toward her I adopted a similar, somewhat callous attitude.

SIX MONTHS INTO my occasional employment with her, Amanda asked me to meet her in front of a Flemish-style villa in an exclusive gated golf-course community in Bethesda. She explained in her usual bloviating style that just a few years earlier she could have sold this place with a snap of her fingers. Tiger Woods had once played here in the U.S. Open, back when these cruise-ship McMansions were considered desirable and before Unfurlings went into foreclosure, but now this was like trying to unload a dead fish, especially given that it had failed to sell in the first three months, or even attract a viable offer. The owners needed to act quickly, she said, and in fact they wanted the house back on the market by the end of the week.

"Brace yourself," she said before punching numbers into the lockbox that hung from the door. "There are photos of the family everywhere you look, and tons of overly eclectic ethnic crap. The owners must travel a lot. Also a lot of hideous modern art."

She paused before opening the door: "Did I mention there are also some problems with a pet? A rabbit, I think? They called me over the weekend; I'm not entirely sure what they were talking about, but it may have escaped its cage and been a little destructive."

No, she had not mentioned this. Nor had she mentioned the smell.

It was the first thing I noticed when I stepped through the door. Vaguely uric, suggestive of cat, it was the sort of semi-tolerable odor that pet owners grow impervious to, apparently no longer even notice after a while, like the sound of a whooshing interstate just outside the master-bedroom window, or the view of a behemoth cell-phone tower from the back deck. Or so they claim to potential buyers of their homes. When people fall in love with a house, they are willing to set aside logic; 95 percent of buyers act on emotion, ignoring warning signs the way one takes on a partner who has a history of philandering, or who is in massive debt.

I looked at Amanda and thought I could see her silently processing the smell as well. I'd recently had another project with a bad-odor issue, a historic row house in Dupont Circle, where the fourteen-year-old Labrador retriever who limped to the door to greet me was wearing a diaper. There had been a long history of bladder incidents in that home, as evidenced by the badly stained wood floors, but by employing the right combination of cleaning products, plug-in deodorizers, and strategically placed throw rugs, I had seen the property go to contract, so I was not unduly worried.

There was always a solution, and that was part of what I liked best about this new job—the way it forced me to think on my feet, to find quick if ephemeral fixes. It didn't really matter if the curtain rod I stabilized with duct tape was likely to collapse in six months; by then the house would be sold, or so we hoped, and the whole thing would presumably be disassembled to accommodate the new owners' tastes. This was the sort of sloppy attitude I would not have tolerated back when I worked in publishing, when any poorly cropped photo or misplaced comma was going to live in cyberspace until the end of days, but the very point of being a home stager was to create illusions, and this suited my current, impermanent state of mind quite well.

The second thing I noticed in the marbled foyer was the pig.

A small, round, winking bronze creature, an impish little potbellied thing that could fit in the palm of a hand. It was poised like a sentry on the green marble console, one of its triangular ears eclipsed by a red tulip that drooped from the vase beside it. Flanking the pig's other side was a tribal figure made of wire and bits of cloth, its belly grotesquely extended. The painting above it was an abstract of black and yellow brushstrokes that had a vaguely Spanish feel. Even as a painter myself, and an aficionado of modern art, I thought it looked like something I might have excavated from my nephew's backpack after kindergarten, crumpled and sticky with the remnants of lunch.

One didn't need to read any staging books to get that all of this would have to go: the last thing you wanted was for would-be buyers to associate the house with swine, starvation, or bad modern art. Before I could commence with a new plan for this entryway, however, I would have to get over the shock of the pig. I knew this pig, or I knew a pig just like it, and at the time of its purchase I had been told it was one of a kind. Bella and I had purchased an identical pig on our trip to Indonesia. We had meant to share it, to pass it back and forth—a pig as an unconventional friendship ring. That I had never had my turn with the pig was not something I had considered until now.

I was almost certainly overreacting, jumping to the crazy and highly unlikely conclusion that I had just stepped into Bella Sorkin's home. For one thing, it was hard to imagine Bella in a gated golf-course community in a faux Flemish villa. When we parted ways, she and Lars had been living in a funky, albeit stunning, Capitol Hill row house in what might be politely referred to in real-estate lingo as a *transitional* neighborhood. Even though Lars had been pulling in major bucks with his endorsements and had wanted to live the more comfortable and, dare I say, flashy lifestyle befitting a professional athlete, Bella had prevailed. She'd still had a dash of Northern California flower child in her blood back when I knew her. She had subscribed to edgy literary journals, dressed with a bohemian flair, and once contemplated a small tattoo on her shoulder, even as she was clearly moving in the sartorial direction of Brooks Brothers and pearls.

Still, there was no reason to jump to conclusions. Washington, D.C., was a very cosmopolitan region, full of international travelers, and souvenir pigs from Indonesia were perhaps not unusual. After reassuring myself of this, I followed Amanda into an enormous living room with light pouring through the stained glass of a cathedral ceiling. The space was gasp-inducing, a potential centerfold for a magazine peddling real-estate porn.

Stunning as this was, there was simply too much stuff: photo-graphs and knickknacks and books, dolls and Rollerblades and field-hockey sticks, all incongruous with the shabby-chic French country furnishings that included a stunning pair of washed hemp cane-back wing chairs and a distressed sage-green-and-white sofa carved from oak. There were also a pair of antique Queen Anne chairs, one of which had an unfortunate gash in the cushion.

Set apart from this flow—at the far back of the room, where it began to bleed into the formal dining room—was a Wassily chair. It faced the wall, forlorn, like a child sent to the corner for fidgeting in class. With its sleek frame and thin leather slats, it looked as stark, emaciated, and weirdly compelling as a heroin-chic model. This chair did not belong in this room. For that matter, this chair did not belong in this house.

We had once done a feature on this iconic chair, designed by Marcel Breuer and named in homage to his friend and fellow Bauhaus instructor Wassily Kandinsky. It was considered revolutionary in its use of tubular steel. One of the designers we quoted in the story quipped that it was "the second most disturbing chair in the world, the first being the electric chair." Another said that sitting in it felt like "inserting a broomstick up your ass."

Amanda noticed me staring at it. "That's going in the attic for sure," she said.

Regardless of its possible value, I didn't disagree.

Turning my focus back to the main area of the room, my eye moved slowly, hesitantly, upward to the gigantic portrait that hung above the fireplace. I was still holding out a flicker of hope that I'd see, there above the fireplace, something else. I don't know what. Just something other than the Sorkin-Jorgenson family of three.

I had never met Lars. And there he was, if not quite flesh and blood, at least rendered reasonably lifelike in oil—blond-haired, blue-eyed, and entirely worthy of his God of Tennis nomenclature. Adding to the surreal nature of this moment was the fact that I had not stopped to consider him as someone who might occupy a home. It may seem silly to say, but I had simply not thought about him as a man who might do things like eat eggs for breakfast or brush his teeth or recline on a sofa or contort into a Wassily chair. The Lars in my head was merely a synonym for something sad and lost and washed-up.

And the child! In this painting she looked to be about five years old. I'd never seen Bella's daughter.

My own daughter would have been her same age.

I stood gaping at the painting for so long my neck began to cramp. The girl looked just like Bella—so exact a replica, in fact, it seemed she might have simply been cloned.

"Out-of-body experience" has always seemed to me one of those phrases so overused it has become devoid of meaning, and yet there I was, having one of my own. I observed myself standing there in awe, the light streaming in blue through the colored glass above, and then I could also see, as if I were watching a split-screen television, the toothless shopkeeper who had sold us the pig in the lobby of the Jakarta Four Seasons Hotel. He was laughing, as if he could see ahead to this improbable moment, many years and many thousands of miles away, like this outcome was preordained. I could even feel a rumble, like the ground beneath my feet when the stirring first began, although this was less portentous—it was simply Amanda, dragging the coffee table to the side.

"Holy Mother of God," she said. We both stared at the asymmetrical explosion of shredded carpet and small brown specks, which had, until a moment earlier, been obscured by the table. Even though I have worked with words my entire life, I'd need a camera to convey properly the nature of this mess. It looked like something Jackson Pollock might have created had he used as his medium animal excrement instead of paint.

"Let me get some paper towels," I said calmly, heading in the direction where I assumed I'd find the kitchen. At the same time, I

asked myself, *What is wrong with me?* What sort of terrible person clinically assesses damage to a rug under these circumstances? Wouldn't
the better woman have already fled this house, the way an animal
bolts upon hearing the sound of a gun?

I suppose I was seized by a morbid curiosity. But also, in my defense, I had the sense that fate had brought me here for a reason, and
until I could figure out why, the thing to do was simply switch to
autopilot and stage—by which I also mean mend and repair—this
home.

This was surely possible. As it was, the job required the ability to
detach. In my own life I was sentimental and superstitious; I kept
messages from fortune cookies with projections of which I approved,
even the ones that were laughably wrong: harbingers of a long, happy
marriage, or of a houseful of children, or of tremendous wealth. But
when it came to other people's homes, I stuffed into boxes, without
remorse, the framed photos on the mantel, the hurricane lamps full of
shells collected at the beach, the family of snowmen the kids had
made from clay. Those diplomas on the wall, the Little League tro-
phies, the photos of the great-great-grandmother getting married in
the shtetl—into a box! Surely, here, too, I could shift into clinical
home-stager mode.

In the kitchen I found a spare roll of paper towels under the sink,
but as I was searching around for some form of disinfectant cleaning
solution, I was hit by a wave of nausea. The smell, which had seemed
tolerable when I'd first entered the home, was closer to rancid in this
room. It was hard to isolate. I couldn't tell if this was the same smell,
or a new smell. The smell seemed to shape-shift, but if I had to guess,
I'd say it seemed to be bubbling up through the floor. I opened the
back door to let in some fresh air before returning to the living room.

As I scooped up the animal excrement (the source of yet another
smell, or the same one, I couldn't say), Amanda reminded me that
this was a rush job, and inquired about my ability to complete the
staging in less than a week.

I asked her why the rush.

The answer was that the Sorkin-Jorgensons had just signed a contract for a multimillion-dollar home in North London, steps from Hampstead Heath, and apparently, even though the homeowners were now raking in big bucks, their resources were only elastic to a point. They needed rather urgently to get their cash out of the Maryland ground.

"The animal—whatever it is, a rabbit, I think—seems to have had quite the party this weekend," Amanda said. We both stared at the damaged carpet. "Any brilliant ideas short of replacing the entire wall-to-wall?"

Bella's messes were always grand, I thought.

I pressed my hand to my stomach, made a loud gagging sound, and ran toward the window, which I opened so I could draw a few deep breaths.

"Something you ate?"

"It's just the smell . . ."

"Deep breaths. You'll be fine in a minute. So—first thing I'd say is, all the clutter has to go."

"Obviously," I said. Did Amanda not find the smell unbearably repulsive? I wondered.

"Also this . . ." I said, with a nod toward the portrait. I walked toward it again and tried to get a peek from behind, but couldn't really see much without a ladder. "I can't quite tell, but my guess is that it's anchored to the wall with toggle bolts, so it could be tricky. We'll have to see what we can do."

Amanda came closer to where it hung, and knocked on the wall. "You're right," she said. "This may have to convey."

We both laughed, but it was true that you sometimes heard stories of such things—gigantic mirrors that were hung with such deeply embedded bolts that it would be easier to remove the wall than to detach the fixture, and often such pieces did convey. Imagine living with a giant oil painting of Bella's family of three!

This struck me as terribly funny, and I began to laugh, perhaps a little too hard. My laughter may have had the sort of maniacal edge that sometimes morphs into hysteria among psychiatric patients. Amanda was staring at me.

"What's the budget?" I asked, trying to pull myself together and behave as if this were an entirely normal situation and not the most shocking thing to have happened to me, ever.

"It's more about time than money. Just tell me what you need and I'll try to make it work."

"I need to take in the entire place first, before I come up with a budget," I said. Although mostly what I needed was time to compose myself, to figure out what to do.

"That's a yes?"

I hesitated. The correct answer was surely no—I should disclose to Amanda my conflict and promptly leave. But I was also thinking this: I could work with the Flemish villa, I could cleanse it of clutter, restore the house to its rightful, faux-Flemish state. I could enable a quick and lucrative sale, and in this way I might make a small private repair, although for exactly what I was apologizing, I wasn't quite sure.

"It's a maybe," I said. It's an 'I'll let you know in an hour, after I've looked around.'" We were parting ways when the most critical question of all occurred to me: "Are the sellers going to be around?" I tried my best to sound nonchalant, although the question wasn't as suspicious as it might have seemed: we'd had an unfortunate incident at another house when the homeowner had burst into tears at my suggestion to replace the entire bedroom ensemble with something more neutral. The woman, a crunchy fifty-year-old artist with wild gray hair and an impressive collection of bird earrings she had made herself from found objects along the C&O Canal, had apparently hand-crocheted the pillows and various throws I was proposing be put on the shelf, and this otherwise minor incident had skyrocketed into such bad tension that we decided it was best if she simply left the premises while I worked.

In this case, for entirely different reasons, I clearly could not accept the job if there was any possibility of encountering Bella.

"They're in London all week."

"Thank God," I blurted with perhaps too much enthusiasm. I felt another wave of nausea taking hold. "How can you bear this smell?" I asked.

"What smell?"

How was it possible that Amanda didn't notice the smell? Was it all in my head? A metaphor for Bella's lies?

That would be overwrought, and as a former editor, I like to keep my prose in check.

IT WAS IN the child's room that I felt the first true chink in my composure. I stared numbly into the closet stuffed with frilly dresses and little patent-leather shoes, as well as heaps of toys and sports equipment of various types. My eye caught on a mud-encrusted cleat, which I studied for a moment, trying to decipher its precise use like it was some alien form: Did these spikes speak soccer, lacrosse, baseball, or field hockey? Or was the footwear for these activities all the same? I shut the closet, only to turn around and confront even more little-girl accoutrements on the dresser to the right of the door: a small basket full of hair ribbons and plastic barrettes, a bottle of sparkly purple nail polish, an impressive collection of eye shadows and lip glosses and face powders, each in a variety of shimmery containers, and all, upon closer inspection, with bits of glitter embedded in the contents.

Elsa's room had been fully outfitted to accommodate the little-girl princess phase, and every object seemed to sparkle. Even the canopy bed, which was perched on a raised platform with drawers underneath, had sheer, floating white curtains with bits of shimmering thread woven into the fabric, a design feature echoed by the dressings for the casement windows. The room was larger than many a studio apartment, or the master bedroom of my house. It also had its own en-suite bathroom, a little library corner with bookshelves and a desk, and a set of armchairs upholstered in a regal shade of deep blue velvet. The best thing to do with this room, given the time constraint, was to embrace the whole princess thing and hope potential buyers had a little girl with her own sovereign aspirations—or at least the imagination to see how the space might look, radically transformed.

The nail polish had me weirdly transfixed; I gave it a shake and watched the glitter dance in the afternoon sunlight before settling back slowly to the bottom of the thick purple slush. At the girl's small vanity table, I sat on the miniature velvet stool and set to work applying two coats of paint to each nail. As I waited for the enamel to dry, I picked up a hairbrush and studied the tangle of light brown hair snagged between the bristles. I then ran, or tried to run, the brush through my hair, but the soft bristles were no match for my wiry, corkscrew strands. A switch on the vanity table illuminated the oval mirror, and, staring at myself in the harsh light, I spotted a mutant gray hair poking through my left brow. Rifling through the beauty supplies did not produce any evidence of a tweezer, which puzzled me until I remembered that the owner of these products was all of ten. I made several attempts to extricate the offending hair with my fingers, to no avail. I then found a small scissor, which proved a bad idea. I inadvertently butchered roughly ten inoffensive hairs, while the gray one remained elusive. As it happens, there are few problems in either home staging or personal appearance that can't be solved, or at least improved, by appropriate illumination, and finally, in frustration, I dimmed the light until I could no longer see the damage I'd done.

Once again I caught a whiff of something foul, but tried to focus on the task at hand. The first thing to do was put these toys away. The Easy-Bake oven; the mounds of stuffed animals; the American Girl dolls sitting at their miniature mahogany dining-room table clad in bathing suits, napkins spread across their laps, the plastic slabs of skewered meat set out on a platter. I walked over to begin disassembling the display, but felt a disarming wave of sadness at the sight of those girls just sitting there, waiting. Waiting and waiting, for the girl to come home from school, to find them compelling enough to sit down on the floor and change them into proper clothing, to help them resume their evening meal.

Did ten-year-olds play with dolls? Did the princess and doll phases intersect, and which was outgrown first? *Ten*. At what age did a girl want to set fire to all this, to paint the walls black and plaster them with posters of scantily clad vampires or of her favorite goth bands? What did I know? Not much. I had missed the opportunity to engage in, or, more likely, do battle with, any Ugg-booted, miniskirted, gum-snapping, cell-phone-texting ten-year-old girls. I felt a headache coming on, or maybe it was just that the sliver of my brain that had been cryogenically frozen with the memory of my pregnancy was undergoing an unfortunate thaw.

I decided this room could wait, and went out into the hall and climbed the next flight of stairs. By this point I was trembling, as if I was about to enter some fraught Jungian landscape marked with totems from my past, and that was before I even realized how apt the metaphor was: until the moment I reached the threshold of the master bedroom, I'd forgotten about the bed.

Bella's distinctive scent emanated from within, fortifying the perimeter like an electric fence. I stopped accordingly. I would not cross this threshold. At least not today. Eventually, of course, I would have to enter, but the idea of touching Bella's things—the wedding picture on the dresser, the perfume bottles, the earrings on the nightstand—felt to me like a moral violation more extreme than the one I was already engaged in.

My head began to throb. The bed. I could hardly believe it. I knew this bed, just like I knew that pig downstairs.

Surely it was possible that I was investing all of these inanimate objects, these mere things from my life, with too much meaning, but ever since Vince and I had separated I'd felt especially sentimental about the matter of the bed.

Toward the end, I said, cruelly and ridiculously, that our bed was at the heart of our problems: It was from IKEA and it was falling apart. I began to obsess about beds I saw in catalogues and in department-store showrooms. Canopy beds with deluxe pillow-top mattresses fifteen inches thick, as lush as wedding cakes. Goose-down feather quilts tucked inside silk duvets. Once, I saw a Restoration Hardware bed that was so sumptuous, with its mounds of pillows and shams, that I crawled inside, just to feel the Italian 50-Year-Wash sheets against my skin. I closed my eyes, just for a moment, and though I don't think I actually fell asleep, the next thing I knew a security guard had come over to nudge me along.

Who can say what that whole bed thing was about? Just one last grasp at the poetry of marriage, at the limp sort of sentiment that makes people cling to something that is clearly dead. Poor Vince. My husband had looked at me, crushed, when, to punctuate my thought, I picked up one of the bolts that had come loose from our sad IKEA contraption and handed it to him.

But *this* marriage bed, Bella and Lars's bed, the bed that should have been mine—this was a sturdy instrument: made of teak, a four-poster, king-sized, low-to-the-ground sanctuary draped in layers of gauzy batiks so elaborate and unusual it seemed to merit some designation apart from "bed." On this bed, there were no loose bolts.

We'd discovered it together, me and Bella, in Jakarta, in a little shop behind the Jalan Kebon Sirih Timur market, and I had instantly fallen in love. Bella had helped me bargain with the shopkeeper to bring down the price, and he was confident he could arrange swift shipment to Maryland. But then I hesitated, and said I wanted to think about it overnight.

Vince and I were in a phase where we managed little more than polite exchanges to do with questions of household management, notwithstanding the fact that I had finally, unexpectedly, conceived.

By that point we were beyond discussing the elephant in the room, the clock ticking on the manuscript he was not writing, the empty bottles in the recycling bin. I was safely past the sixth month, and determined to embrace this marriage, to try to believe in the future.

Vince had been intensely negative about my decision to go with Bella to Indonesia. I decided to ignore his objections. It was true that buying a round-trip ticket to Jakarta only three days before departure was obscenely expensive, but, then, the hotel room was free, and, really, how often do these sorts of travel opportunities come along? Besides, I saw this as my last hurrah before being constrained, happily so, by a child. On top of which, Bella was having a rough time of things and she needed me along. Or so she said, and I was a sucker for Bella, easily seduced by the idea that I, her trusted confidante, could soothe her through this troubled patch.

As I stood in the market with Bella that day, I'd thought, optimistically, that perhaps the very thing we needed to go with a new baby was a new bed. This was no ordinary bed; it was huge and worthy of Homeric epic, which seemed to me exactly what it would take to get me and Vince to turn the corner. I had blissful if delusional visions of us parked here for the next few years while we slept, or tried to, and the baby fed, and we healed. Maybe Vince would even plug in his laptop, prop himself up against the oversized batik pillows I'd buy, and finally write his book. That said, I wasn't sure that the headboard, even disassembled, would fit through the awkward angles of our hallway, and it seemed prudent to call Vince to consult about the dimensions before arranging to ship this behemoth piece of furniture. I told the shopkeeper I'd come back the next day. That had been our first afternoon in Indonesia, before Raymond Branch showed up and the ground shook and there would be no going back to the market, at least not for me.

We were by then two years and six months into the Raymond narrative, and eighteen months since it had theoretically come to its conclusion but had not. Forget the memoir that I'd likely never write,

I could write a book about the Bella/Raymond affair! I could even provide a time line to help readers locate events lest they become confused, fleshed out with detailed field notes and a sketch or two. Even though my talents lean toward capturing the nuances of furniture—the dimple in the cushion, the worn fabric on the armrest, the gash in the woodwork made by the child who'd rammed it with the toy truck—I had, in fact, done more than a few rough profiles of Raymond. I am fascinated by that cratered, weathered penny of a face that some women find attractive, and I have always been a little bowled over by that hand.

Even that first night at the garden party, I found myself unable to stop staring at him, and when I went home, I'd drawn a picture of him and Seema, wrapped in her exquisite shawl. I made records of his face on each of the three occasions that we met, admittedly rendering him a little more craggily than was fair. That I laid eyes on him so few times is hard to believe, in retrospect, given how much of my mental real estate the man has always occupied.

Of Bella I have many records. I am not so indiscreet as to broadcast this horror show, but if I was, hypothetically, to attempt some transcript, the narrative actually lends itself quite well to discrete chapters.*

1. The garden party: love at first sight, ominous weather conditions, etc.
2. The Ritz-Carlton: liaison number one, room-service champagne, rich desserts, endearments, projections, empty promises, etc.
3. Repeat chapter 2 with slight geographical variations: Paris, Rome, New York, Malaysia. We settle into an almost dull routine, even though it has only been three months.

*I have deliberately left myself out of the rough chapter outlines, because this story is not about me.

4. Bella learns of Raymond's other affairs: tension, drama, tears, six-month breakup.

5. Coincidental meet-up in Brussels: resumption of affair, repeat chapters 2 and 3. (Shake, stir, and yawn.)

6. More tension, drama, tears over the discovery of some poems Raymond has been exchanging, full of innuendo, with his financial adviser. (How she could deduce the sexual implications embedded in a stanza to do with property index derivatives is beyond me—she read it to me twice, and it went completely over my head.)

7. Bella sleeps with Guillermo Peña, the Yankees first baseman.

8. Pregnancy ensues.

9. Deductive reasoning points toward Raymond.

10. Guillermo disappears. A café in San Salvador was the last place he was reportedly seen.

11. We go to Indonesia!

I watched and counseled with a mix of both genuine concern for my friend and a clinical fascination. It was educational, in its way. Though I loved Vince, I realized I had only ever really known Vince, and had never been in the grip of anything quite like what I saw. Passion, lust, desire: those are the words one typically uses to describe a love affair, I suppose, but Bella's behavior appeared to me more like illness, and I considered myself fortunate to have been spared such torture in my personal life. A grown woman, a professionally successful woman, a married woman, checking her cell phone every five minutes for Raymond's texts, then lapsing into despair and paranoia when one failed to arrive. She would reroute her own travel to coincide with his, would invent stories that needed to be reported in obscure cities. And the lies she'd concoct were shocking in their detail and complexity. She once told Lars that she had to make an overnight trip to Boston to accompany me to a doctor's appointment at the Dana Farber clinic because I'd had an ambiguous mammogram, and asked me, on the off chance Lars should contact me (as if he would—we'd never even met), to go along with the elaborate lie. I don't remember agreeing to that, but I was also too much in her grip to push back, and was there for her twenty-four/seven, even if, by chapter 8, I was beginning to experience a bit of crisis fatigue. I was involved in a love triangle in which I had no role, and the whole thing was becoming a grind. That the affair had run its course was obvious to me, if not to the central protagonist.

If you have ever been to the movies or read a book or seen an opera, you know the stuff of chapters 1–11: the self-absorption, the deceit. All pretty run-of-the-mill. Frankly, it's beyond me what all the fuss is about, given that the endings are all largely the same. The only thing that makes this story special is that few have the gall to drag into the mess their pregnant best friend. At least I assume I was her best friend. She never spoke of any other friends, best or otherwise.

Bella was seven weeks along, evidence of her pregnancy visible only to those who knew her well—unlike me, so enormous by this point that I looked like I might tip over when I walked; in fact, I nearly did on a couple of occasions when I ill-advisedly wore high heels. I was sick much of the time, and my skin a spotted, hormonal mess. By way of unsurprising contrast, pregnancy made Bella even more radiant. She actually had that glow I had thought apocryphal.

When we arrived in Jakarta, Bella had insisted that we waste no time; after checking into the hotel, we'd gone directly to one of the old markets. I'd pleaded for a bit of rest first, but she said that jet lag was all in the mind and that the best way to address it was just to soldier through the day and ignore it. Yes, but what if you have just spent some thirty-plus hours in travel on two separate flights, and you happen to be more than six months pregnant? I didn't have the nerve to ask.

The heat, the cars, the scooters, the honking horns, the pungent smells from the food stalls lining the narrow streets of the bazaar, the shopkeepers pressing beads and scarves and small carved Buddhas into my hand, the heat, the heat, the heat. I felt like I'd been blindfolded and spun in circles, as in some children's party game. I was growing profoundly disoriented—unsure, even, of what we were doing in Jakarta. I knew only that it had something to do with a series Bella was working on, investigating the shady financial trail of certain extremist factions in Indonesia. I actually believed this, although in retrospect I'm ashamed to have been so gullible. For one thing, although Bella had been plucked from the intern pool and hired as a reporter by then, it was nonetheless unlikely that such a plum assignment would have landed on her desk so early in her career. I certainly didn't question it, however; by this point in our friendship, like a long-married couple, Bella and I didn't spend a whole lot of time discussing certain things, and one of them was work.

After an hour, I actually thought I might faint. I took Bella's arm, and she steered us to a quiet, shady spot behind one of the stalls, where she instructed me to lean against a craggy brick wall. My heart was racing, and I was soaked with sweat. Bella pointed out that I was likely dehydrating, so she left me for a moment and went to get water. When she returned (without water), she said she'd noticed a shop with breathtaking furniture that she insisted I see. We were immediately swept in by the shopkeeper, who mercifully pressed cool bottles of Coca-Cola into our hands and led us toward the back, where I gravitated toward an aged window air-conditioning unit, but it was only wheezing out more hot air. At least the sweet syrup helped me revive, and a few moments later, I found myself ogling that bed. Then Bella appeared by my side to help me begin the process of claiming it.

IF WE WERE going to *do* Jakarta, why not do it in style, at the swankiest place in town? This was what Bella asked, rhetorically, an hour or so later, as we lay side by side in lounge chairs at the pool. She looked like she'd been planning this outing, or at least packing for it, for a lifetime, with a batik scarf wrapped around her head (fashionable, yet useful for religious-sensitivity purposes), oversized sunglasses, and a sarong hiding her minuscule bump. She ordered us a pair of Niçoise salads and virgin piña coladas and commenced comparing and contrasting the virtues of this particular poolside setup with other luxurious accommodations around the world. Dubai rooftops had the funkiest views, which I'm not sure she meant in a good way; Florence the most romantic; Delhi was too smoggy; ditto on the pollution in Bangkok and Beijing; Singapore was perfect, but why would you want to go there, really; and Tokyo . . . Mexico City . . . Jerusalem . . . I listened with feigned interest; since I was never going to any of these places, she might as well have been describing the surface of Mars. Only Bella could rattle off these names, these rooftops, these fabulous hotels, and make it seem so matter-of-fact. This was simply her life—it had been for the brief time when Lars remained on the tennis circuit, and now, through her own work, she was managing to find ways to continue to roam in relative style. She wasn't bragging about this, exactly; or, if she was, I was too enthralled by her to see. At the time, I took at face value that she was simply mentioning these places the way a motorist might name-drop rest stops along the New Jersey Turnpike, debating which ones had cleaner bathroom facilities. If anything, she'd tell you that she found it all pretty tiresome, that what she really longed for was a little boredom in her life, a small, quaint house with a garden and a picket fence, a slobbering dog, that sort of thing. I think she was talking herself into, or out of, the bad decision she was about to make, finding a way to bridge mentally the fact that she'd made a hot mess.

I remember, lying by the pool, the sensation that I was swaying, as if I had just stepped off a ship. I put my hands on my belly and waited for a kick, which had become my way of grounding myself lately, but when it didn't come, I didn't think too much of it. She was a peaceful infant, whoever she was, and not much of an acrobat. I could see her already, although I tried not to see, having grown up with the sort of Old World superstition that caused my grandmother literally to spit and throw salt over her shoulder to ward off the evil eye, *kein ayin hara*, whenever someone muttered anything the least bit nice about her, or about me, or even about the lovely weather. She'd shush all compliments should someone comment on my fledgling signs of talent—as if saying it was so, even just a throwaway comment about my ability to draw, would make the skill evaporate or actively invite disaster. Whether she ever paused to consider that the absence of encouragement might have its own detrimental effect, who knows? So I tried not to think about her too much, this person growing inside me, and yet felt I knew her, a little bookish introvert with unruly black curls. I'd swaddle her in the receiving blanket Vince's mother had already bought. It was adorned in cheerful blue and red bears.

Because my husband's family knew nothing of persecution, of superstition, of spit and salt, Vince thought it strange that one might wait to prepare for the baby until it arrived, and so he planned to paint the nursery while I was away. Even though I would have preferred to wait, I didn't give this too much thought; I just assumed that, like every other project he said he would undertake, it wouldn't get done.

The skinny boy whose job it was to stand sentry by the pool came over every few moments, offering to spritz us with Evian and refresh our supply of drinks and towels. I listened to Bella continue to namedrop exotic cities, but I was feeling heavy and depleted and was melting into my chair. Bella seemed to have more stamina; maybe she was just the better traveler. This was the farthest from home I'd ever been, and, at least where I came from, this was the sort of journey people spent months planning, reading guidebooks about what to see, what to wear, and how to eat, rather than just jumping on a plane three days after a friend makes an idle suggestion. I hadn't even given thought to the climate this time of year, had only heeded Bella's advice to pack a bathing suit. Who knew what the exchange rate was, or what the currency was called? Until we arrived at the airport and Bella led us toward an ATM, I hadn't contemplated the existence of the rupiah in this world. As I lay there sipping soda water, trying to quell my unease, I assured myself that my reaction was the normal one—that at some basic physical level this sort of travel was fundamentally unsound; the human body wasn't meant to step off an airplane after flying halfway around the world and slip right into the new time warp without a hiccup or two. Perhaps there was something wrong with *Bella* for being so adaptable. Maybe Bella was so unmoored by the mess of her life, or just so restless generally, that she occupied most comfortably the space on hotel rooftops, where there was minimal connection to reality.

Me, I needed a nap and a guidebook and several days to adjust to this unfamiliar landscape, to get my mind around this skyline that looked like it might have been haphazardly assembled from a template in an urban-design class. The assignment: create a modern, soulless metropolis using an assortment of asymmetrical and incongruous skyscrapers while paying lip service to the Old World bazaars. This was so disorienting that I was weirdly comforted by my own sweat, relieved that it was still with me, that it had managed to transport all this way.

Not only was I disoriented, but I truly felt unwell. I locked into the familiarity of Bella's voice as she moved on to comparing the virtues of various Niçoise salads she'd sampled around the world. If I squinted, I could make believe we were in Miami, and the palm trees, the pulsing electronic music pouring from invisible poolside speakers, and all of the stylish fellow hotel guests made this easier than I might have supposed. Even the family of what Bella said were Libyans, with the women in abayas, did nothing to detract from my decision to pretend that we were simply in South Florida.

After Bella ran out of travelogue, we read for an hour before returning to our room. We showered and dressed, and by then it was time for dinner. I agreed, even in my woozy state, that since we had so little time in Jakarta we ought to dine outside the hotel, in an effort to continue to explore the city. Not that there was much to explore: from what I could tell and from what I had heard, apart from the few old markets like the one to which we had already been, the place seemed to be dominated by shopping malls. We nevertheless planned to ask the hotel staff for dinner recommendations. I hoped we wouldn't wind up anywhere too fancy, because I felt positively bovine in my only seasonally appropriate maternity dress. Bella looked gorgeous, of course. She wore a blue sleeveless shift accessorized by another fabulous batik scarf. Before Bella adopted the more conservative wardrobe of a banker, she was always draped or wrapped, like a princess, or a gift. We had just alit from the elevator and were headed toward the concierge when it caught my eye, beckoning to me in the same way that bed had done a few hours earlier: the pig.

I tapped Bella's shoulder and pointed toward the gift-shop window. Her eye went straight to the pig, too, even though it was one of many objects on display, and one of the tiniest at that, dwarfed by a couple of sinister-looking shadow puppets on either side. The pig, a tiny bronze orb, was compact and self-contained, like a vacuum cleaner that needs no attachments. An all-in-one pig, its face etched right onto its body.

Bella and I, too, were back to all-in-one: a pair of giggling girls locked arm in arm, determined to have that pig. I won't pretend to recall our actual dialogue—I'm always suspicious of those who claim to remember in detail events from long ago—but I know that we went inside the gift shop and purchased that pig, and we decided on the spot that we'd keep it forever to commemorate this trip.

And what of this trip? To the extent that the reason for it might have seemed even the least bit fabricated, which it genuinely did not, I figured the only excuse for deception might have been because Bella needed to get away and reboot. A few weeks prior to our departure, she had been in full crisis mode. She had shown up unexpectedly on my doorstep on a Tuesday night at midnight, woken me and Vince up, scaring us both half to death with her maniacal ringing of the bell. It would be an understatement to say that Vince was not happy about this, or about the fact that I sat with her, talking, until 4:00 a.m. She had just discovered she was pregnant.

Vince had become one of those well-meaning but suffocating spouses; he wanted to micromanage my pregnancy. He read *What to Expect When You're Expecting*, and tried to regulate my sleep and diet and exercise. He had come into the kitchen at least three times that night to suggest that whatever drama was unfolding could surely wait until morning, and that I should send Bella home and get some sleep.

I was exhausted, and of course he was right, particularly since I had only recently begun my new job at the magazine and needed to be in for a meeting by 9:00 a.m., but I'd been through a lot with Bella over the last couple of years, and I'd never seen her this wrecked. Discovering her condition should have been a good thing, given that she'd been trying to conceive since around the time I'd first met her, but her life had been so *eventful*—her word, I assure you, not mine— these last few weeks that she wasn't sure who the father was, even though the timing pointed toward Raymond. Still, it could have been Guillermo. And maybe the outside possibility of Lars, but she couldn't remember, with any accuracy, the date when they'd last had sex. Before winding up hysterical and wretched at my kitchen table, she'd gone first to Raymond, who'd been in New York, and then, the next day, to Guillermo, who'd been en route to the ballpark for practice. Neither one of them had seemed particularly animated by the situation. Raymond had been on his way to the theater with Seema, and he told Bella, somewhat dismissively, to calm down and go back to D.C. and suggested they talk by phone later. Guillermo didn't speak enough English to understand, or at least that's what he indicated, even though Bella was pretty sure she was saying the Spanish word for baby correctly (wasn't it *bebé*?!), and if she had it wrong, pointing to her belly and indicating a mound with her hand ought to have gotten the message across. I didn't know what to say. This was the stuff of daytime soaps, not the sort of thing that was supposed to happen to a highly educated woman who knew her way around birth control. But she'd been trying to get pregnant for so long she'd basically given up hope, and, hard as it was to believe, she said she'd sort of forgotten about this potential outcome. Meanwhile, Lars had seen the pregnancy test in the bathroom trash, pressed for an answer, and gone straight to the store for champagne.

Complicated backstory notwithstanding, we were both pregnant in Jakarta, and were determined to enjoy ourselves. This would be our own pre-motherhood, chick-flick-style getaway, and we decided on the spot to memorialize this with the pig. What we'd really wanted was two pigs, but in the shop there was only one. The shopkeeper, who wore a lurid neon-yellow polyester shirt, and who told us as we entered that his cousin lived in Nashville, Tennessee, set his cigarette in an overflowing ashtray that already had another butt alit, and put both hands on the counter to lean in hard to close the deal. If we paid for two right now, he said, he'd get us another by morning. In the next sentence, however, he let on confusingly, and in reference to the extortionist price of four hundred dollars, that the pig was one of a kind. We bargained him down to $220, which still seemed obscene, but we bought it anyway, rationalizing that we were feeding the economy like good tourists. Anyway, the steep price tag would make the pig feel special, and would invest the pig with extra, if illusory, value. As he wrapped it in newspaper and bound it in twine, he mentioned that he had a brother who owned the new, hot, excellent seafood restaurant just a mile up the road, on the twenty-second floor of the brand-new Malia Intercontinental, and that if we wanted the best view of Jakarta, for another fifty rupiah, he would call ahead and see that we were treated like VIPs. We shrugged our shoulders and smiled. We were already in deep, so why not?

A HOTEL LIMO was summoned, and forty minutes later, traffic being even more hideous than the Capital Beltway at rush hour, a ridiculous fuss was made over our arrival. Someone was actually waiting for us in the lobby to escort us up the elevator. This was either a sidebar benefit of having paid about ten times the going rate for a bronze pig, or the effect of having pressed Bella's business card into the shopkeeper's hand. We were given such VIP treatment that heads turned our way as we were led to a corner table, and I suspect people thought we were celebrities. Or maybe they thought that Bella was a celebrity and I was her celebrity escort.

We accepted complimentary bubbly apéritifs, our pregnancies notwithstanding, and clinked the tiny glasses. What was it we were celebrating, exactly? That Bella was going to make the best of things, because there was nothing else to be done? Probably that was the decision she had reached, but I'm not sure, since we had stopped talking about it. We were now simply embracing her pregnancy as the reality that it was. I only sipped the alcohol to be polite. I didn't want to drink while pregnant, on top of which I was still feeling ill. The queasiness and nausea were evolving into something more like stomach cramps. I'd eaten so little since arriving that I couldn't pinpoint anything that should have been making me feel unwell, unless it had been something in one of the airplane meals. I tried to block out the voice in my head—Vince's voice, to be exact—telling me this trip was a terrible idea. He had cited a list of concerns ranging from hijacked planes to malaria, dengue fever, and typhoid. He invoked the possibility of terrorist attacks and typhoons. I was surprised he didn't add alien abductions to his list of potential catastrophes. He had even tried to forbid me to go. Usually, in my experience, the exercise of overthinking bad outcomes serves as a sort of balm. It's only in the most rare instance that the neurotic fears prove right. Just because you're paranoid doesn't mean they aren't after you, etc.

In a vivid slow-motion loop, the rest of our time in that restaurant still runs through my head on an almost daily basis, like some particularly bad PTSD. My back was to the doorway. The sun, bleeding a surreal orange from the chemical air, was in its final stage of setting, and the city lights were just beginning to flicker on. I flagged the waiter and ordered a Coke, hoping it might settle my stomach as it had back at the shop in the market earlier that day. I began to tell Bella a funny if convoluted anecdote to do with a photo shoot in the current issue of *MidAtlantic Home* that had gone horribly awry; it involved finding a gun in the vegetable crisper of the homeowner's refrigerator, and having to call the police. Midway through, I realized that Bella wasn't listening to me, which was mostly okay—it was a stupid, meaningless story. I was slow to realize something was wrong. Even slower to realize it involved Raymond. The idea that Raymond, of all the people in the world, might have been in Jakarta, at this moment, at this restaurant, would never have occurred to me as even an outside possibility. He was seated at a nearby table, with another woman.

"Who is she?" Bella asked, as if I might have the answer. As if the answer mattered. They were all the same, from the financial adviser to whom he sent bad poetry, to the stewardess he'd accidentally slept with after one too many beers. Bella didn't understand this, that they were all the same, and she wasted a lot of time and energy parsing their different attributes to understand how she, my otherwise beautiful, confident, talented friend, failed to line up.

Even at that moment I was slow to realize that I had been set up. I would soon come to understand that Bella knew Raymond would be in Jakarta, reading from his new collection at an international literary festival, and that the reporting trip had been devised to get us here. But that he would appear at this restaurant? That part would prove coincidence, although not really *that* coincidental, given that this was evidently the hot new restaurant in town, and that it had just been written up in all of the tourist and airline magazines.

Even as I absorbed the fact of Raymond's presence, I was still slow to process the implications. Or maybe not slow. Maybe my radar was more finely tuned than I appreciated, but I was distracted by two other things: by the cramping in my abdomen, which had now grown a notch more intense, but which I now interpreted as the only reasonable response to vile Raymond's presence, and by an attractive young man in a blue-and-white track suit and a Marlins baseball cap who had just walked into the restaurant and was conferring with the receptionist. He looked to be in his late teens or early twenties, and was having issues growing facial hair, as indicated by his wispy beard. Had we been in Washington or New York, I might have identified him as a bicycle messenger, although whether they had bicycle messengers in Jakarta I had no idea, but the baseball cap caught my eye, and something about him made me think he was a courier of some kind. On these particular details I confess to being a bit fuzzy now, but he might have had a package, or he might have asked to speak to someone, or maybe it was the way he was dressed that made me think he was a messenger. Messenger was now morphing into terrorist in my feverish mind as I replayed Vince's crazy list of fears. I saw him speak to the hostess, and she went to get someone, and some commotion ensued, but it was developing into a night of confusion. Bella got up from the table, walked over to where Raymond was seated, and in a not very Bella-like way (in her defense, not that I'm inclined to defend her, she was seven weeks pregnant and very hormonal) threw her drink at him and let loose with a string of overly loud invectives about his being a two-timing cad. (A wildly amusing understatement, I might point out.) I didn't know what to do, but as her friend, I felt I should do something to save her from further humiliating herself. I walked toward Raymond's table and put my hand lightly on the small of her back to lead her back to our table. Her scarf was coming unwrapped, and I picked up a piece of the fringe to keep it from falling to the floor. She pushed my hand away, which was more upsetting than perhaps it should have been. Then my body was seized by a full-on contraction, and I let out a little moan. Raymond stood up, and for one delusional second I thought he was going to help me, but instead he took Bella's arm and led her to the door, and they left the restaurant.

Raymond's companion and I exchanged strained, awkward smiles. If there was an appropriate thing to say in these circumstances, some etiquette governing the exchange between the current mistress and the former mistress's best friend, it apparently eluded us both, but she at least had manners, and she stood up to shake my hand. She was tall and dark and surprisingly plain—not half as beautiful as Bella, or even Seema—and this may be difficult to believe, but she was pregnant. Somewhere, I'd say, in the fifth month. Again I was racked with a contraction, such a ferocious one that I nearly doubled over. After it passed, I asked the alarmed pregnant mistress if she knew where the bathroom was. She told me, in a British accent, that it was to the left behind the bar, and asked if I needed any help. I thanked her and said no. As I made my way there, I noticed the messenger turn to leave, but he had forgotten his bag. Now I was certain something was wrong, and I thought about flagging someone, but I was about to double over. I would later reflect on this man, on the coincidence of my premonition and its possible meaning. He was, in fact, only a messenger, but perhaps his message was that there was something else sinister in the air.

I had only just walked into the bathroom and turned the lock in the stall when I felt the ground begin to shake. The building was brand-new, and the bathroom was elegant, with marble floors and stalls like little private offices, which is not the sort of thing you notice until you are essentially locked inside the cubicle because a piece of the ceiling has just fallen on the door, and you hear mirrors shatter and the sound of water surging from pipes and then, a moment later, the electricity fails. I still didn't know what was going on. I was now in the pitch-dark, thinking thoughts that didn't add up. If this was a bomb, was I already dead? If this was a quake, might there be a tsunami to follow? I found myself calculating, in the screwy way one's mind works when in shock, that we would be okay because we were high up, on the twenty-second floor.

Perhaps the place was imploding from the coincidence of three pregnant, volatile women under one roof, was my last coherent, or maybe incoherent, thought before I passed out.

The news stories focused on our collective good fortune. It had been a relatively small quake, but the building was so flimsy, and so many aspects of the construction were below code, that the infrastructure crumbled and the walls came crashing down much more easily than they should have. Four people died. *Only* four. That's how they spun it, as if this were a thing to celebrate, four being so much better than, say, five. That one woman miscarried alone in the dark did not merit any ink.

That was the last time I saw Bella. She tried to visit me in the hospital. She wanted to help arrange my travel back. I refused to see her, even though I almost softened when I heard her voice and picked up her scent in the hallway when she came by my hospital room with a sprig of jasmine. Later, back home, I saw her number a few times on my caller ID, and she once left a message. After that, I never heard from her again. She might have put a little more energy into seeking my forgiveness. She had, after all, found the resources to stalk Raymond Branch halfway around the world. Given all that effort, I think she might have tried a little harder to stalk me.

VINCE AND I separated within a year, which was both easier and harder than I'd anticipated. It was a relief to detach from his sluggish and debilitating rhythms, which had begun to wear me down, and yet in their absence I found that my own movements nearly ground to a halt. For a time I worried that I'd misunderstood the dynamic—I'd thought the parasitic nature of our relationship was grinding me down, but after he left I realized, belatedly, that it might have been the only thing spurring me along.

The price of my friendship with Bella had been unusually steep. I wondered if my outcome ever weighed on her, or if she ever even thought of me. I couldn't see any evidence of remorse from what I glimpsed of her on television, nor did I sense remorse inside her house. There was nothing here but the trappings of success embellished with a nice messy normalcy. Was it really possible that Bella's actions had had no consequences at all, for anyone but me?

I STOOD FROZEN in the doorway of the master bedroom, staring at the bed. *My* bed. It was madness enough to want to sit on the floor and feed the dusty dolls their plastic food, but the sudden desire I felt to climb into the bed was surely certifiable lunacy. Because I was, in fact, feeling rather mad, and because it really was the very definition of madness to be in this house in the first place, I decided that the only counter to this crazy situation was to leave immediately and never come back.

I thought I was leaving, actually, when, on my way out the door, I caught a whiff of that horrible, rancid smell again, and felt obliged to at least to see what was going on. For all I knew, there might be a body decomposing in the cellar, which seemed to be the direction from which it was emanating. I descended hesitantly, in part because I couldn't find a light switch at the top of the stairs, but also because I was a little afraid of what I might discover. After locating a switch at the bottom, I flipped on the light and could see instantly that the word "cellar" had no place in the lexicon of this house. "Lower-level luxury suite" would be the better description for this basement, with the exception of a rather dark, depressing, windowless bedroom. A nanny's room, most likely. A glimpse inside suggested that it was being occupied; there was a pair of Converse sneakers on the floor, some clothing items on the unmade bed, and a whiff of perfume, or maybe just of some lotion or hair conditioner, lingering in the air, a few of its fragrant molecules still miraculously isolated from the larger stench.

Immediately past the bedroom was an expansive room with mirrors on every wall that looked like an exclusive-membership gym. There was a rack containing a full range of free weights, as well as two elliptical machines, two treadmills, and two flat-screen televisions. Off to the right of this was a separate room with a shower and a sauna. Sliding glass doors led to the garden, with a pool, beyond which appeared to be a cabana.

I continued to explore, flipping on light switches as I walked, pinching my nose in a hopeless attempt to filter the stench. Heading back in the other direction, I found a playroom with buckets full of toys, as well as a little faux-grocery-store area with a cash register and shelves full of cardboard food. One might reasonably suppose there was some sort of group day-care program being run in this house, given the quality and quantity of toys.

If there was a way to quantify the degrees of badness of a very bad smell, I would say it was getting worse, doubling in intensity just about every second, to the point where it was now close to unbearable. The smell led me to the utility room, where I found the washer/dryer (one of two laundry rooms in this exquisitely renovated home!), the hot-water heater, the furnace, and an enormous freezer (also one of two in this double-everything distinctive residence, within walking distance of excellent public schools, not that anyone in this neighborhood would deign to use the public schools!).

Then I saw the freezer, and knew, suddenly and without question, that the smell was coming from within. I should have left, and yet there I was, grabbing a dish towel from the pile of neatly folded laundry resting in a basket on top of the clothes dryer, pressing it to my nose. I closed my eyes and opened the top, anticipating some horror inside. Raymond Branch might be in there, for all I knew, cut up into tiny pieces. (Does it make me an awful person to confess that the thought, ridiculous as it was, gave me some sly satisfaction?) I found nothing quite as dramatic as a corpse in there, however. In the split second before I began to gag, I glimpsed dozens of gallon-sized freezer bags of the sort one uses to preserve leftovers. And there was the usual assortment of freezer foods—those colorful ice pops that Zed used to like, frozen lasagnas, and, for reasons I didn't want to explore too fully, especially since I had already entertained the thought of dead bodies, a couple of naked Barbie dolls, which, though amusing, frankly seemed disrespectful of the vast investment in this child's playthings. All of it stank indescribably. I slammed shut the lid and ran to the garage, opened the door, braced myself against a Mercedes, then stumbled out into the driveway, where there was a Lincoln Navigator SUV, and gasped in air like a dying fish.

Obviously, all of this putrid food was going to have to be removed from the freezer and hauled to the trash. Although in my handful of previous commissions I had gracefully performed, without complaint, many a task more properly suited to a maid than to a stager, emptying this freezer seemed firmly outside the realm of my job description. On top of which, I thought I had already decided to quit this job. Nevertheless, I pulled my phone from my pocket and tried to reach Amanda; the call went straight to voice mail.

After a few deep breaths, I decided that there was little choice. Simply walking away and leaving the putrid contents in the freezer felt unethical, somehow, or at least lazy, like leaving your shopping cart blocking a parking spot rather than wheeling it back to the front of the store. I gave myself a little pep talk, and went back inside.

As soon as I re-entered the utility room, it all clicked. Crouched beside the freezer was a rabbit. It looked unwell. Large tufts of hair were missing, and its eyes were glassy and unfocused. It looked a little psychotic, which is not to suggest I knew rabbits well enough to determine the status of one's mental health. Then I saw the cord, the plastic casing gnawed, the electrical wire exposed. The animal must have chewed through the freezer's electrical cord during this same weekend of debauchery in which it had consumed and then regurgitated the living-room carpet. This had caused all the contents of the freezer to become defrosted, stinking up the house.

The animal was quivering as it cowered between the freezer and the washing machine, and I paused to consider the effect on a rabbit's stomach of two square feet of white Berber carpet, as well as an unknown amount of electrical casing and wire. Did it look sort of guilty, as if it was aware of the consequences of what it had just done, or was I imagining this? Then again, the rabbit had a nose, so maybe he—or she—was simply delirious from this smell.

Rummaging around, I found rubber gloves and some heavy-duty trash bags, and, without further contemplation as to how I had descended so quickly from being the managing editor of a prestigious shelter magazine to being Bella's de-facto cleaning lady, I went to work emptying the freezer. Over the course of the next hour, I hauled three giant green plastic bags to the edge of the property, where they would, I hoped, be taken away by the sanitation department without any close scrutiny as to whether I had violated the county's byzantine trash and recycling rules, which I probably had. My own refuse had once been rejected for mixing in some plastic with the cardboard, and it was surprisingly dispiriting to fail at being able to get rid of one's own waste. Then I went back inside and used every spray cleaner within reach to scour the inside of the freezer and, I hoped, to counteract the smell. After opening the basement windows, I turned off the lights, picked up the animal, and ascended the stairs.

The door from the basement opened directly into Bella's stunning if chaotic kitchen. Cleaned up, it was the sort of kitchen that would have merited a spread or, like her living room, a come-hither centerfold in *MidAtlantic Home*. Among its amenities was a Sub-Zero refrigerator with a glass door, generally an elegant design feature, but in this case not such a good idea: you could see fingerprints all over the glass, plus you could peer straight into the jumbled mess inside. The rest of the kitchen was outfitted with the full orchestra of gleaming, high-end stainless-steel appliances: a restaurant-grade Viking range, a Miele dishwashing machine, a refrigerated wine rack, soapstone countertops, a mosaic of glass tiles for the backsplash, and the perfect, elegant touch of a crystal chandelier. The distinctive beadboard cabinetry was recognizable as almost certainly the work of one of the magazine's advertisers. Or, rather, *former* magazine. *Former* advertisers. It was breathtaking. Was I so shallow a person that what I envied most about Bella was not her beauty, or her almost unfathomable success, or the fact that her marriage had endured despite the disrespect Bella had shown the institution, or her obvious wealth, or her daughter, or her possession of both my pig and my bed, but her kitchen?

No. But. Still. This all seemed blatantly unfair. It wasn't as if Bella even cooked! Back when we'd been friends, she'd had trouble using a can opener, and I'd once had to talk her through microwaving a cup of instant soup. Expensive finishings didn't mean this kitchen was quite ready for prime time, however—it was as cluttered and overly lived in and in need of staging as any of the other rooms in this place. The countertops were jammed with at least a half-dozen high-end small appliances. Was there a personal barista who made cappuccino in the mornings? Was there so much puréeing going on here that the Sorkin-Jorgenson family required not one but two fourteen-cup Cuisinart Elites? Also on display were so many canisters of breakfast cereal it seemed she might be running a bed-and-breakfast. All of this would have to go.

With the rabbit in my arms, I opened the door to the enormous refrigerator, not just grimy with fingerprints but streaked with what was clearly the wrong sort of cleaning formula. I then pulled out the vegetable crisper to see if there was any lettuce I could give the animal, assuming its digestive system wasn't fried. No lettuce, but I found a bag of wilted carrots, and pulled one out. I wasn't sure if I needed to wash and peel it first. I decided probably not. I offered the carrot to the rabbit, but it didn't so much as blink. I tried to insert the carrot in the animal's mouth, but it wouldn't unclench its teeth.

I heard voices, and to say that my heart stopped would not technically be to employ a cliché, because I believe that, for a moment, it actually did, and I thought I might faint. Before I could catch my breath and announce my presence, two people, a young girl and a young woman, moved toward the kitchen.

She looked just like the girl in the portrait, except that she was a few years older and now a little on the heavy side. She was clad in a field-hockey uniform and holding a stick. Her long brown hair was pulled back in a ponytail and affixed with a ribbon, and she had bold blue eyes. Maybe I was projecting this, but she looked to me like a girl who knew exactly who she was and what she wanted from this world, and who would consequently smash you over the head with her hockey stick to get it.

The young woman carried with her the pleasant scent I'd detected in the downstairs bedroom. They were discussing the amount of homework in the child's backpack, and how long that would take to complete.

I was on the verge of squeezing out the word "hello," but before I could speak, the girl spotted me and for a split second we locked eyes. She looked at me like I was an ax murderer, or someone who knew the extent of her mother's capacity to lie. The girl charged at me and screamed the name "Dominique"; the rabbit fell from my arms. The young woman came in behind her and began to scream, too. We all stared at the animal, inert on the floor.

PART III

POOLS
OF LIGHT

LARS

n the fine print of the five pages of warnings that accompany the Praxisis refill is the following disclaimer: "In extreme cases, the first-person narration may be told as a story within a story, with the narrator appearing as a character in the story." I don't know what this means, but it doesn't sound good.

Like a neurotic who begins to twitch just hearing about the existence of Tourette's in the world, I realize this is precisely what's happening to me—I'm stuck inside my own story and I can't get out.

"Lighten up, man," says Dominique, pulling on a Marlboro Light. He scratches his head with his foot, demonstrating an impressive, if unsurprising, limberness, and generates a couple of perfect smoke rings. It has not previously occurred to me that my rabbit might smoke, and his voice, too, is utterly unexpected—not just that he has one, but that he speaks with a slightly Southern accent, and in a frankly grating tone.

"I know it's bad . . . It was bad for me, too," he says. "That's why I had to get out of that house."

"It's a nice house. And we treated you well. Sure, maybe we could have done a better job, but I mean, we did our best. We fed you, we tried to cuddle you. We put little toys in your cage. Let's be honest— you weren't a very good pet."

"Oh, *please*. Let's not go there, okay? I mean, I get that you guys aren't bad people. You're just . . . *people*. Self-absorbed, stuck in your worldview, unable to think outside the box. That's all I'm saying."

Hay and grass, plus the fecal smell of fresh mulch, mingle with the incongruous aroma of fresh-baked sugary things. My stomach rumbles. I'd had dinner on the plane, but I'm still hungry. Losing six hours means I really need dinner twice. Or is it the opposite? Maybe I ate twice but should've eaten only once? The math is confusing, especially in my current state; plus, these kinds of complicated logic problems have never been my strong suit. Have I mentioned I was a tennis star once? A whirling dervish in Tretorns? The only math I'd ever needed was to count my cash. Anyway, it hardly matters; whatever time it is in whatever country I'm in, I'm hungry, and I have the sense that here, in the dark, in a field, there will not be a stewardess bearing a tray of food.

It's a beautiful night, with clear stars and a slim crescent moon. I stick a piece of straw between my teeth and, staring up at the sky, I try to identify the constellations, which is difficult without my glasses. I fumble through my pockets and realize it's possible that I've lost them along the way, probably back at the pharmacy, when I took them out to read the literature that came with my Praxisis. But I'm not going to stress; I'll take the rabbit's advice. I'll lighten up, go with the flow, shed my angst, and pop another pill.

To Dominique I say, "I thought you were . . . French. Also, I thought you were . . . I hate to say it and don't take it the wrong way, but I was under the impression you were dead."

"Just because you gave me a French name doesn't make me French. If you'd named me Kyung Don Park, it wouldn't make me Korean. If you'd named me Veronica, it wouldn't make me a girl. If you'd named me Honda Odyssey . . ."

"Okay, I get it. Fair enough, and many apologies. I really don't remember how you wound up with that name, but I assure you it wasn't my call. Nothing in that house is ever my call."

"Oh, poor self-pitying you! But you've got no one to blame except yourself for that, man. No one is making you stay with your controlling, cheating wife. But back to my problems—lest I remind you that you wanted to name me Thumper?"

"*Me?* No! That was Elsa!"

"Yeah, but you backed her up. I mean, I probably could have lived with Thumper—at least it's not pompous. Still, you might have lobbied a little harder for something strong and masculine. My dignity was at stake."

"I have no memory of this debate."

"Well, you wouldn't, would you? Your brain is fried, my friend. And you let your wife run the show, so let's face it, Dominique was a fait accompli. Fancy a spot of tea?"

"You are one asshole rabbit. But I guess we already knew that about you. I assume the tea part is a joke. Unless you have a kettle out here in the middle of wherever it is we are."

"I can make that happen for you. And I'm not an asshole rabbit, I'm a fucking *wonder* rabbit, my friend. There are many things you don't know about me. Many things you don't know about the world, for that matter. You've been too lost in yourself, Lars. It could be a television show: *Lost with Lars.* Tonight's episode would begin:

"Suburban streetscape at night, quiet but for a single taxi, from which our protagonist emerges. He moves with difficulty, obese, arthritic in the knees. He stands before his front door, his shirt untucked, scratching his head, looking extremely confused."

"As I was saying, you are one mean rabbit. Could I at least point out that I'm not obese? Also, I don't have arthritis. I blew out my meniscus on the left and . . ."

"Well, you can have some editorial input, I suppose, given that it's your story and I don't want you to sue me, but I think that, clinically speaking, I'm really sorry to say it, you're obese. I'm just talking facts, Lars, so don't take it personally. Anyway, back to our regularly scheduled programming: I'm not big on the narrative device of having characters talk to themselves, but in this case it might be unavoidable. We have some problems of exposition, so we need some way to let the audience know that the door to your house—well, *our* house, right?— has been painted a different color, and then, when you turn the key in the lock, you're even more confused because it fits, but when you look inside, everything is different. You'll have to say something like 'Wow, this door used to be the color black! And what happened to my beloved painting? This is my house, but it no longer looks like my house!' And then you can do something physical to emphasize this, like maybe look confused or scratch your head or . . . what else do humans do? Maybe put your finger on your chin and raise those furry things above your eyes."

"My eyebrows?"

"Yeah, those. They need a trim."

"I don't want to be mean, but that's all pretty clunky and forced. I think you want the dialogue to sound more natural. Maybe try using some contractions? My father was a writer, so I know something about this."

"Yeah, everyone's a critic! But you try it. It's a lot harder than it looks. Also, we'll have to find a way to let them know that Lars is a wreck already. Backstory is hard to weave in, but you can do little, subtle things to convey that he can't hold down a job, his wife is worried sick about him, and he's totally stuck."

"Two interjections, if I may. First of all, I can hold down a job, it's just hard to find one right now. You know, the recession, the financial crisis, sequestration, all those problems with mortgages, houses underwater, banks failing, high unemployment—don't you follow the news?"

"Yes, we all know how that impacts the tennis world."

"Well, it does, in a way. Have you heard about a trickle-down economy and other economics stuff? Or is your little rabbit brain unable to understand such financial complexities?"

"Yes, I've heard that millionaires can't afford their country clubs."

"It's true. I was giving private lessons for a while, you know. Maybe that was before your time."

"Ah, so your students couldn't afford you anymore?"

"Well, it wasn't that. It was more my knee. If I can't play, how can I be an effective teacher? And sidebar point—I've just picked up some construction skills. When we move to London, I may apprentice as a roofer. Hey, what's that strange noise? Are you okay? Are you choking on something?"

"No, sorry, it's cool. That's just me being amused. You might not know this, but rabbits can't really laugh. Just the idea of you doing manual labor . . . Sorry. Actually, I am choking. I need another sip of tea."

"You have a mean streak, did you know that? Really, what did we ever do to deserve this sort of treatment from you?"

"Okay, seriously, let's not have this conversation. It's not going to lead anywhere productive."

"If you weren't my pet, if it wasn't for Elsa, I might pick you up and strangle you."

"It's possible, you know, that I'm already dead, so if the spirit moves you . . ."

"Don't push me. But if I may back up, in my own defense I'd just like to say that I have a lot going on in my life right now. I'm in the middle of moving, and I'm dealing with some major things."

"Okay, that's great. Very helpful, very deep. So we need a way to convey, instantly, that this guy is, like, not only completely paralyzed but in total denial about it. He can't seem to extricate himself from a lousy situation, because he won't even admit that he's in one to begin with. It's clear to everyone around him that his marriage is killing him, almost literally, and he really needs to get away and reboot, but he can't. Or he won't. I mean, any other man would pack his bags and go climb a mountain, or enlist to fight a war, or go on a rampage, maybe kill his two-timing wife, put her body parts in the blender, or just do something totally radical . . ."

"So you're proposing I put Bella in a blender? *That's* your solution?"

"You're putting words in my mouth. I'm just saying the guy, if you want the audience to root for him, needs to have some sort of epiphany and finally take action. And maybe this guy—by which I mean the fictional you, the superhero you (not actual schlubby, pathetic *you* you)—is on the verge. Maybe, when he arrives at the house on this particular evening, it's the turning point. You are supposed to begin a story like that, with a sort of *why now*. You know, like on Passover, when you say, "Why is this night different from all other nights?"

"Are you Jewish?"

"Three of my possible fathers were. What? Don't look so shocked! There are a lot of things you don't know about me. But this is not about me."

"No, it's just that I didn't ever think about rabbits having religion. Also, I didn't know you were a screenwriter. And, no offense, but since we seem to be speaking freely, I just want to say that if you're a screenwriter it sounds like you're kind of a hack."

"I'd take offense if I wasn't feeling so mellow right now. Here, have a cup of tea. I insist."

Weirdly, I haven't noticed until just now that he has a little table set up, with a teapot and two cups, painted in cabbage roses, resting in saucers.

"You have Bella's china!"

"She won't mind. I borrowed a few things. That crazy Stager woman working in your house, she put it in boxes anyway, so I figured you didn't want it anymore."

"That belonged to Bella's grandmother."

"Don't have a coronary, Lars. I said I'd just borrowed it. Anyway, quality tea demands quality china. And this is not just any tea, my friend, this is Unfurlings Tea. Totally organic. No sugar, either, not that you look like someone who cares. But I'm telling you, you'll see the world in a whole new way."

"Thanks, but I'm more of a coffee drinker. I'm really into the new Blonde Roasts. Anyway, I'm already feeling pretty mellow. I can almost see the light, I'm getting so close, even right now, here in the dark . . . which reminds me, I have a question for you. Well, a few, really."

"Fire away."

"Well, this isn't really my main question, but how did you even make the tea? I mean, like, actually *make* the tea. Because we seem to be in a field, and I don't see a stove. Or even a campfire. Or a kettle. But I smell food."

"Seriously, *that's* your question? When I'm in the position to answer so many more important things? If a genie gave you one wish, would you ask for a hamburger?"

"Maybe. I'm pretty hungry right now, so maybe I'd ask for a platter with fries and a milkshake."

"Get serious, Lars. Aren't you the least bit curious to know how it is you are talking to me?"

"Ah, that. No. I'm all over that one. The ability to converse with you is one of the lesser-known side effects of mixing too many medications containing the letters x and z, but if you read the footnote of the fine print down where it refers to omniscience, it does suggest, in so many words, that if you take more than a thousand milligrams of Praxisis combined with seven tiny bottles of gin and then, from thirty-three thousand feet, you see your wife standing in front of the house of Raymond Branch, who may or may not be the father of your child, and who you thought was actually ancient history—your wife told you that much, again and again—and then, and then, well, then you order a few more gins—then it is not at all unreasonable to think you might find yourself standing in a field, talking to the family pet, who seems, the more he talks, to be stoned. Were you always stoned, or am I just noticing this now? Because something about this feels weirdly normal."

"Well, you heard Bella say that your definition of normal has become rather elastic. And, no, I was never stoned at your house, although I would have had a better time of it had I been. It's the tea."

"How did you know about that conversation? You weren't even there. And if you know everything, can you explain to me everyone's fascination with that Raymond cad?"

"You're transparent, man. You've got so much transparency flowing, it's like you're permeable. I can see right through you. You're just jealous of that guy. He can write, he can make things rhyme. Women like shit like that. But he's kind of mean, or at least a little cutting. I once heard him comment on Bella's weight."

"Bella? She's perfect. I'm going to go beat him up . . . Okay, really, please don't start choking again."

"I'd like to buy a ringside seat for that! I'm telling you, but you're not listening, that if you had some tea you might actually have the power to do that. Anyway, this is no longer optional. I insist. It's part of why I brought you out here to our control center. We're doing some tests before we start selling it commercially. Whole Foods is interested in being an investor, which would be a huge coup. Also, the lady in that house over there, she's a real sweetheart, she might be able to get them to sell some of her baked goods, which would be great. She's a good person, just down on her luck."

"Okay, if you insist. I am thirsty, and maybe if we put some sugar in the tea, that will help with my hunger. I should probably try to sit up, but . . . well, it seems I can't. What are you talking about, anyway? What lady? Did you say baked goods? Is that what I smell?"

"Yes. Marta—she's living in that model home right there. Her husband, he returned from Afghanistan last year and he's wrecked even worse than you, man. I mean, you're just wrecked in the head, and a little in the knees, but this guy lost a leg and he's out of his mind. He thinks she was fooling around with his friend, and in fact he did beat him up. And he beat her up, too. She had to leave, and she took the kids. She's been living here for about six months now. But don't tell him."

"Seriously? Man, that's bad stuff. Was she actually fooling around with his friend?"

"Who cares? You humans, you get totally tripped up by the whole fidelity thing."

"Okay, well, look, I hear you. It shouldn't be important. I keep telling myself that. But it's hard to get over, especially when you mix in the DNA question."

"Yeah, but, really, is it so important? I mean, look at me: My mother had seven hundred and fifty-six related offspring in one mating season. It could have been seven hundred and fifty-five but we were never sure if my sister Lakshmi was part of the fifth litter or if she just got lost and wound up in our brood; we let her in anyway, and my mother raised her like one of her own, which is the way it should be. And we're all close, or we were close until I was kidnapped by some hustler who sold me on Craigslist, but that's another story. Do you think my mother cared that she never even knew the names of half the fathers? I mean, at the end of the day, we're all rabbits, right? Two ears, cute little tails. We hop."

"Bravo for you. But we're not rabbits. Maybe the fact that we care about these things is what makes us the higher beings."

"No, actually, I read somewhere that it has to do with sweat. Animals that sweat—like you—can outrun animals that pant, like me, so, in pure Darwinian terms, that makes you the boss. It's all about sweat."

"I'm not sure that's true. Over distance and time you might out-sprint me."

"That's not entirely the point, Lars. Your higher beingness is certainly not about brains or good judgment, because frankly, in this day and age, do you really expect me to believe you don't know who Elsa's father is? That not a single one of you knows? If I had to bet, I'd put my money on Raymond rather than Guillermo. Or you. Raymond's a shady character, a bit of a rapid breeder himself. This ain't the first place he's left his mark, if you know what I mean. Also, I mean, come on, Lars, let's just face reality. Haven't you noticed your daughter has his cleft chin?"

"Maybe. But you know this gene stuff can be confusing. There's, like, dominant traits and recessive traits. You just never know what's going on. My grandfather might have had a cleft chin. Anyway, how do you know about Raymond and Guillermo?"

"You keep asking me the same question over and over. How do *you* know what you know?"

"I read some e-mails. Plus, someone sent me a messed-up Facebook message."

"Ah, well, that's a little more pedestrian. Me, I just . . . know. And once you get this tea flowing, you'll know, too. A little advice, my friend, is that shining some light on this might help. You've got, what, four highly educated people involved here—although I take that back, who knows if the baseball player can even spell his own name—but you're all pretending you don't know who the father is? All you have to do is take a piece of Elsa's hair down to Walgreens."

"I think that's oversimplifying how it works, but I get your drift. Still, at the end of the day, what's the point? It's not like I'm going to walk away if I find out she's not my kid. I mean, maybe I would have left if I'd found out at the start, but to learn this now? What do you even do with that information?"

"That's what I'm saying, man. You have to transcend this stuff. Plus, there are some problems you can't solve on the ground. You've just got to take some of this stuff to another level. That's what the philosophy shit is all about."

"Oh, you're not just a talking stoner rabbit, now you're a philosopher rabbit?"

"Tea. Tea. Tea."

"It's still too hot. I think it's better to just live in denial. You know, to hold on to the possibility that she is mine."

"Oh, like you're doing so well with that decision."

"Well, you say that like you'd know what to do."

"Hop away while you still can."

"It's complicated. I love Bella and she loves me. I forgive her."

"Maybe you forgive too much. If she loved you, would she continue to cheat on you? Maybe she just loves herself. Maybe she loves you because you're an adjunct to her own self."

"How would you know anything about this? You're a nasty rabbit who doesn't seem to have any love in him. You don't understand what you're talking about. Bella feels terrible about what happened, and I know she loves me, and that's why she takes such good care of me. But it's true, I can't deny it, the whole thing is wrecking me. Sometimes I feel like I'm bleeding to death. You can keep telling yourself the whole thing shouldn't matter—you have a beautiful family and a nice life—and yet it's a hard thing to live with. Sometimes I feel like I've really fallen down the rabbit hole."

"Watch it, okay? I get really tired of all of the innuendo. You guys are so sensitive to anything that appears to be racist or sexist or ethnically offensive, and then look at all the speciesist rabbit slurs."

"Why, what did I say? I open up my heart to you, and then you attack!"

"Oh, don't get me started. You even insult the way we live. Like a rabbit hole is some dark place."

"I'm not familiar with the deeper meaning of that expression. You forget I grew up in Sweden."

"And let's not get started on the whole fertility thing, Playboy bunnies—so offensive! It's true, yes, we are rapid breeders, like your Raymond friend, and just how rapid is a little embarrassing, and not something I particularly want to discuss, given that I haven't had much activity myself for three years. Also, now that I've broken out, I just learned that twenty-seven of my siblings were eaten by badgers."

"Oh, Dominique, that's bad. My condolences."

"Duly noted. Thanks."

"And the other thing I want to say—and I don't expect you to understand—but I'm staying for Elsa's sake. She's a fragile kid, and these things can really . . ."

"Oh, please, Lars. Elsa is the strongest point in your tepee. She's about ten times more together than you or your wife. I think you'll see this if you just step back. And one thing that is going to help you with the clarity is the tea. I'm only going to say this one more time, Lars. Drink your tea."

"It's still too hot."

"Blow on it."

"I'm blowing. Do you have some ice?"

"Does it look like I've got a freezer out here, man? Do you have a screw loose? Here, I'm going to pour some down your gut. Open up. Let's just raise your head a bit. Okay . . . isn't that good?"

"It's not bad. A little more . . . You're spilling it on my shirt."

"Not to worry. It evaporated already. Listen, since we're friends, and I'm feeling so mellow, and, really, Lars, I'm just so fond of you— I mean, we've been together a long time, you and me—can I talk to you frankly?"

"I think we've been pretty frank already, don't you?"

"Let me just say this: there's such a thing as being a little too patient. As my grandfather used to say . . ."

"I don't think your grandfather thought of that himself."

"I didn't even say what it is yet, man. Look at us, we're totally mind-melding! I was going to tell you it's a losers' game. We're all playing a losers' game. You're just losing more than most."

"This tea is a little . . . weird."

"Weird is good. Yes? So you see, Lars? Are you getting ready to do something? Are you ready to change your life?"

"Yes. Yes, I am, Mr. Rabbit. What's in this tea?"

"Remember back when you were a kid and you smoked some hash that your cousin Pieter got from his Pakistani friend and you could totally understand each other without even using words?"

"Exactly. How did you know that?"

"For God's sake, Lars."

"Oh yeah, the transparency Vulcan mind-meld stuff."

"Interestingly, I never watched *Star Trek*, but I know the reference."

"It's getting so advanced that it's like we've reached another level. It's like . . . we're beyond mind-meld. I think we're actually one."

"We are, man. We are. Listen, Lars, I think you should try a little harder to sit up."

"I'm trying. I'm really trying, but I can't seem to move anything but my hands."

"Here, let me give you a little help. Whoa! I see the problem, man. You're bleeding. Didn't you just say you were bleeding to death? And you are! Put your hand here to stanch the wound. What's this wet, squishy thing? Is it a kidney or a liver or an intestine of some sort? I don't really know the human anatomy very well."

"Good God! You're right. I think it's my spleen. It seems to have fallen out!"

"Your spleen? I've never heard of a spleen. Anyway, I wouldn't worry too much: you look like you have a lot of blood to spare, so a little letting is probably good. Just think of it as lightening your load."

ELSA

The Stager is back in our house very early Saturday morning, even though she's a thief. Don't ask me how she pulled it off, but she talked her way out of it, made up a story about the pig having been in her bag only because it had been a convenient place to stick it when she had her hands full and needed to move it to the table on the third-floor landing.

"Why in the world would I steal this silly little pig? With all of the beautiful objects in this house, would this be the thing I'd risk my job to take?" That's what the Stager asked, and Nabila thought she had a good point, so don't ask me how this is possible, but *I* wind up being the one who gets in trouble. Nabila warns me to be careful next time; she says that, where she comes from, accusing someone of being a thief might result in chopping off her arm.

When I come downstairs, the door, which is open, is still streaky white with the black seeping through, and my dad's keys are dangling from the lock. The small silver tennis ball that hangs from the key chain that we bought him for his last birthday makes a clanking sound as it bounces against the brass part of the knob. I call my dad's name, but he doesn't answer. I worry that something bad might have happened. His phone is on the bottom step, and his suitcase is belly-down on the walkway below. It looks like a bug that got stuck upside down and couldn't flip itself back over. The two new flowerpots the Stager brought yesterday are tipped over, and there's dirt and flowers all over the pavement. The flowers are red. New red flowers to match the soon-to-be new red door.

I call Nabila, and she comes upstairs from her half-room in the basement with a basket of clean laundry. I point to the door. We both look at the keys and the suitcase and the flowers, and then at each other.

"What do you think this means?" Nabila asks.

I shrug my shoulders. "I guess it means my dad is back from London?"

"Yeah, but where is he? Is he in the house, do you think?" She sets the basket down and begins calling his name. "Mr. Jorgenson?" she yells up the stairs.

"You can call him Lars. He won't mind."

"Mr. Jorgenson?" she yells again, moving up the staircase.

I follow her all the way to the top floor, but there's no one in my parents' bedroom, and it looks exactly like it did the day before. Nabila pulls her phone from her pocket and pauses to read a message. "Stupid tea guy," she says. "I already told him I don't want any more."

"Who is the stupid tea guy?"

"The guy who sold me that tea from Unfurlings."

"The marijuana?"

"Stop saying that, Elsa. You are going to get me deported, like you did that cleaning lady."

"What are you talking about?" I ask. I'm not sure what "deported" means, but I can guess, and I definitely don't want that to happen. I'm completely terrified about the things that go on in the place where Nabila comes from, wherever that is.

"All I said was that the cleaning lady broke Molly's horse's stirrup! What does the tea guy want?"

"No idea. He keeps calling and texting."

"Maybe he likes you, Nabila."

She makes a face. "Enough of that. Let's pretend we're detectives. Let's try to figure out what might have happened here. Obviously, your dad came home—he probably took a taxi from the airport, right? Then he put his key in the door, and . . . did you hear anything strange last night?"

I shake my head no.

"Weird," says Nabila. "And creepy. I'm going to call your mom."

We stand there while Nabila calls my mom. For some reason, Nabila doesn't have her on speed-dial, and she screws up the number. The first time, she reaches a Chinese restaurant and gets a message asking her to press "1" if she wants to make a reservation and "2" if she wants to order food for delivery. She hangs up and tries again, and when she finally connects, my mom doesn't answer.

"Maybe we should call the police," Nabila says.

"I don't know; my mom likes to keep stuff private," I explain. "He's probably fine. Maybe he went to Starbucks. That's where he usually is when we can't find him."

"Yeah, but something isn't right. Like, how would that have worked? He puts his key in the door, his suitcase falls down, he decides instead of picking it up he'll go . . . to Starbucks? Besides, his keys are here, and, look, his car is still in the driveway. And what happened to the planters? None of this makes sense. Do you think your dad was mugged?"

"Probably not," I say, "because, remember, his phone was lying on the ground? Plus, I'll bet his laptop is still in his suitcase."

"Let's go see."

We walk down the stairs and back outside. I see a van pull up and park across the street. It says "HGTV" on the side.

"I thought my mom said they weren't supposed to film anymore."

"That's what she told me."

"Well, why are they here again?"

"They're not actually here, are they? I mean, who knows why their van is there. I can't really say anything if they're just sitting in their truck, right? Do you think? I mean, I could walk over, I suppose."

I shrug my shoulders. "Maybe you should ask Amanda."

"Good thought."

I flip the suitcase over, which isn't easy, because it's ridiculously heavy, and unzip the front pouch. Dirty laundry spills out, and underneath the dirty socks and T-shirts is his computer.

"See? I told you! It's still here!"

"Well, you may have a point," Nabila says. "But, on the other hand, who would bother to steal any of that? The computer is, like, a hundred years old, and that phone is pretty pathetic, too. I think they stopped making those about five years ago. Still, if he was robbed, they would have come inside the house, right? I mean, the door is open and the keys are right there!"

"Is that *blood*?" I shriek.

Nabila and I squat on the ground beside the suitcase.

"I don't know. It could be," says Nabila.

"Or maybe he was drinking something red?" I say. "Cranberry juice? Or he also likes that Tazo passion-fruit tea at Starbucks."

"Good God. Let me try your mom again. I'll call her office directly. At least I can talk to her assistant."

"My mom will be in a meeting, and anyway, she'll tell you not to panic."

Of course I'm right. My mom is in a meeting, but when we say my dad is missing, and then mention the word "blood," her assistant says she'll interrupt her and give her the message. Then she calls back a few minutes later and says my mom said to tell Nabila to wait about an hour, and if he doesn't turn up, to call back.

———

THE UPSIDE OF my dad going missing is that Nabila seems to have forgotten to take me to field-hockey practice, which is good because the coach had told me to be prepared to run two extra laps today to make up for the ones I've skipped out on all week. He says I'm lucky it's only *two* extra laps, given that I've used the "just going to get my inhaler" trick three times. He insists that I bring my inhaler from now on; he wants to see it before practice begins. I tell him this might be illegal. Or harassment. Or something. And that my parents are paying a lot of money for me to go to this school—the annual tuition is more than the chair my dad once bought on eBay that had belonged to some famous dead tennis player. I heard my mom say this once when they were having a fight.

He looks unimpressed.

I haven't bothered to complain to my mom about the coach, because I know she'll just say that I should listen to my teachers and that a little exercise is probably a good thing. I sent a text about this to my dad, figuring he'd be more sympathetic, but he never replied.

I try to remember if Nabila was living with us the last time my dad disappeared, or if that was Adriana. Probably Adriana, because otherwise Nabila wouldn't be so freaked-out. He goes off every once in a while, and then he comes back and adjusts his meds and everything is fine until it happens all over again.

The only thing different this time is that Dominique is missing, too. Our family members are disappearing one by one. I wonder if this is my fault. It makes me think about disappearing myself, maybe going back to Unfurlings to get another snack.

DIANA RECENTLY TOLD me about something called blackmail. I liked the sound of this. It means that you know something that someone wishes you didn't know, and you can make him do things for you so you'll keep the secret. Here's how it worked for Diana: She promised her mother she wouldn't tell her father about the Golden Goose boots she'd just bought that cost twelve hundred dollars and came pre-rolled in dirt to make them look broken in. Her mother got her a new iPhone in return. *Then* she promised her father she wouldn't tell her mother that she found his boxer shorts in the stable, even though she didn't understand why that needed to be a secret, and he got her a pony that she named Iris. I couldn't believe I'd never heard about this before, and when Nabila finally announces it's time to take me to practice even though it already began, I decide to try something like this myself, even though I know there's no pony in it for me.

"If you let me stay home, I won't tell my mom about the bag of leaves," I try.

"My goodness, Elsa. That's pretty wicked. You're totally obsessed with that bag of leaves, even though I've told you it's just tea. Someone gave it to me. I didn't remember I'd slipped it in my pocket until you swiped it. Where is it, anyway?"

"I don't know. I think I threw it away."

"You threw it away? First you steal it, then you throw it away without asking?"

"Well, if it's only tea, why do you care?"

"So you think tea has no value? Maybe I want to drink it."

"What kind of tea is it?"

"That's kind of the point. I can't answer that, because you went snooping through my things and then stole it before I even got to taste it."

"I wasn't snooping, I was cleaning. Anyway, who is this guy who gave it to you? Is he in love with you? How do you know he's not a drug dealer?"

"Not that it's any of your business, but his name is Eton, and I already told you he's that guy who sells wildflowers and produce outside the gate at Unfurlings. Your mom told me to pick up some fruit and honey there a few days ago, and he gave me the bag of tea. He said it's compost tea, and he wanted to know if I thought it was any good."

"Is it?"

"I don't know. Remember what I just said?"

"Oh, right. Well, maybe can we try some later?"

"Maybe. Although that's kind of your call, since you took it and I don't know where it is. For now, let's stop talking and get in the car."

"I have a much better idea. Let's have a tea party! Maybe the Stager can come, too. It will be like that Mad Hatter's tea party."

"The what?"

"Don't you know *Alice in Wonderland*?"

"Vaguely. Anyway, can we please stop talking about the tea already? I'll be honest with you, I'd rather just forget about the whole thing, okay?"

"Okay. I'll forget about it if you let me skip practice and play with the Stager again."

"I told you, she's only here to finish the front door and fix the flowerpot situation. She just got here a few minutes ago, because she had to swing by the garden store first. Your open house is tomorrow. Your mom said under no circumstances should you be playing with the Stager. They are paying her a lot of money to fix up the house, and she doesn't have time to play with you. Your mom thinks there is something kind of strange about the whole thing. Plus, not to pile it on, Elsa, but given that you almost caused her to lose this job, why do you think she'd even *want* to play with you?"

"Fine. Maybe she doesn't want to play with me, but she needs to fix my rug."

"What are you talking about? She's done with the inside of the house."

"Did you see my rug?"

"No. Elsa, please don't tell me . . ."

"Sorry! Sorry! My God, don't get all mad about it. It's just got some red paint spilled on it."

"Did you do that on purpose?"

"That's mean, Nabila."

"I wouldn't put it past you."

"You are supposed to be my friend."

Nabila and I lock eyes for a while, like we're in a staring contest. Then she goes outside and asks the Stager if, when she finishes painting the front door, she'd mind coming upstairs to my room to take a look at my rug.

I CAN'T DECIDE if the most fun thing to do with the Stager will be to bake, paint, or play with the dolls. She's taking a very long time with the door. I go downstairs and ask how long she thinks she'll be, and all she says is "a while." She doesn't even look at me. I wonder if there's anyone in the world who isn't mad at me.

I go back upstairs and stare at the mess. Molly is slumped over again, falling right back into her dinner plate, even though I sat her up straight last time we played. The American Girl food is still spread all over the floor. Maybe the Stager will be less mad at me if I clean up my room. It's pretty bad, but maybe it's like homework: Once you start, it doesn't always wind up taking as long as it seems like it might. Except sometimes it does.

I open the toy box and scoop up a handful of plastic food—a fruit basket, some sunny-side-up eggs, a carton of orange juice—and drop them inside. Plastic food landing in a toy box does not make very much noise, however. I go to the other side of the room and begin to toss the pieces in one by one. When that doesn't work, I shout to her.

"I'm cleaning up my room!"

"Good girl," she says.

"Do you want to come see?"

"In a few minutes."

"Why? What's taking so long?"

"I don't know, this paint isn't the best. I'm not sure what's going on. They may have mixed it too thin or something. It's just not going on smoothly, and I'm having trouble getting the red to even out."

"Do you want help?"

"No, thanks."

"Do you want me to Google anything about how to make the red even out?"

"No, thanks."

I turn on my iPad and Google "painting the door red." Some of the same stuff the Stager has already told me comes up, along with a lot of stupid questions (if you paint the outside red, do you have to paint the inside red, even if the color doesn't match?). Then, on the side of the screen, an ad pops up. It's for an app called Staging 101.

"Oh my God, you've got to come see this!" I can't believe there's a stager app. Four days ago I hadn't even known there was such a thing as a stager, and now there's an app?

"In a few minutes, Elsa."

"Hurry! You are not going to believe this! I'm going to download the stager app."

"Okay, just behave. It's hard to hear you from out here. Just give me a few minutes."

It takes a long time to download, but when it does, the first thing I see is something called a cost calculator that tells you how much money you can make, or save, by hiring a home stager. I play with that for a while, but I don't really understand how it works. Even though I'm good at math, this doesn't make sense. If you spend between three and four thousand dollars on home staging, you can make between fifteen and twenty thousand, it says, which sounds like a mistake. I put in some more numbers to see what happens if you spend between thirty and forty thousand. Before it finishes calculating, a box pops up on the screen and a beautiful lady in a red dress who looks a little bit like Amanda Hoffstead but with blond hair and big earrings appears and says, "Let me stage your home and I guarantee you will make a five hundred and eighty-six percent return on your investment or your money back."

I hadn't thought about there being other stagers in the world, or ones that come with money-back guarantees. I wonder if Eve Brenner comes with a money-back guarantee.

"Do you come with a money-back guarantee? Can you promise a five hundred and eighty-six percent return on investment?" I shout.

"Elsa, I can't really hear you. Just give me a few minutes, okay?"

I wonder if the staging app has anything to say about the Rule of Three, or crazy ladies with nail guns, or no toasters on the kitchen counter. I don't see anything about that, but I do see a button that says "Stage Your Own Virtual House!"

I click on that, and, my God, it's amazing: you can do anything you want in the virtual house! First you can pick the outside of your house—anything from a small house that's all on one level called "a rambler," to an enormous house with turrets that looks like a castle. I pick the house that looks the most like ours. It's called a Tudor, even though our house is a lot bigger and more modern-looking. Then, inside the house, you can add on rooms, and you can even create extra levels. I add a room to the top floor, just like where my parents' room is, and I make a room like Nabila's in the basement. It goes well until I try to put the swimming pool in the backyard. I'm having trouble dragging it into the right spot, and it winds up on the *side* of the house, which looks pretty weird. I fool around with it for a while and I can't get it to move. When I click on it to drag it, it just gets bigger. Soon I've accidentally created an Olympic-sized pool between the house and the one next door. When I try to make it smaller, the whole thing freezes, so I leave it there and go back to the part of the app that lets you fill the house with furniture.

"Do you know if your mom keeps any spare potting soil?" the Stager calls from downstairs.

"I don't know. We have a gardener named Alejandro who usually does all that stuff. You should ask him. You've really got to come see this!"

"Okay, just give me a few more minutes. I'm going to go look in your back shed."

"Okay. I'll finish making the virtual house, and then I'll put some furniture in it."

"Please promise me you'll behave while I pop around to the back for a few minutes."

"Yes, I'll behave. No problem."

Staring at the screen, I decide that what the house needs first is more windows, especially since my dad likes a lot of light. There's a toolbox on the left side of the screen, containing things like doors and windows. Then, when you click on the item, it gives you a choice of which kind. Who knew there were so many different types! For doors there are slab, French, Dutch, sliding, and bifold. For windows there are single-pane and double-pane, casement and block-glass. Also accent, picture, and bay bow. There are all sorts of different ways of opening them, too—sliding to the side, pulling open from the top, or just normal. It seems like you could spend an hour trying to decide which kind of doors and windows to put in your house. And then there are all sorts of different doorknobs, which I've never even noticed before! I decide to do one of each kind of window in the master bedroom, but then I run out of space on the wall, so I have to enlarge the room. But to get it big enough to fit every kind of window, the master bedroom starts to grow, and soon it takes over the whole upstairs. I have to get rid of all of the other bedrooms on the top floor, but once I do, I make it the biggest, most light-filled master bedroom in the world.

Then I decide that the downstairs needs to be just as bright, but this means that, instead of staging each room, I'm going to have to do some *destaging*. I wonder if that's even a word.

"Do you *destage* something, or do you *unstage* it?" I yell.

She doesn't answer. I take out the stove and the sink and the countertops and put in some sliding glass doors. It makes the room look much bigger. I add three windows on the side that's looking out onto the ginormous pool, then three more, and then another three. Now the kitchen has nine windows. I begin destaging the bathrooms and adding windows to them as well. I wonder if I can keep doing this forever, or if at some point the program will run out of windows and shut down. I'm so busy with this, I don't see the Stager standing at my door. She has her arms crossed and she has dirt on her pants. Like everyone else in the world, she seems to be mad at me.

"My God, Elsa, what happened to the rug? And the toys! I thought you were going to clean this all up." She walks over to the part of the rug that has the most red paint and squats down to look more closely. "Seriously, what are we going to do about this carpet? It's too late to get it replaced." Now she stands up and glares at me again. "This room is a disaster."

"I thought it was the best room in the house!"

"Well, it *was*. But look at it now!"

"It's just the carpet. Are you sure it's too late to get it fixed? Have you seen those commercials for Mrs. Karpet? I think they can do same-day installation!"

"Really? Is that your plan? Just make a huge mess and let someone else take care of it for you? *Like mother, like daughter.*"

"What did you say?"

"Nothing."

"You said something about my mother."

"You're hearing things. So what's our plan?"

"Our plan is, we use some soap . . . or maybe shampoo. I'll get it. But let me just show you something first—it's a stager app."

"A what?"

"You know, an app for the iPad."

"You have an iPad?"

"Don't you?"

"No."

"Oh, well, I only have an iPad 2, so it's not that big of a deal. Here, look. Really, I promise we'll fix my room right after I show you. I'll start you a new house, since this one is pretty messed up. It's all windows."

"People in glass houses . . ."

"What?"

"Nothing. It's just an expression."

"You are saying a lot of weird stuff. Do you want a colonial, or a rambler, or a studio apartment . . . What's a studio apartment? What's this mean, a Murphy bed?"

"A Murphy bed is a bed that folds up into the wall. It's for small spaces like a studio apartment, which is an apartment that's just one room."

"The whole house is one room and the bed is in the wall? Why would anyone live that way?"

"Housing can be expensive, especially in cities, and sometimes that's all people can afford."

"So they sleep in the same room where they eat and play?"

"They do, but that can be kind of nice. Not everyone needs, or wants, lots of space. Some people like to minimalize."

"That's kind of sad. Especially when we have so many extra rooms. If your staging doesn't work and we move to London and no one is living in this house, maybe some people who only live in one room could move in here."

"Well, that's a nice idea, but the world doesn't really work that way. Also, it's really the case that some people want to live in smaller spaces. They feel it's liberating to spend less time and money taking care of their homes. There's even something called the Tiny House Movement now. People deliberately build tiny little houses, even smaller than this bedroom."

"My God, I've never heard of such a thing. I think you're making that up. Do they have tiny houses at Unfurlings?"

"No, but maybe if they did it wouldn't be in foreclosure. The thinking behind that place was kind of backward. It was built on the premise that we're not living the right way, that our houses are too far apart, and too far away from anything, and that this fosters loneliness and isolation. And yet the houses are monstrously huge and on big lots, which is kind of retrograde thinking. There's no dancing in the streets anymore, the way we live."

"What are you talking about?"

"That the houses are . . ."

"No, the dancing-in-the-street part, I mean."

"Oh, just an observation about the way we live these days. Back in the old days—or even now, in other countries—there's much more communal activity. More joy. There are bands, mariachi bands playing outdoors, outdoor theater, festivals, there's just a lot more playfulness. People literally dance in the streets. Now we have shopping malls and highways."

"People do Zumba at my mom's gym."

"Yeah, I guess that's the modern-day equivalent, which is a little sad."

"It's not sad. I've watched them do it, and it looks like fun! Also, we went to New Orleans once and there was dancing in the street."

"That's true, Elsa. Good point. Maybe we should all move to New Orleans."

"Anyway, nothing is stopping us from dancing in the street. Right? We can go outside and dance right now!"

"Sure, we could, but we don't."

"Why not? Let's just do it! There's not that much traffic. We can bring my phone, maybe hook it up to some speakers and live-stream some music."

"I'm not even sure what that means. But whatever. Listen, let's first clean your room, then we'll talk about dancing. Now, tell me once and for all, what are we going to do about the carpet?"

"I'm sure we can get the paint out. I wouldn't worry about it."

"I *would* worry about it. I *am* worried about it."

"I have an idea. Let's just move the bed over the big part of the splotch. Then maybe we can scrub the footprints out with carpet cleaner."

We both stare at the bed, and stare at the red splotch, and stare at the trail of red footprints leading to and from the bathroom.

"That looks like one very heavy bed! Even if we manage to move it, the bed will be sort of floating in the center of the room, which is a little strange, but we can work with that, I suppose. There aren't a lot of better options at this point—that huge blotch of paint isn't going to come out, although you may be right that we can get the footprints out. Better to try than to postpone the open house. But . . . I don't know, if we move the bed there, not even taking into consideration the question of how we would do it—that thing is a monster—where would we put the dresser, and the end tables? That left one might have to go in the attic."

"This is exactly what the stager app is for. Let's make a room just like mine, and then move the pretend furniture around."

"You know, that's not a bad idea. Let me see that thing."

The Stager stares at it for a minute like she's never seen an iPad before, and then the screen goes dark. "You have to push that button," I explain. "It works just like your phone! Now slide your finger across the lock. Okay, pick a kind of house. I think we have the one that is called a Tudor, right?"

"Technically a Tudor. A perverted Tudor."

"What does that mean?"

"Nothing, just that it's not a very classical Tudor. Okay, now what?"

"Well, let's pretend that room is my room. Put your finger on it. You can make it bigger by tapping that button there . . . Great . . .

Perfect . . . Now you can drag in furniture, so maybe take that bed and drag it into the middle of the room, like we might do in here."

She moves the bed into the center of the room and sets it at an angle. Then she moves a side table over, and sets a lamp on top of it. She stares at it and begins to laugh. "This is amazing!"

"Maybe you should put a picture on that wall."

"Do they have pictures, or do you draw your own?"

"I don't know . . . Wait, tap that button right there—'household accessories.'"

Up pops a range of categories: rugs, art, throw pillows, pets.

"Pets?" the Stager says.

"Pets?" I repeat. We look at each other and start to laugh. She taps "pets." Then she taps "rabbits." She drags a rabbit and puts it on the bed. Then I drag another rabbit onto the bed. We take turns for a minute dragging rabbits onto the bed. We must drag about a hundred rabbits.

"Do you think it's possible to run out of rabbits?" she asks.

"No, I think the Internet just keeps sending the rabbits from somewhere. Not sure where they are coming from, but I'll bet we can keep dragging them forever. I never ran out of windows in my other house. But let's see." I tap and tap and tap, and the rabbits just keep coming, and soon you can't even see the room. We look at each other, and then we both start laughing again. Soon we're laughing so hard that it's like the first time we met and read the Max books and I had to go get my inhaler, which actually happens again.

"You okay?"

"Yeah, I'm fine. Just a little wheezy."

"Maybe we'd better call Nabila."

"No, I'm fine. Sometimes it just takes a minute for the inhaler to kick in. You know what helps sometimes?"

"What?"

"Food."

"Why do I have trouble believing that?"

"No, really. Well . . . caffeine helps. It really does; the doctor says it gets the heart pumping faster and that helps dilate the airwaves or something like that. And, actually, I have some tea I want to try. It's a new kind. It's organic tea from Unfurlings. Can we try it?"

"Sure, but if it's organic, it might not have caffeine. Or maybe it does—it's not like I'm some tea expert."

"Me, neither, but let's give it a try. Maybe we can bake some fairy cakes to go with it?"

"That's a little ambitious right now, given that we need to put your house back together and your room is a complete wreck and the open house is tomorrow, but I'm sure we can find something else to eat."

"LET'S USE THE red kettle," I tell the Stager when we get downstairs. "It has a nicer whistle than the silver one," which is the one she has just found in the cupboard and put on the stove. I still don't understand why everything in the kitchen had to be put away—the toaster and the Cuisinarts and the kettles and pretty much everything else. Don't people want to imagine themselves preparing food?

"I'll get the teapot ready so we can make enough for Nabila and my dad, once she finds him. My mom told me that you're supposed to warm it up first with hot water, so that it's ready when you pour the super-hot water in. I'll bet they're back soon. My dad is pretty easy to find. Do you know my dad?"

I can't find the teapot, either. It seems ridiculous that she's put everything away while we are still living in the house and trying to do normal things like eat breakfast and have snacks and drink tea. I need to find the tea cozy, too, to keep the pot warm, and I start to dig through the drawer where we keep stuff like tea cozies and aprons and dish towels.

"Okay, easy does it, Elsa. You don't have to take everything out from under there. No, I never met your dad, but I feel like I know him."

"What do you mean?"

"Just from being in this house, seeing his pictures, being around his things. But I also feel like maybe it would be better if I get out of here before he and Nabila get back, assuming she's found him. He's coming home after a long trip, and he'll be tired. The last thing he needs is a stranger in his house."

"You're not a stranger. You're the Stager! The Stranger Stager!"

"Hmm . . . that doesn't necessarily sound like a great nickname, does it? It's been a while, though, since Nabila left. Do you think we should give her a call?"

"No. Really, like I said, this happens all the time. Sometimes my dad goes away for a bit just to clear his head. Sometimes he does that in his room. But sometimes he has to go somewhere. It has something to do with the light. It's no big deal. He always comes back. And Nabila will find him. He never goes anywhere very far away."

"Was he always like this?"

"Like what?"

"You know, sort of . . . sensitive?"

"Only since . . . Oh, I don't know. Maybe about three years ago. Around when he hurt his knee the second time and had an operation and it got infected, and he wound up in another hospital, and then another. Then it finally got better but he couldn't play tennis anymore. Then, one day, he got worse, with the mean reds, and they never went away."

"The mean reds?"

"It's from a famous book my mom loves. It means he got depressed."

"Yes, I know. I'm so sorry."

"Yeah, well, it's okay, because my mom started to make more money than my dad did, so we didn't become poor or anything. Now she has to work all the time and she's always away. But I get that it's not so bad, because we have some kids at our school whose parents work all the time, too, and they don't even have any money, like Zahara. She's a refugee from somewhere, and her mom works at a restaurant, but they let her go to our school anyway but I don't know how she pays because my school costs more than a chair on eBay."

"She's probably on scholarship. It's nice that your school does that. What do you mean, a chair on eBay? The Wassily?"

"The what?"

"The chair in the corner of the living room?"

"Oh yeah. Yes. Where is it, anyway?"

"I moved it to the attic."

"My dad is going to freak out."

"It's just temporary. We can move it back downstairs as soon as we sell your house."

"No one wants to buy our house."

"Just watch. They will this time. Here, I think the tea's ready. It's kind of hot, though."

"Put some milk in it to cool it off. That's what people do in England, where I have to move. We should have some scones, whatever those are. Tea and scones and crumpets!"

"Well, no scones or crumpets lying around, but how about some rice cakes?"

"Yuck. Just tea, please."

"So do you play with this girl, Zahara?"

The Stager pours some milk in my tea and sets out the rice cakes on a plate, even though I just said I didn't want one.

"Diana says we should be careful around her because she's from a country where they have a lot of problems and maybe her parents are going to blow up our school."

"That's a horrible thing for Diana to say! What did you say to her?"

"I didn't say anything. Diana doesn't always let me sit with her, either, so I need to be careful not to get on her bad side."

"Maybe you don't want to be on her good side, if she says things like that."

"I know. I've thought about that, but she almost didn't invite me to her birthday party this year, and we've been best friends forever."

"Well, things change; maybe you should just move on. Why don't you invite Zahara over sometime?"

"What's the point? I have to move to the stupid house in London anyway."

"Well, you never know. Life is long. Things come around."

"What do you mean?"

"I just mean that people reappear in your life, strange things happen, you reconnect unexpectedly. So maybe someday Zahara will wind up in London. You just never know. Invite her to sit with you at lunch on Monday, maybe."

"Yeah, maybe. I'm just afraid of Diana."

"It sounds like maybe you shouldn't worry so much about Diana. It sounds like she thinks she's sort of superior to everyone. That's not the kind of friend you need."

"Yeah, my mom says that, too. She says it's not good to judge people. She said she used to have a friend who was always judging her, who thought she was morally superior."

"Really? What else did your mom say about the friend? Wow, this tea is . . . weird. It tastes like flowers. And licorice."

I blow on it and take a sip. "Yuck! It's horrible!" I run to the sink and spit it out.

"I don't know, I kind of like it. Try another sip. It's like lavender, but with a little . . . I don't know, maybe a little hint of yarrow? It tastes like flowers."

"Flower tea."

"Yes. Flower tea. That's a good name. It makes me think of the 'Flower Duet.'"

"What's that?"

"It's from an opera. It's a stunning aria. It's one of those pieces of music that, if you carry it around inside of you, it feels like you've been transported to some holy place."

"My God! I want to hear it! Are you okay? You look a little funny." The Stager's eyes are getting kind of glassy, and she's slumping in her chair, like Molly upstairs. She looks like she's drunk.

"Can you get me my bag?" she asks. "It's by the front door."

I go to get it. It's on the table where the naked starving person and the pig are supposed to be. I give it to her, and she digs around inside and pulls out her lipstick. She puts it on, but she doesn't do a very good job, and it smears below the bottom lip, making her look a little like a clown.

"Why are you putting your lipstick on? Are you going somewhere?"

"My lips are dry," she says, smacking them together loudly. She pours herself another cup of tea and drinks it straight down, even though I can see the steam coming out of the cup.

"Stranger Stager?"

"Yes, my darling?"

"Are you okay? Isn't that really hot? Did you burn your tongue?"

"I'm so okay, you have no idea. What did your mom say about the friend?"

"What friend? Zahara, or Diana?"

"No, the judgmental friend."

"Oh, my mom's friend, you mean? My mom said she made one mistake, just one simple mistake, and the friend would never speak to her again."

"A simple mistake? Only one? Is that really what she said?"

"Why? Do you know her?"

"Know who?"

"The friend?"

"I feel a little like I'm floating. Do you?"

"No." I suddenly realize it's the tea. I was right. The tea is not tea. Or maybe it's not just tea. The tea is drugs, and the Stager is pouring herself another cup.

"No more tea for you," I say. But she picks up the cup and drinks it down quickly, even though it's very hot.

"What else did your mom say?" she asks.

"Something like that the friend was bitter and jealous and not very attractive, and she couldn't get over the fact that my mom was beautiful and happy and successful."

"I can't believe she said that! It's so not true. On top of which, well, there are different ways to measure these things, right? What about someone who lives an honest life? Is there any reward for that? Probably not, it seems. I mean, look at these people who just keep on going, taking whatever they need, and never look back at the wreckage along the way?"

"Are you okay? I think you should try to sit up."

"I'm starting to get upset."

"I see that."

"I need another cup of tea."

"That's not a good idea. You've had too much already."

"No, tea is very comforting. You'll see when you get to England. Whenever anything bad happens, anything at all, they say, 'Here, love, let's have a cuppa.' Even if something terrible happens, like someone gets hit by a car, or even dies, they say, 'Put the tea on.'"

"I believe you. But I think you've had enough."

"But the tea is making me very happy."

"What else makes you happy?"

"Music. I love music. Sometimes I just put my headphones on and blast music. It's like a drug."

"Okay. Great idea. Let me get my iPod and we can play some music."

"You have an iPad and an iPhone and an iPod? That's a lot of iThings."

"Only three! What do you want to hear?"

"I totally want to hear the 'Flower Duet,' to go with the flower tea."

I run upstairs to get my iPod and live-stream the "Flower Duet."

When I come back downstairs, the Stager is lying on the kitchen floor. I put my iPod in the dock with speakers, and the music starts to play. It sounds almost like perfume. Or like a perfume commercial.

"Whoa . . . I'm dancing."

"You're not, actually. You're lying on the floor."

When we talked about marijuana in our DARE class, no one explained it would be this bad. I thought it just made you hungry. Maybe this isn't even marijuana. There are other, worse things, but we are going to discuss those when we get to middle school, and since I'm not going to the middle school, I don't know if I'll ever learn. Who knows what kind of drugs they have in London.

The Stager tries to sit up, but she's having trouble. I take her hand to help, but she's heavier than she looks, and I can't get her to move.

"I have an idea," she says. "Let's go dance in the street."

"Sure," I say, even though she doesn't look like she's going to be able to dance in the street for a while.

"Oh, Elsa. Elsa, Elsa, Elsa, this is such a brilliant idea! We're dancing! We're flying!"

Actually, she is lying spread-eagled on the ground. "You really don't look so good," I say.

"Why? Is it my hair? My hair is so unfortunate. I didn't have time to dry it, and it's still damp."

"No, your hair is fine. You just look kind of . . ."

"Wait, I have an even better idea. Before we dance, let's paint! And then let's bake! Let's just do everything you've ever wanted to do in your whole life!"

"How about let's finish the picture of Dominique in a chair? His ears are really crooked, and he looks kind of insane. I don't know what to do to fix it."

She seems motivated to get up. She grasps the table leg and pulls herself into a sitting position, and after that, I take both her hands and pull as hard as I can. We get her almost up, but then she falls down again. The second time is easier, and we finally get her on her feet, even though she looks like she's not very steady.

"You look a little wobbly."

"Me? No, I'm fine. Not wobbly at all."

She gets up the stairs by hugging the banister, and at one point, halfway up, I worry that she's going to fall asleep and fall down, so I keep talking to her, coaxing her along.

"Do you want to lie down?" I ask, once we reach my room.

"No, I want to paint. Let me see what you have so far." She stares at my crooked rabbit. At first I think she's going to say something negative, but then her face lights up.

"I have an idea. Instead of just painting on the canvas, what if we paint some rabbits on the wall? It can be kind of a Dominique memorial."

"Um, I really like that idea, but since the open house is tomorrow . . . I don't know . . . Didn't you say we were supposed to *depersonalize* the house? Isn't this sort of the opposite?"

"No, Elsa. It will just make the house more special! I mean, how many houses have rabbits on the wall?" She's already opening the lid on the paint, and then she stops and says, "I should probably do an outline first." She takes a black Sharpie pen and draws an outline of a gigantic rabbit on the wall. It's amazing how good it is. I could have spent the entire day trying to get the ears right and the tail right, and in five minutes, she's drawn the largest, most perfect rabbit I've ever seen in my life.

"That's *fabulous*," I say. "After we finish painting the rabbit, can we dance in the street?"

"You know we can, honey. We can do anything you want. This is your special day."

We both start laughing again, and I really can't remember having ever met anyone who is this much fun. The Stager is such a happy person, and I'm lucky that, of all the stagers in the world, she's the one who has come to stage my house.

LARS

The minor subplots and broader themes are bleeding out. All that's left is memory, spare and sepia-toned: me and Bella on a rusty swing set at dusk in the weedy back garden of a motel. Because we are partial to five-star hotels, I'm having trouble locating this scene. Why are we here? It must be family-related, a random stopover along the way from there to here. A funeral, perhaps? A visit to one of her cousins in the Midwest? I can't say for sure. But I do know there are fireflies, and they are just beginning to light. We swing high, me and Bella, legs pumping, synchronized. Cicadas sing in the background. I don't know at the time that in the end it may be that this is all that's left of our marriage.

We always think there will be more—a nice assisted-living suite, a connected burial plot—but it's possible the whole thing will implode and we'll be left with only disembodied memories, as indistinct as the loose change that rattles in your pocket, with no reminder of when and where you split the last dollar bill. That said, tender memories are nothing to sneeze at. It's not nothing, a firefly memory, even if the narrative is thin.

"You okay, Lars?" The rabbit is standing on my chest, slapping me. "You look a little pale. I think you should try to get up."

My spleen has grown cold. It feels like a hunk of liver you might acquire from the butcher. Surely this is just a bad dream.

"I'm actually not feeling so well."

"Oh, Lars, quit complaining. Just get a grip."

"You seem weirdly unconcerned about my physical condition. It makes me wonder if you really care about me. You're as bad as Bella that time I couldn't stop throwing up and she didn't even have time to drive me to the pharmacy. Do you have anything to at least help stanch the bleeding?"

"Oh, Lars, enough with the self-pity. Don't break my heart. I care about you deeply, my brother. That's why I brought you here. I have this towel you can use, but it's kind of dirty. I wouldn't want you to get an infection."

"I appreciate that—thanks for caring. I think, actually, that fighting infection is part of the point of a spleen, and since I no longer have a spleen, or at least it's not where it belongs, I guess I have a choice of bleeding to death or getting an infection. Do you think you could call a doctor? Or at least get me out of this place, wherever we are? I don't really want to die alone in a field. I think this scene may actually be a little dialogue-heavy."

"Not really. You began with some boring descriptive digression about fireflies that did little to advance the plot, and I'm the one trying to move the action along, but if you like, we can slow this all waaaaay down and go back to the fireflies and such. We can contemplate the years of small, perfect moments that add up to—to what, Lars? To some comforting memories of glow-in-the-dark bugs that will convince you your entire marriage was not a lie?"

"That's a little harsh. Not all of it was a lie. She was faithful to me in the margins. I'd say for about fifteen percent of our marriage she was fully there, which is more than many people get in their lives. There were a lot of good things along the way. There were fireflies."

"Yes. Fireflies. That's been established. I get it. I have my own firefly moments, too."

"Any happy memories that involve time spent with our family?"

"Let me think about that for a minute. No."

"Not even with Elsa?"

"Still thinking. Okay, done: No. Zero. None. Zilch. Sorry. Look, the sun is coming up, and there's a certain poetic lightness on the horizon: I see yellows and blues and a whole palette of pastels. I smell wheat and hay and the earthy scent of farm animals, and also of marijuana and baked goods . . ."

"Do you see any fireflies?"

"Well, no, but it's almost morning, so it's the wrong time of day."

"Anyway, yeah, I see your point. The descriptive shit can bog down. Let's get on with the action. Speaking of which, did you hear me suggest you should call a doctor?"

"There's a good thought, but I don't have my phone. It was getting too expensive, and I'm in the process of switching to Sprint. I want to get an unlimited data plan. I just haven't had a freaking free minute to go in and deal with all of this. Let me use yours."

"I don't think I have mine, either. But I wish you'd said something. Had I realized you were struggling, we probably could have added you to our family plan."

"That would have been nice, Lars. I really would have appreciated that. It's a little late now, obviously. Maybe if you'd treated me with love and kindness, with the sort of affection and respect you might have shown a dog, even if there was inevitably going to be some mild condescension involved, things would be different now. For us all."

"What, you honestly think the problem is that I didn't love you enough? For God's sake, you bit me so badly once, I needed stitches. You caused massive property damage to my house!"

"Oh, come on, man. There are two sides to every story. You stuck me in a cage and stole my dignity."

"You want to talk about stolen dignity?"

"Okay, look, I don't want to fight with you, and it's not like we're making much progress anyway. We sound like an old married couple, arguing about whose turn it is to take out the trash. I think you should sit up, Lars. Really, have a proper sip or two of tea; you need fluids. I'll hold on to the spleen for you."

"I don't know, I feel I should hang on to it. It's kind of . . . personal."

"I know, but I'm family. Look, I'll tuck it right under my hide. I'm going to keep it warm, the way the penguins do with their eggs. I'll give it back to you after you've told me your story."

"What story?"

"Precisely."

"What are you, the Wizard of Oz?"

"I hadn't thought of that. Interesting, but, no, I'm just your pet, and I'm trying to help you out of this bad loop. Remember that one of the side effects of all of your x's and z's and the general mess of your life is that you are stuck inside a story and you can't get out?"

"Yes, but I don't understand what story that is."

"It's Bella's story. That's the problem! You're living life on her terms. You do everything she says. And you even believe her version of events. Like, she's probably even put some sort of happy spin on the current situation. You get all of ten percent fidelity out of her, yet all she has to do is put out a press release with her own version of the story and then she controls the narrative."

"I think we said it was fifteen percent, didn't we? Maybe she controls the narrative, but we don't even have her voice."

"What would be gained by having her voice? What is it that you need to know about her? She's complicated, I'm sure. Everyone is complicated, right? All you humans and your problems. You're all very special and important, and you each have a story. I get it. But we can also just assume she's a modern superwoman, one of those *Lean In*, you-*can*-have-it-all, you-*can't*-have-it-all, Wonder Women types who juggle too many things. Her telling detail is that she's a sucker for Raymond Branch. And she's thrown you under the bus for him. God knows why. Talk about bad choices."

"Talk about controlling the narrative: that's what *you're* doing right now, and you have all of your facts wrong. You don't know the first thing about Bella."

"Okay, this is good, in its own sad way. And now it's time to reclaim your narrative. It's the only way out."

"My God, that sounds so profound, even if I don't really know what you're talking about. I'm not one for therapy or yoga or any of that touchy-feely stuff."

"Did you ever notice that your voice is not very clearly defined? Sometimes when you talk you sound like Elsa. All those 'My God!'s— like a little girl! And sometimes you sound like Bella."

"Isn't that what family is about? You take on each other's mannerisms. You merge. Besides, you tend to forget that I am from Sweden, so I absorbed most of my English from my family."

"Phew. That makes sense. I was starting to worry that you simply had no definition. That I had utterly failed in getting your voice down—maybe I hadn't thought about you enough before my attempt. But the truth is, you are no one right now, and you haven't been anyone since the day you met Bella."

"Ouch. Are *you* writing this story?"

"It's complicated, Lars. But let's just say, at this point, *you* are writing this story. From henceforth."

"That's a heavy burden. I'm not sure I'm up to this."

"No, Lars, believe me. This is the only road to recovery. It's practically a scientific, or at least an empirical thing. You need to remember who you are, and where you began, before you lost yourself."

"I really can't remember. It involved tennis, that's all I know. But the more urgent question is: What if this is the end of my story? What if I'm genuinely bleeding out?"

"It's true that this could be the climax, but let's not allow it to be. Let's make this the turning point."

"So what do I do?"

"In order to push past this, to a better place, you need to excavate something positive to bring forward. Otherwise, it's too easy to look back and see nothing but darkness."

"I've excavated the fireflies. That's a good start, isn't it? Maybe I chose fireflies because I abhor the darkness? I need a lot of light."

"Yes, Lars, we are all painfully aware of this. It's *your* telling detail. And fireflies are a nice start. But let's do a little more work. Here's what we're going to do. You are going to tell me your story, and somewhere along the way we'll pick up some things real and true that will be our clues to figuring out who Lars is—or at least who he was. It's like a video game where you have to get from point A to point B but along the way you need to pick up powers."

"Oh, like Sonic the Hedgehog? I used to love that game!"

"It was a clever game, but a little exploitative and degrading to hedgehogs—a few of my stepbrothers are hedgehogs, but don't get me started. Let's just agree . . ."

"You have hedgehogs in your family? Jeez, I'm not sure I want to think about that one."

"Yeah, it's a piece of my family history I'm not so proud of. Let's not get derailed here, let's just begin."

"Beginnings are hard. Do you go back to the very beginning? Like: I was born on a frigid night in a small clinic outside Stockholm?"

"Probably not. I mean, that's true enough, and that *is* your story, but you really want to begin somewhere more dramatic, and I'd recommend mid-scene, possibly even in the present tense, which is quite fashionable these days. You don't really want to spend pages and pages getting from your miraculous conception to here."

"Where is here, anyway? And what's that lovely smell? Like burnt sugar. Or like cake."

"Those are fairy cakes. From the grow house."

"The grow house? There's a grow house out here? A grow house like in that TV show *Weeds*?"

"What planet are you on, Lars? What do you think is going on out here in these houses? This development debacle that is called Unfurlings. The place is in foreclosure. People lost their deposits. We've got to make the best of things, we've got to at least use the land the best we can, man. It's an almost biblical thing; it's our mandate on this earth."

"That house right there? Is that the grow house?"

"No, that's the finance office. It's all locked up pretty tight. No way in, not even for a rabbit who can tunnel. It's all concrete foundation, and then, inside, a maze of hallways, locks on every door. It's alarmed up the wazoo."

"That one there?"

"Maybe. I don't want to get anyone in trouble. But over to the right, that's the model home for this place. Or it was, before it went into foreclosure. Now it's where Marta lives with her kids. It's tough. You think you've got it bad, man—although I guess it's true, you do have it pretty bad. But she's a single mom who had to take the kids and disappear. She bakes all day. Sells her stuff to one of those fancy bakeries where the people stand in line for an hour just to buy a stupid cupcake. Fairy cakes, she calls them. It's the next old new thing."

"So that's the grow house she's living in?"

"It is, they're just letting her work there. She's a good front, you know. She's squatting illegally, but whose gonna care about a pretty lady and her kids? Especially when her old man has been beating her up? Anyway, there's precedent. I think there's even some movement about this, people squatting in houses and saying it's a religious thing. I think they're Moorish Nationals or something."

"There's a movement for everything now, isn't there?"

"Seems to be."

"That's horrible, that any man would put a hand to a woman . . . Man, that smells so good! I'm trying to imagine what fairy cakes are. I'd really like one."

"Yeah, sure. We can hook you up with one. But you do realize you ought to go on a diet at some point. And start exercising again."

"My knee . . ."

"I think I've heard that riding a bicycle might be good for the knee."

"Am I really getting health advice from a rabbit? I feel almost like I'm in a fairy tale. Or maybe a nightmare. Or a slasher film. Isn't there a talking rabbit in that movie *Donnie Darko*? Isn't he a serial killer or something?"

"Frank. Yeah, I met him once. He's a friend of a friend. He's got some issues, but let's not get off-track here. The point is that you are trapped inside a story. But it's become the wrong story, and in order to find your way out, you need to recover your own story. I keep telling you the same thing over and over and over, but you seem very resistant to this idea."

"Not really, it's just that I have no story. Or, if I did, I've lost it."

"It might not be that hard to recover your story. Just find a place to begin."

"'When I was a kid, my brother and I used to . . .'"

"Once again, no."

"Sorry, I guess I don't understand this at all. I'm a tennis player, not a writer."

"Remember what I said about ten seconds ago? You want to begin in the center. Mid-scene. Action. Suspense. You want them turning the pages. You want to begin in the Four Questions spot."

"Still *no comprendo*."

"You know, remember the Passover seder conversation? The 'Why is this night different from all other nights?'"

"You're Jewish?"

"Good God, Lars, you really are stuck. We've already had this conversation. What I'm trying to suggest is that you begin in a meaningful spot. Why now? Why is this the moment you need to reclaim your life?"

"Because I've hit the wall?"

"Good job. And this is signified how?"

"By the fact that you're sitting on my spleen?"

"Well, that's clearly of significance, but not what I'm really going for. Try it in the third person, to get a little distance."

"'Bella stood in front of Raymond's house, staring at . . .'"

"Man oh man, are you going to be a lot of work. Enough with Bella's story already. Tell me about Lars. Look, just start tonight. That will totally qualify as mid-scene."

"'When Lars emerges from the taxi in front of what he thinks is his own front door . . .' Is that the sort of thing you have in mind?"

"Excellent. Go on."

"'. . . he finds himself confused. The number on the house is the same, as is the somewhat emasculated shrubbery, but something's wrong. At first, he thinks that the door is simply the wrong color, but since it's late at night, and the light on the porch is dim, he can't tell for sure . . .'"

"Bravo! Continue."

"'But then, when he opens the door and stands in the foyer, he can see that something even stranger is going on. Nothing is as it should be. It's as if the house has become possessed. Because Lars Jorgenson is disoriented generally (although he's not sure if the problem is being magnified by too many bottles of mediocre airplane gin or the fact that he's lost his glasses somewhere along the way), he freaks out when he opens the door and observes that things are different.'"

"Like what? Give us detail."

"'The pig is gone! The African tribal figure is missing! The expensive yellow painting, nowhere to be seen! It's so disturbing that he can't even step inside!'"

"Too many exclamation points, but good. The detail is good. Now might be the time to loop back and pick up a thread of something that will provide a hint as to how we got to where we are."

"You're really throwing me off here. I'm not a very complicated guy, you know. Just give me a loving family, some food and shelter, a tennis racquet, and a ball, that's all I ever needed in life. I never asked for all this drama."

"Well, that's kind of a cop-out and you know it. You made your choices. I mean, they were bad choices, obviously, but no one made you stay."

"But my . . ."

"Please. Don't get started about your knee . . ."

"Look, I didn't sign up for psychoanalysis here. And anyway, what I was going to say was not about my knee. I was going to say, 'but *my daughter . . .*'"

"Ah . . . well, that's completely different, then. That's a good sign."

"My daughter is my life. I can't walk away from her. Whether I'm her real father, or whether she's the spawn of the rapid breeder, or whether she's yours, for that matter."

"One thing I can assure you is that I am not the father. She's older than I am, for one thing. Plus, I don't think it's biologically possible. To be honest, we were even surprised about the hedgehog thing working."

"I was just speaking metaphorically. Although I suppose she does have your coloring. On a different subject, and this is a little embarrassing to ask, but I really need to use a bathroom. Do you think there's one around here? Maybe in that house?"

"Well, it's late. It's four a.m., so maybe I should say it's early. I don't want to wake Marta up, but actually, if you're willing, I know a way in. It involves a little tunneling. And you're a big guy, so it could be tricky, but . . ."

"Yeah, well, do what you've got to do, but I really need to pee."

"You only need to pee? Lars, may I just point out that we're in an open field and you're the only human who's awake in the radius of about a mile."

"I know, but, still, that's kind of who I am."

"That's ridiculous, but it's also good, since we need another telling detail about you for your reconstruction. The light thing is distinctive, but it's also part of the whole insanity thing that we really need to lose. So this is a much better start: Lars is a man who does not like to pee outdoors."

"I wish it could be a little more romantic, somehow, like that I can bench-press a hundred and seventy pounds, or that I play a mean bass guitar."

"Can you? Do you? You don't need to answer that, since I think I know. We want this to be a truthful reconstruction. Okay, listen, mate, scrape yourself off the ground and follow me. We're gonna do a little hop over to the grow house . . ."

"But . . ."

"But nothing. No worries. Just do it, as they say in Nikeland. I've got your spleen right here."

ELSA

We have just finished filling in the color on the rabbit's tail when the Stager crumples. First she sinks into a squatting position, then she leans forward, and even though it looks like she's going to collapse onto her stomach, her body contorts as she falls, and she winds up sprawled on her back. Her eyes are wide open, but when I ask her if we should mix some white paint in with the beige to brighten the color, her answer comes out as gibberish. Then her eyes roll back, the lids close, and she begins to snore. I have to shout her name and then kick her a couple of times until she stands up so I can help her onto my bed, which we somehow managed to move to the center of the room before we started painting.

The bed now covers up the worst part of the carpet stain, but it looks awkward in this spot, and we haven't entirely solved the problem, since you can still see small red footprints leading to the bathroom. We agreed we'd clean those up after we finished our mural, but nothing is going quite as planned. The bed is big and heavy, and as we pushed it, a couple of the boards under the mattress collapsed, and now it's sloping down on the right, like a boat in the process of capsizing. I get the Stager onto the mattress but wonder how long she'll be able to stay where she is before she'll start to slide off.

Her limbs are splayed all over the place, like she's fallen down in the middle of dancing. Her shoes are still on her feet, so I take them off and then try to get her into a more organized position. I cross her arms, but that makes her look too stiff, like she's dead, so I try to make her look more casual, with one arm up and one arm across her chest, but that makes it look like she's doing the Pledge of Allegiance. It also doesn't help that the bed has just made a loud creaking noise and the mattress sloped down even farther. I stare at her for a minute, trying to think what I might do to help her improve, and remember the lipstick in her bag. It's a beautiful color—a bright shade of red called "Lust," and I apply it to her lips, but it's harder than it looks to apply lipstick to a person who is asleep, because to put lipstick on properly it's helpful to open your mouth a bit, and then smack your lips together on a tissue, like my mother does. My attempt to fix it with the lipstick pencil in her bag only makes it worse. I really don't know what I'm supposed to do at this point, either with the passed-out Stager or my messed-up room or the giant unfinished rabbit on my wall, so I recalibrate, and decide to go outside and do a little dancing in the street. But first I put on my blue ballerina tutu, even though it's from three years ago and it's too small.

I take my phone and the speakers and plug it in by the front door, and turn up the volume as loud as it goes. Then I go into the street and begin to twirl. The Stager was right—it really is a beautiful song, almost magical. I close my eyes and think of fairy cakes and of the animals at Unfurlings and of the Stager, how fun and happy she is. I twirl and twirl until I'm dizzy. Then I stop until I feel better, and begin to twirl in the other direction.

I remember how much fun we had in New Orleans, when everyone was tossing beads and dancing and singing and being friendly, like the whole city was having a party and everyone was invited. I wonder why it can't be like that here at The Flanders.

I'm having fun, but there's still something a little weird about twirling by myself in the middle of the street. I wonder if people are staring out the windows at me. I wish a marching band would come along, or even a dog or a family with a kid, but no one in my neighborhood ever walks anywhere. Even on the golf course they ride around on little carts. Although there are no people, there are more cars coming down the street than I would have thought, and they all keep honking at me. When I shout to them that they should stop and dance in the street, they just honk again. Someone even leans out the window and gives me the middle finger and tells me to get out of the effing middle of the road.

Then a fancy black car with tinted windows pulls up and stops. The door opens, and out comes a leg with a red high heel. I wonder if a movie star is coming to visit our neighborhood, or maybe even to buy our house. A second later, I find myself staring at my mom, and all I can think to say is "Wow, I love your new shoes!" But then I stop, confused.

"Wait, how could you be here? You were just talking to Nabila on the phone! I thought you were still in London."

"No, sweetheart. I just landed at Dulles. When I spoke to Nabila it was from the airport."

"Oh, I see," I say. But I don't, really, and I wonder if it would be that difficult for someone, every once in a while, to tell me what's going on. I hadn't realized my mom was on her way home, and maybe if I had, I wouldn't have tucked the delirious Stager into my bed.

"Anyway, the real question is, what are you doing out here in that old tutu, spinning around in the middle of the road? It's dangerous. And the tutu is too small."

"I'm dancing in the street. The Stager says the thing that's wrong with the world is that no one dances anymore. Or at least they don't dance in the street."

"But they do Zumba!"

"I know, right? That's what I said!"

"It's dangerous to dance in the street. That's why you don't see people doing it so much."

"I know, but I'm looking out for cars, so don't worry. The Stager says dancing in the street is a way to be joyful."

A minivan comes speeding down the road and honks at us, and my mom shoots me a look that means "I told you so." She leans back into the black car and signs a credit-card slip; then the driver gets out of the car and comes around to the trunk to get her suitcase, and we go to the front of our house.

"Wow, the door is very white and . . . *streaky*." My mom doesn't sound happy about this.

"Well, it's going to be red. The Stager just hasn't finished yet. That's primer."

"Oh. Well, that's good news, I suppose. But, still, it's getting a little late to be painting, isn't it? The open house is tomorrow."

"Yeah, she's just super-busy, Mom, but she'll do it. She's great. You'll love her."

"I thought she was finished."

"Well, she is, almost, but she just came back to fix the flowers and finish painting the door."

"I love those geraniums," my mom says. "I should have thought of putting planters by the door. Funny how people wait until they are selling their houses to fix them up. It's really a waste, if you think about it." Then she opens the door and steps into the foyer. "Holy Mother of God, what is that smell?"

"What smell?"

"How can you not smell that smell?"

"I don't smell anything. I mean, I did—it was really bad before the

Stager came, but she fixed the smell. It turned out Dominique had chewed through the . . ."

"Yes, I know all about that, but it still smells rancid."

"Really? Weird. I mean, it still smelled bad after the Stager cleaned out the freezer, but then she opened all the windows and the doors—that was how Dominique ran away—and it got better. I guess it's true, it did get bad again the next day, but we all figured it was still part of the same smell that was just kind of . . . well, doing whatever smells do. And then maybe we just all got used to it?"

"I don't know how you could get used to this!" My mom starts opening windows and she makes a gagging sound. Then she stops and stares for a minute at the green table in the foyer before stating the obvious: "The pig and the yellow painting and the tribal elder from Botswana are gone."

"Yeah, the Stager said we had to *depersonalize.*"

"I suppose that makes sense. Where is this Stager? I'd like to meet her, and also talk to her about fixing this smell."

"She had to leave early," I lie. "Also, even though she can fix smells and stuff, she's not a cleaning lady, you know. She used to be a journalist! She'll be back later to finish up. Can we play a game?"

"She used to be a journalist, eh? Listen, sweetheart, I can't wait to catch up properly, and to hear about your week, and play games. But right now I'd like to get this Stager person out of our lives, plus I'm worried sick about your father. Where's Nabila? I've tried to call her, but she isn't answering her phone. Is she upstairs? We'll play a game later."

I'm not sure what to do. I don't want to get Nabila in trouble for leaving me alone, even though I wasn't alone, obviously, but I also don't want to draw attention to the Stager in my bed, so I lie a second time. "She's here somewhere. Maybe she's just taking a nap."

"Well, she shouldn't be napping when she's supposed to be looking for your father and watching you. Let's rouse her!" My mom speed-dials Nabila, and we hear a sound emanating from the kitchen. My mom and I walk into the room and stare at the phone as it lights up blue and vibrates, skittering along the table.

"See, she's here somewhere," I say.

"Okay, well, I think the first thing I want to do, before I set out to find your dad, is change my clothes."

"No! Don't change, Mom, you look beautiful!" She does look beautiful, but my real reason for saying this is that I don't want her to go upstairs.

"Thanks, sweetheart, but I'm really uncomfortable in these heels, and it's already been a pretty long day for me. I had a meeting at eight a.m., then a quick TV gig, then this flight. My God, what a long day. Really, what a long *week*! I think blue jeans are just the thing."

"No! You look terrible in blue jeans. You're not a blue-jeans kind of mom."

"I'm not sure how to take that," she says. "But I'll just take it as a compliment. I'm not sure what I think of all those blue-jean moms you see out on the field-hockey field."

I'm sure how to take *that*. Some of those moms actually seem pretty nice. She begins to walk toward the staircase. I throw myself at her and hold her tight. "Please, just stay here for a minute. You've been gone forever. At least sit down and have a snack."

She looks annoyed, but then says, "Okay, I'll sit for a minute and we can catch up. Actually, I'd love a cup of tea. Is there anything in that teapot?"

"No."

But there is, and she feels it and says, "It's still warm." Then she gets out a mug and begins to pour it.

"No, Mom! That's bad tea. You really don't want any."

"What are you talking about?" She takes a sip.

"It's herbal tea. From Unfurlings. It doesn't taste very good."

She spits it out into the sink. "My God! Get that tea out of here!

Pour it down that drain! There are rumors that they're growing and selling opium over there. I seriously hope you haven't been drinking that stuff!"

"Me, no! I hate tea. Isn't opium a perfume? Is that why it tastes like flowers?"

"Do you have the tea leaves?"

I hand my mom the baggie with the leaves, and she opens it and dumps the tea leaves—or, rather, the opium leaves—down the drain. Then she pours what's left in the teapot down the drain, too. "It comes from poppies, which, yes, are flowers. How did you get that stuff, anyway?"

I shrug my shoulders and think of blackmail.

"Okay, look, sweetie, I'm going to run upstairs to change clothes, and then I'm going to look for your dad."

"Nooooo! Please, Mom, you just got home, and I want to spend some time with you!" I haven't planned to start crying; I don't think I even realized until that moment how much I've really missed my mom. I throw my arms around her waist and hold her tight.

"So sorry, Elsa. This has been a really rough patch, I know, and I promise I'm going to make it up to you. There's a lot going on, and I've been distracted. We need to get your dad some help, and watching all of this is not something a ten-year-old kid should have to do. On top of which, this move is unbelievably hard, and I'm sorry to have been away this week—horribly bad timing, but unavoidable. I should have brought you along, but I really thought you'd be happier here. I travel all the time, and you and Nabila usually do just fine, and you're so busy with your friends and school and field hockey that I figured a week would just fly by like *that*!"

She snaps her fingers, and I notice that the red nails could use some fresh polish.

"I can see now that Dominique running away just triggered a whole bad series of events."

Hearing her say all this, plus mentioning Dominique, makes me cry even harder. My mom continues to hold me, and she keeps rubbing my back and kissing me on the head, and after a while I feel better. Still, I need to do something to keep her from going upstairs, but I can't think what, and I'm lucky I don't have to figure out a solution, because just then Nabila walks through the door.

"Oh, hey," she says, acting nonchalant but looking at me, alarmed. I try to tell her with my eyes that I haven't said anything that will get her in trouble, like that she left me with the Stager or that the bag of opium belonged to her. But she can't tell what I'm trying to say, so we just stand there making weird faces at each other. Then she says to my mom, "Um, wow, I didn't realize for some reason that you'd already be home. I thought you were . . . in London. I'm really confused!"

It's helpful to not be the only confused person.

"Anyway, I looked every place you suggested, and tried three additional Starbucks as well. I showed his picture to the baristas and to some of the people sitting in the cafés, and no one has seen him. I was going to call you, but . . ."

"You forgot your phone!"

"Exactly. And I wasn't sure what you wanted me to do next. I'm glad you're here. And I'm really sorry."

"There's no reason to be sorry, Nabila. I'm sorry we've put you in the middle of this mess."

There is a noise outside the window, a rustling of the bushes, and then voices. My mom goes to the door to look. "What the hell . . ."

She opens the screen door and goes outside. "I told Amanda to tell you not to film this house. I'm going to call the police and get a restraining order. I'll give you one minute to get off my property." She starts to count: "One . . . two . . . three . . ."

While she's counting, Nabila's phone starts to vibrate again. She picks it up and listens and keeps nodding her head. Then she puts her finger up in the air, which I think means that she has something interesting to say, which she does: when she finally hangs up, she explains that her friend Eton has found my dad, that he's apparently been drinking the tea, and that he is bleeding and we should come over quick.

THERE ARE TWO ways to get to Unfurlings if you are walking. One way is to stay on our street, then turn left at the first intersection and go downhill, then turn right at the bottom of the street and head back up on a different street. You have to be careful at the fork; it's easy to get confused, since all of the houses there look exactly the same, and sometimes you might go the wrong way and wind up going in a great big loop. If you make the wrong choice, you end up back where you began. If you make the right choice, you will get to the little thatched gatehouse where a man sits in the booth to tell you whether or not you are allowed to come into The Flanders. If you are on your way *out*, you don't need to stop, because anyone can leave The Flanders. You only need permission if you want to come in.

Next is the trickier part: Unfurlings is right across the street, but there are six lanes of traffic, and the cars go very fast. The nearest traffic light is a quarter of a mile up the road, which is a long way to go to cross the street, especially since, once you get to the other side, you have to walk a quarter-mile back to get into Unfurlings. My mom once told me they were trying to get a traffic light installed, but it had been two years already and they were still having meetings about whether or not this was a good idea.

There's another, better way to get to Unfurlings, which is what I learned the first day I went chasing after Dominique. You have to sneak into the Mehtas' backyard, which is a little tricky; then you have to make sure that at the BEWARE: GUARD DOG ON DUTY house the dog is not in the yard, and then you have to go to the very back of the property, behind all the flowers and bamboo, and then find the hole in the chain-link fence and squeeze through. The next thing you know, you're at Unfurlings; the houses look completely different from The Flanders, and there's lots of land, and the last time I was there a llama even came up and licked my hand.

My mom hasn't changed out of her work clothes, since I absolutely refused to let her go upstairs, and I feel kind of bad that she's still wearing those red high heels. As she squeezes through the fence, the sleeve of her shirt gets caught on a piece of sticking-up wire and makes a tear in the sleeve. "It's a brand-new shirt," she says. "Theory!" I don't know what she means by "theory," but my mom is really into fashion, so I guess she's talking about the shirt.

"Isn't it beautiful?" I say, pointing to a lake with ducks floating on the surface.

"It's a little strange, I admit, to have this completely different universe right behind us. It's even a little disorienting. What's that delicious smell?"

"That's the fairy-cake house! There are three colors of icing, but they all taste the same."

I take my mom's hand, and then I take Nabila's hand, and I pull them toward the house. "You have to meet Marta!"

"Wait, Elsa. You don't just knock on someone's door unannounced. Plus, we're not here to eat cupcakes. We're here to find your dad."

"Actually, it's possible this is the house Eton called from," Nabila says, pulling out her phone. "Let me check the address . . . 54 Naomi Wolf Lane."

"No way."

"Yes, we seem to be in the Contemporary Nonfiction division of the Literature compound."

"I hope we're not in *Vagina*."

"Mom!"

"It's okay, honey. It's a book."

Nabila is already knocking. Marta opens the door. She looks a little like an angel, with flowing blond hair and a lot of bangles on her wrists. She throws her arms around me. "Elsa! Thank God you're here. I really don't know what to do. I think I've got your dad here, of all the coincidences in the world. He's only semi-conscious, but he keeps saying your name. I don't even know how he got in here, but I came home from running errands just a few minutes ago and there he was, lying right there on the floor, talking to himself. I was totally panicked, because I didn't want to call an ambulance since I'm not supposed to be here . . ." She stops talking and stares at my mom. Maybe my mom looks like the sort of person who might call the police.

"It's okay, Mom," I explain. "It's the model house. That means it's supposed to look perfect so that people will want to live here and they'll want to buy one just like it. Look, it has fake everything, even dishes and a coffeemaker. I mean, it's pretend, but it's real. But since no one is going to buy a house here anymore, Marta is staying here so it doesn't go to waste. Right, Marta?"

My dad makes a noise. I squat down beside him, but I can't tell what he's saying. His hair is a total mess, matted with sweat and sticky with something that looks like blood. His shirt is full of stains, and the zipper on his trousers is down; I'm embarrassed to see him like this. My mom sits down on the floor on his other side and runs her fingers through his hair. "Wake up, Lars," she says softly.

He mumbles some more, and it sounds like he says, "Once upon a time there was a man named Lars . . ." And then he stops. And then he starts again and he says, "Once upon a time there was a man named Lars." And then he stops.

I go over to him and say, "Dad, finish the story!" And then he starts again with the "once upon a time" part, and then his eyes open and he tries to sit up, but he can't. He looks around, then puts his hand on his stomach and says, "Oh my God, where's Dominique? What did he do with my spleen?"

"Jesus, Lars!" my mom says. "You're hallucinating."

"Do you want some water?" Marta asks.

"Just more tea," my dad says.

"Enough with the tea!" my mother shrieks. "How much did he drink already?"

Nabila shoots me a nervous look.

"I have no idea," Marta says. "As I was saying, I just got home and there he was. I don't even know how he got in here."

"What's the rest of the story you were going to tell, Dad? 'Once upon a time there was a man named Lars.' I think that's what you said. Is there more? Is Dominique in the story?"

"My God, where am I? I was in the middle of a dream about . . . You know what, I think you're right . . . I think I was actually dreaming about Dominique, and he wanted me to tell him a story."

"What did you tell him?"

"I don't really remember, but he really wanted to hear about my life, and I think all I could talk about was *you*."

"Is that good, or is that bad?"

My dad doesn't answer. He's staring out the window, mesmerized.

"Of course that's good," my mom says. "Right, Lars? Tell Elsa that any story about her is a good story, no matter what. It's important that you tell her that."

I don't know why my mom says that. I already know that any story about me is good, unless it's one about me not running laps or spilling paint or eating too much or doing something else that's bad, which makes me remember the Stager in my bed and the red paint on the floor and my broken bed and the half-finished six-foot rabbit on my wall.

"You are the light of my life, Elsa," my dad says. But the words come out slurred, and then he asks me if I have any idea where his spleen is.

"We should really get him home," says Nabila.

"Actually, what I think we should probably do is get an ambulance," says my mom. "Let's first wipe up all that blood . . . Do you have a cloth or something?"

"Please," says Marta, returning with a bowl of water and a cloth. "Please, I'll do anything I can to help, just don't have anyone come here. Anyway, these look like superficial wounds, just scratches on his head and all over his arms. Maybe from the barbed wire on the fence?" She wipes his forehead with the cloth and puts some iodine on the cuts. "I've also got to get busy baking. I have a big commission for tomorrow. I was just hired to bake cupcakes for some realty firm, to serve at open houses, and I can't afford to blow it. So, as much as I want to help, I really need you guys to get out of here. No offense."

"They give cupcakes out at open houses?" I ask. "We should totally do that!"

"I think maybe we are," my mom says. "It was either that, or Amanda was going to do some sort of cash giveaway to whoever guesses the sale price, which seems to me a little tacky, so I voted for the marginally less tacky cupcakes."

"Did you say cupcakes?" my dad asks.

Nabila puts a hand under his arm, and my mother does the same thing from the other side, and Marta puts her hands around his waist, and they pull him up onto his feet. He peers down at his side.

"Hey, weird. Somehow the wound has closed up, but it's still pretty tender, and it's not quite healed. Do you think my spleen is back inside? Or do you have it? Did someone say something about cupcakes?"

"Lars, for the love of God, what's wrong with you?"

He pulls up his shirt and points to his side, but we can't see what he's talking about. Then he looks out the window and then back at me, and he smiles hugely and says, "My God, Elsa, look at that gorgeous sun poking through the clouds!"

THE HOSPITAL SEEMS to take forever. We're there all afternoon, and then all night. The good news is that I get to watch television in the waiting room, and no one tells me to do my homework or practice the violin, but the bad news is that the only thing to watch is CNN, and they run the same stories over and over and over. Most of the stories are terrifying.

First, the ground has opened up and swallowed a grocery store in Louisiana. A lady who had been pushing her shopping cart down the cereal aisle disappeared, and then most of the food in the cereal aisle disappeared, too. They're bringing in drilling equipment and men with flashlights and goggles to try to find her, but she's been gone for half the day and they seem to think she's unlikely to be alive. They interview the chief of the fire department, and then they talk to her husband, who cries and says she'd just gone in to get some Diet Coke and sliced salami. They also interview the manager of the grocery store, who says nothing like this has ever happened before. Then they interview a lady who had just been standing outside the store with her dog while her daughter ran inside to buy paper towels, and then they interview the daughter, who had just been getting her change from the paper towels, and she's really relieved that she hadn't dawdled, because she'd actually been thinking about maybe getting some cereal, too.

The next story is about a crazy man who has a lot of guns and has kidnapped a boy and put him in a box. That story is on a lot, too, and the CNN newswoman says, "Wow, it's a busy news day, and a grim one at that!" For the boy-in-the-box story they talk to the police, the FBI, the boy's mom, who says he's a very good boy, and then they talk to another person, who's just standing there with his dog and doesn't know what's going on, so he doesn't have very much to say.

Then there's a story about the government not having any more money and how that's going to mean people are going to lose their jobs and some schools are going to have to close because they can't afford teachers. For that they interview a senator who's the head of the budget committee, a lady who's the head of the teachers' union, a teacher, and a mom holding the hands of two children. There's no dog in that story.

I ask my mom if the ground is going to swallow our house, and my mom says, "We should be so lucky." When I ask her what she means she says, sorry, she was just making a bad joke. Then I ask her if Mademoiselle Shapiro is going to lose her job, and she says "Don't be silly, Elsa," but I don't know why that's silly. Then, when I ask if the boy in the box is going to be okay, she tells me the news is too gruesome for a child to be watching, and she asks the nurse to turn the channel. When the nurse says that's not possible, my mom suggests I close my eyes and try to take a nap.

I try, but it's impossible to take a nap with the other people in the waiting room talking and with the bright fluorescent lights. There are a lot of other distractions, too: like, the woman across from us is crying and moaning and rocking back and forth, and someone else is throwing up, leaning into the garbage can. Outside, I can hear ambulance sirens and then a helicopter. My dad wakes up every once in a while and starts talking, too. Twice he taps me on the shoulder and asks me if I have his spleen. My mom goes to the admitting desk to complain a few times, but the nurse says there's just been a nine-car collision on the Beltway. My mom says she understands, but explains that we've been waiting to see a doctor for over three hours, and the nurse says, "People literally bleeding to death take priority over people who simply *think* they are bleeding to death."

Finally, in the middle of a really interesting news story about the discovery, in Florida, of a dolphin with three extra fins, it's my dad's turn to see the doctor. I'm allowed to come in, because Nabila has gone out to get us food and my mom says she can't leave me alone in the waiting room.

I watch the doctor listen to my dad's heart and ask him a bunch of questions, and then he sticks a fat needle in his arm and draws blood. We all watch it snake through a plastic tube. Then, after another hour, the doctor says that my dad's okay, all things considered, although he talks about cholesterol and weight and blood pressure and depression, but the doctor says what he really needs to do is go into rehab. My dad sits up and says, No! The problem is that he's lost his spleen. The doctor says that's impossible. My dad says he's certain. They go back and forth about this for a while, and finally the doctor agrees to order up a sonogram, mumbling to the nurse something about malpractice and having to give in to the nutty patients sometimes. But this means we have to wait for the radiologist, who isn't going to come in until 4:00 a.m., which is more than three hours away.

We wait what turns out to be more like five hours to discover that my dad still has his spleen. When the doctor tells him the good news, my dad says, "Thank God, I thought Dominique took it!"

"Who is this Dominique?" the doctor asks.

When my mother explains that Dominique is our missing and possibly dead pet rabbit, the doctor looks at her meaningfully and writes a prescription for something called Zanziflexxx. He suggests we stop at the pharmacy on the way home, and says to give my dad five of the green pills ASAP but to keep a close eye on him, because the side effects can be very intense and sometimes involve something called *disambiguation*. Also, he says to be sure to get the triple-*x* version, and not the double-*x*, since the double-*x* is for peptic ulcers, not for severe disorientation, and the two medications are frequently confused. Then he writes out the name of a psychiatrist on a different sheet of paper and says my mom should be sure my dad sees Dr. Benghazi, who is very good with this sort of thing, right away.

"What sort of thing, exactly?" my mom asks.

"Talking to animals, depression, missing internal organs, the whole shebang."

AFTER WE STOP at the pharmacy, I float a bunch of ideas to keep us from going home. I suggest we go out for breakfast to celebrate that my dad still has his spleen, but my mother just says, "That isn't funny,

Elsa. The open house is in two hours and I think we'd better stop home to make sure everything is in good order. Honestly, I don't know what to do with your dad."

"We could just tuck him into bed and hope the people looking at the house won't notice him," I say.

"Or we could get some things and go to a hotel," Nabila says.

"Probably that's best," says my mom.

Home is the opposite of where I want to go, because I'm terrified about my mom finding the Stager in my bed. I can't say why I feel like everything to do with the Stager is my fault—it's not like I hired her to come into our house. Plus, I don't want my mom to see the mess in my room. I try a couple more ideas, ranging from stopping at the grocery store (even though I'm now terrified of its being swallowed by a sinkhole) to going to 7-Eleven for Slurpees, but my mom says that in our family we don't have Slurpees for breakfast, and that I should understand that my dad needs to get into bed.

TWO AMAZING THINGS are going on in front of our house when we arrive: First, the door is finished. It is painted red, and is no longer streaky. This almost certainly means that the Stager is no longer asleep in my bed. Also, there's a rabbit sitting on the front stoop.

"Dominique!" I shout. I try to open the car door once we stop in the driveway, but it's locked. I bang on the window and tell my mom to hit the unlock switch, but she doesn't listen. My dad leans forward, and it seems like he's trying to say something, but he's having trouble forming words. We'd given him the five Zanziflexxxes, and I guess they made him sleepy. I think he's trying to say "Dominique," too.

"All these rabbits look alike, you guys," my mom says. "And Dominique has gone to rabbit heaven, remember?"

"*Dominique*," says my dad, this time more clearly.

"Mom, you heard him. Open the door."

"He might just be disambiguating," Nabila says. "Remember what the doctor said about the medicine?"

"What's 'disambiguating'?" I ask.

"It's the present participle of 'disambiguate,'" Nabila explains.

"But what's 'disambiguate'?"

"I don't know," she replies, "but I see it on Wikipedia all the time."

My mom finally turns off the ignition. "Don't even think about going after the rabbit, Elsa. I'm warning you, I'm completely out of energy, and I can't deal with any more drama." She finally unlocks the doors. As we're getting out, the rabbit hops away. I want to go after him; he looks exactly like Dominique, and if I had to guess, I'd say it really *is* Dominique, but I don't dare. Besides, I'm genuinely concerned about my dad and this whole disambiguation thing.

"Why do you think my dad is disambiguating if you don't know what it means?"

"Because the doctor said it might happen, right?"

"I know, but still . . . How do you spell it?" I tap it into my phone. "Here, I've got it: 'In computational linguistics, word-sense disambiguation (WSD) is an open problem of natural language processing, which governs the process of identifying which sense of a word (i.e., meaning) is used in a sentence, when the word has multiple meanings. The solution to this problem impacts other computer-related writing, such as discourse, improving relevance of search engines, anaphora resolution, coherence, inference et cetera . . .' That doesn't sound like what my dad is doing," I say.

"I think the doctor was suggesting that your dad might be having some double meanings."

"I still don't understand."

"Like, maybe he's splitting in two? Or something like that. It's one of those words that sound good but no one really knows what they mean."

"So why did the doctor say it's a side effect?"

"I don't know, darling. Maybe because then it covers a broader range of possible side effects? Or maybe because . . . Who knows? No one really pays attention to these things."

WE ALL STARE at the new red door before my mom turns the key in the lock. "It does look nice," she says. "Don't you think?"

We all agree. Even my dad.

"I must say," my mom continues, "that's a fabulous shade of red. It's so . . . assertive! It's like it's saying, Buy me! Or even, Buy *me*! Why didn't we think to paint it red while we were living here? Why do people always wait until they're moving to make their homes look nice?" I start to tell my mom that she's already asked that question but decide it's probably better not to.

"Be careful of the paint, everyone," she says as we go inside. "It looks wet." As soon as we step into the foyer, I double over. I feel like I'm going to be sick. My mom and Nabila also begin to gag.

"Holy Mother of God," my mother says. "I thought I smelled something foul yesterday, but it's twice as bad now."

"It's true," says Nabila. "I mean, I sort of thought there was something bad in the air the last few days, but I figured it was just the remnants of the first bad smell. Unless maybe it's just that, once you leave for a while and then come back, it seems worse just because you've been away?"

"No," says my mom, "I think it's just metastasized. It's sort of quadrupled in intensity since yesterday." The Stager must have noticed it, too, because all of the windows in the living room are open. I wonder if she's still here. I didn't think to look to see if her car was on the street when we came in. I guess I was too distracted by the door and the rabbit.

"I don't smell anything," says my dad. He looks, and sounds, like he's drunk. He's swaying back and forth a little. "I need to lie down," he says, and walks toward the stairs.

"I don't know, Lars, why don't you stay down here? I'll go up and change and get some of your things. We can go to a hotel for the afternoon. You'll be more comfortable."

My dad ignores her and begins to climb, but he's wobbly, so Nabila goes over and puts an arm around his waist. It looks like they are both going to fall backward, so my mom goes over and grabs him from the other side.

"It smells worse up here, I think," Nabila says as they approach the second floor. They stop for a minute while my dad catches his breath.

"How long, once we figure out the source of the smell and remove it, will it take to clear the air?" my mom asks Nabila.

"I have no idea," says Nabila.

"But in your experience?"

"I'm not sure what you mean by that. I'm not really experienced with smells. Is there some reason you think I'm a smell expert?"

"Jesus! Hold on to the bannister, Lars!"

My dad says something no one understands.

"Try enunciating, Lars," my mom instructs.

He tries, but we still have no idea what he's saying.

Everyone is in a really bad mood.

They move up, slowly, a few more steps, all three of them linked together. Now they're on the landing just a few feet from my room, which is the absolute worst spot for them to be pausing. There's no way my mom is not going to turn her head to look inside. When she does, she gasps.

"I would never have thought to put the bed there!" she says. "I mean, it's completely counterintuitive, to move a bed to the center of the room, to make it ever so slightly askew like that. This Stager person is causing me massive anxiety—there's definitely something unsettling about this situation, and I have a really bad feeling about this whole thing—but I'll give her credit for knowing her stuff."

I run up the stairs, relieved. I don't know how she did it, but the Stager has fixed the mattress and made the bed, and she's picked all of the doll food up off the floor and put it away, and she's even changed the girls into normal clothing and cleared the soup and pie and ke-bobs and set out the tea service. Molly has a cookie on her plate, and Kaya has one in her hand, which is poised about an inch from her mouth. I want to help her eat it, but I don't dare move.

Even the red footprints are gone. Everything looks pretty normal, except that there's a gigantic rabbit painted directly on the wall. The rabbit is sitting in a red velvet wing chair, and it's the most beautiful rabbit in a red velvet wing chair that I've seen in my life. My mom evidently disagrees.

"I take it back," Mom says. "That woman is a complete menace. What is she thinking, defacing our home just before the open house? This is as bad as graffiti! I'm going to call Amanda Hoffstead, and I'm going to figure out who this woman is, and then I'm going to hunt her down and kill her!"

I run to my mom, throw my arms around her waist, and dig my head into her stomach, hard. "No, Mom! Please! Please don't kill the Stager!"

THE STAGER

The brush is not quite fine enough, or, frankly, of the quality to which I'm accustomed, but it will have to do, because this rabbit needs a whisker revision. I let the girl take the first pass at this earlier, and held my tongue as she turned out whiskers as thick as pipe cleaners. Sad to say, but with that heavy hand, this is not a child destined for a future in the arts. Still, I gave her nothing but praise and encouragement. Had I been a mother, which I am not, I would have been a spoiler. I would have given my kids rewards for every just-missed field goal, for every atonal note, for every almost-A. Or so I like to think. I'm told that mothering wears a woman down, that ideals go by the wayside as you try to get through each day. But still. I told the girl her whiskers were the best whiskers I had ever seen, and she beamed.

Now that the child is gone—off somewhere with Nabila, I can only assume—it seems wrong to leave the rabbit this way when it's within my power to make a quick, easy fix. Leaving those too-thick whiskers is like declining to tell a friend that she has something stuck in her teeth or that her zipper is down. After re-creating the whiskers, I begin to layer some depth into the rabbit's tawny hide. The child resisted my suggestion that she add a bit more brown to the pool of paint she dumped, indelicately, onto the mixing tray; hence, the rabbit has come out looking too monotone. Ditto for the eyes, which the child had also made a thick, muddy brown, but which seemed to me more appropriately hazel—not that I am all that familiar, to be honest, with the color of a rabbit's eye.

At some point along the way, I find myself reflecting on, and then quickly agitating about, the fact that I am wasting my talent. Maybe not just my talent, but possibly my entire life. I was, at one point, a better-than-average artist. I could have really made something of myself. I always thought it was Vince, with his drinking and his apathy, that threw me off, but now I decide that what stood in my way was Bella. Call this irrational thinking, I know, I know, it doesn't really add up; I can't blame Bella for my decision to apply for that internship, to switch gears from illustrating to writing, to take the job at *MidAtlantic Home*. I can't even blame her for my bad decision to have boarded that plane, although, sometimes, I do.

Yet she was, in some ways, responsible. If I couldn't *be* Bella, I at least wanted to be more Bella-like, and in my mind, at the time, this meant I needed to be more wordsmith than furniture artist. You may say this is revisionist history, and maybe it is. But, then, maybe it is not. What history, I ask, is not revisionist? I'm told some people pay therapists more than two hundred dollars an hour to help them rewrite history, or at least to make it conform to the stories they want to tell themselves. What a waste! Those of us who are more self-realized are able to achieve enlightenment for free, paintbrush in hand. Behold, the giant rabbit of wisdom!

I'm not feeling so well, and I consider lying down again, but time is of the essence. Also, I'm in the midst of forming an uplifting thought, and they are so rare these days that it seems worth staying awake for, to savor: even if I've been reduced to digging through and making sense of the detritus of other people's lives, somewhere deep inside this middle-aged, too-thin, bristly, somewhat damaged woman lies the spark of what once was, or almost was, a different me. Unfortunately, I can't carry that thought much further, because I am under the influence of something very powerful. I feel like I was drugged. I'm not sure what day it is; it seems the sun has set, and the sun has risen. But how many times? Who can say? God alone knows these answers. Or maybe my iPhone knows, too. I look at my screen and see the date, but this doesn't help, since I can't remember what day it was when I began. Whatever day it is, it's that much closer to the Sorkin-Jorgenson open house, which means I need to whip this place into shape *and*, at the other end of the spectrum, it's definitely time to change those poor dolls out of their swimsuits and give them something new to eat.

Also, a completely unrelated thought: There is a very bad smell in this house. A new very bad smell. Or could it be a mutant strain left over from the original smell event, some speck of smell that has survived and has now gone rogue? This seems impossible, since I personally emptied the contents of the freezer and disinfected the inside, and a couple of smell-free days occurred in between.

Whatever the source of the smell, the headline is that it has gotten worse in the last twenty-four hours. *My God*, as the child would say, is not one bad smell in a house enough? I try to focus on smells. There are run-of-the-mill bad smells, from spoiled milk, animal excretions, trash left too long in the bin, soiled diapers, expired fruit. There are more extreme bad smells of the *Psycho* variety: corpses in the shower, the attic, or the bed. By now I know this house so intimately that I can eliminate these particular causes of the smell. Unless, like bad breath, the smell is emanating from within.

Could there be something beneath the floorboards, or perhaps inside the walls? Maybe something embedded in the drywall, or in the attic? The smell is so pervasive it's going to be difficult to isolate, like trying to find the source of a pinhole leak in the hull when the captain's bridge is underwater.

Another lucid thought emerges: A blind person is said to have sharp ears. Or a refined sense of taste. So maybe I should block my other senses to make the smell one more acute. Certainly it's worth a try.

I look for a scarf to wrap around my eyes, but fail to find one among Elsa's things. Quickly improvising, I use a pair of purple fishnet tights.

I press my body against the wall, wormlike, to guide myself through the house to isolate the smell. It's a large house, and therefore a laborious process. In contrast to the first bad smell, which came from the bottom up, this one is oozing top-down. At least, that's my working theory after the first blindfolded pass, but I'm not yet certain. Perhaps the thing to do is to eliminate one more sense? I push the tights up from around my eyes for a moment and—eureka!—the first thing I see, now back in the kitchen, is the child's iPod, sitting on the table. I put the buds in my ears and figure out how to replay the song, and the "Flower Duet" is injected into my brain. I turn the volume up, pull the tights back over my eyes, and press my belly back to the wall to make my slow journey upward.

There are certain details of this portion of the narrative that are rather mundane, but suffice it to say that, after a lot of olfactory detective work, I wind up eventually back in Bella's bedroom with a golf club in my hand. The process involves the conviction that the smell is in the still-unfinished portion of the attic, where luggage and excess artwork and old birdcages and the Wassily chair and various other superfluous objects from an overstuffed life now reside. Inside this part of the attic is a wall that presumably divides the storage area from the rafters and insulation, and I am pretty sure the problem lies within.

I go in search of a blunt instrument, but as it happens, this is not a DIY house. I can only presume, from the lack of tools, that when projects require screwdrivers, or lawnmowers, or things with which to break through wood, others are called upon to do the job. A golf club will have to do, and, thus armed, I go back upstairs one more time to the attic. Again I don my blindfold and earbuds so that I can better focus when it comes time to break through the wall at the precisely right spot, so as to minimize the damage.

Because I am, animal-like, attuned to my environs, even with my back to the door and my senses largely deprived, I know I am in the presence of others. Instinctively I bring the golf club over my head and into assault position and pull the tights from my eyes. The first thing I see is Lars.

Lars. My first flesh-and-blood Lars sighting. Blond and bloated Lars. Lars with glassy eyes. I can see, beneath the ruin and general disintegration, the bones of a very handsome man.

"What's my chair doing up here?" he asks, walking toward it and squeezing himself into the seat. He barely fits; his flesh oozes through the slats.

"It's just temporary," I say.

"You're holding my five-iron the wrong way," he says. "What you want to do is move the right hand down a bit . . . Well, wait, are you right- or left-handed?"

I hear a cell phone ring, and Bella's voice answers. I tense. Red alert. The same physical response I'd had that first night, many years ago, when we'd first met at the intern party. Bella is in the other room, and she doesn't know I'm here.

"Nabila, I have to take this call," she says. "It's Amanda. She says it's urgent . . . Of course it's urgent. It's always urgent. But actually she says we might have an overseas buyer willing to take the house sight unseen. Can you imagine?! Keep an eye on things for a minute, okay?" I hear her moving toward the staircase.

"I'm right-handed," I say very softly, in case Bella is not yet fully out of hearing range.

"Okay. Move your right hand down about an inch . . . Great, yes, just like that. Now take the thumb of your . . ."

"For the love of God," I hear Bella say from the landing. "Is he talking to himself? Nabila, please deal with him. Honestly, I don't know how much more of this I can take."

"No worries. Everything is under control, Bella."

Nabila is on her way into the attic to retrieve her charge. She's a footstep or two away, and I brace myself for the scream I'm certain will be forthcoming, not because I am particularly frightening, but because Nabila can be a little high-strung. But I guess the sight of me pales in comparison to the smell, because, instead, she doubles over and begins to gag. "Oh, dear Lord, there must be something dead in here."

"Agreed," I say.

Elsa hears my voice. "Stager! Stager!" she cries, as she runs in and throws her arms around me.

"Yuck! It's horrible in here," she says. "It smells like something dead."

"Precisely," says Nabila.

"Squirrels," says Lars, still sitting in the chair.

"Squirrels?"

"Dead baby squirrels."

This is a little creepy. "Dare I ask how you know the aroma of dead baby squirrels?"

"I don't. I'm just speculating. I can't actually smell anything in here, to be honest, but this happened once in my house in Sweden. The mother squirrel had a litter, then she went outside to get food and she never came back. The babies starved to death and died."

"That's so horrible! What happened to the mother?" asks Elsa. The child looks completely stricken.

"Who knows? Probably she was eaten by badgers."

"Badgers? Do they eat squirrels?"

"Well, I don't know for sure, but they eat rabbits. They ate a bunch of Dominique's siblings."

"My God! Really? How do you know?" she asks. I wonder if I ought to call Child Protective Services to keep her from having to hear any more about this bloodbath.

"He told me. But sometimes badgers and rabbits can be friends. Some of Dominique's relatives are even badgers."

"I'm really confused."

"Life is complicated, Elsa. Sometimes it's best not to think too much."

"I think you should lie down," Nabila says.

"Why? Do I look tired? I'm getting a second wind."

"It's true, you do seem better. Maybe it's the medication."

The girl's face is screwed up in a mixture of pain and confusion. She looks, again, on the verge of tears, but fortunately she surprises us with a more academic inquiry.

"There are squirrels in Sweden?"

"Yes."

"Are they scrawny, like the rabbits where Nabila is from?"

"No, they are very healthy. But we do have some interesting variations. We once had a red squirrel in our yard."

"No way!"

"Yes. Well, not bright red, like the door, but a sort of orangey color. And once we had a squirrel with white spots."

"No way! A spotted squirrel?"

"Well, not spots like polka dots, but more like white blended in with the brown. It's not that unusual, really. I saw one in Maine once, too."

"What if the smell isn't squirrels, but Dominique? Or what if Dominique had babies? What if there are dead baby rabbits in the attic?"

"It's not Dominique. And Dominique is a boy, so he can't have babies."

"But his wife can. But never mind, Dominique doesn't have a wife, right?"

"Not to get too technical, Elsa, but you don't have to be married to have a baby. We can talk about that someday. More to the point, Dominique wasn't doing any breeding."

"How do you know?"

"He told me. That's been part of his frustration."

"Dad, what are you talking about?"

"Also, he missed his family."

"Mr. Lars, you should really lie down," Nabila says again.

"Enough with lying down! I'm wide awake!"

"Nabila, you can call my dad just plain 'Lars'—right, Dad? She doesn't have to say 'mister.'"

"You can call me anything you like. You can call me a whirling dervish in Tretorns."

Lars grabs the golf club from my hand and begins to poke at the rafters. "A hundred bucks says it's dead baby squirrels."

Lars fails to make a dent. The noise produces Bella, however.

There she stands, long legs in red heels, hair mussed yet perfect somehow, ditto for the ripped shirt and artfully crumpled skirt. With the cell phone still pressed to her ear, one hand on her hip, her eyes wide as she takes me in, she looks like a whimsical rendition of herself, playful and full of color. Bella Sorkin as rendered by Maira Kalman. Or perhaps I have imagined this improbable moment for so long that it has become in my mind a tangible thing, something you can frame and hang on the wall.

"Mom!" Elsa exclaims. Now she detaches from me and throws her arms around her mother's waist, confused, or nervous, about her allegiance. "I'm so excited you can finally meet the Stager. Remember, I told you about her, how she used to be a journalist like you? Now she cleans houses."

I'm prepared for anything at all. Bella could pull a gun from her rumpled pocket, press it to my temple, pull the trigger, and end the scene right here. I'm so terrified that, for a fleeting moment, I think that particular outcome would be fine by me.

Another possibility briefly occurs to me—potential outcomes are racing through my brain the way one is said to revisit highlights of a life while passing through the tunnel of death. Perhaps Bella will not even remember me. Although she has loomed so large in my own life that her memory has nearly destroyed me, it's possible I have been but a blip on the crowded Bella Sorkin time line.

No such luck: from the way she's looking at me, I think she remembers.

Lars seems oblivious to the explosive drama unfolding around him. He takes the golf club and this time, instead of just clutching it and jamming it straight up and down like a pogo stick, he pulls it back like he's teeing off and somehow, still glued to the Wassily, he delivers a concentrated, powerful swing. Bits of rafter crumple, and splintered wood sprays down, along with fluffy pieces of insulation. A fresh blast of chill spring air instantly provides relief from the smell, and the light streams in.

"Light!" Lars says, redundantly. "I think I see the light!"

"I think he's beginning to disambiguate again," says Bella. "Nabila, please give him another pill."

"I see the light, but I also see the light."

"See? There he goes."

"But I thought the pill is what's causing him to disambiguate," says Nabila.

"Then give him a different pill, for God's sake. Just get him out of here. Take Elsa, too. She doesn't need to see this."

Then she turns her attention to me, like I'm the next appointment on her jammed-up calendar today: "So you are the Stager," she says. "That's just what I suspected."

A mere statement of fact. The confirmation of a theory. Although Bella is calm, I get that this is not going to turn into a happy reunion of girlfriendy screams and long embraces and oh-my-God-how-have-you-been-you-look-exactly-the-sames!

"No, Bella. *You* are the Stager," I say. "The master manipulator. I just take out the trash and move the furniture."

"I would like you to leave my house, and cease all contact with my family."

"You're welcome, Bella."

"I'm supposed to thank you? Please, let's not go there."

"I'm taking my pig."

"It's not your pig."

"No, it's not. It's *our* pig. You've had it ten years. Now it's my turn."

"Keep it."

And so we come to the end. I'm not sure what I expected after all these years. Maybe I wanted blood. Silly as it sounds, I at least wanted her to fight me for the pig. I wanted it to be important enough to get her riled up. I wanted the bounce of Indonesia, and the toxins of her secret, to have as much of a grip on Bella as they do on me. But not all endings are dramatic. Once you let a secret go, it loses steam. Your uncle was a cross-dresser, your great-grandmother half Cherokee, your brother-in-law did heroin in college. At the end of the day, after the news is absorbed and everyone gets over the shock, who cares?

I say goodbye to the girl and then walk down the stairs and out the front door. I don't need to retrieve the pig, because I've already taken it home.

DOMINIQUE

don't know what became of them.

I understand that this lack of clarity will disappoint, but I'm an honest rabbit. I could medicate or drink a little tea and give you a more satisfying dénouement, but after the time I spent with the wreck of Lars, you will understand my reluctance. Even Advil gives me pause.

What occurred within my line of sight is therefore all I can relate. The day after the Stager drove away, a placard that said UNDER CON-TRACT was affixed to the FOR SALE sign. It hung from metal hoops, and swayed whenever the wind blew. Once, during a powerful storm, it blew off and landed across the street, in the neighbor's yard; I watched Elsa retrieve it, and then, later that afternoon, Amanda Hoff-stead came to hang it back up. A few weeks later, a Japanese family arrived to look at the house they had purchased sight unseen. Their car had diplomatic plates.

One steamy summer day in June, I watched a Salvation Army truck back into the driveway. It clipped the rosebush, breaking off a stem. Two men went in and out of the house several times and put some boxes and furniture in the truck. Another day, an old guy with a scruffy beard came and kicked the tires of Bella's car a few times, looked under the hood, wrote her a check, and drove it away. Finally, the first week of July, the moving trucks appeared. The day after that, the family got up at dawn and climbed into Lars's SUV, and then they were gone.

I GET A glimpse of my old life sometimes, in the wee hours of the night. The house is featured in a series called *Suburban Celebrities* that airs on cable television, and I even have an off-screen cameo: "A stager was employed, in part to repair the damage inflicted by a pet rabbit," the voice-over says. I read in the newspaper that Bella filed a lawsuit to get an injunction against airing the rest of the footage, so there's not much more substance than this. We are all reduced to sound bites in the end.

That's all I know. There are many things that confound me. What did they do with Lars's car, for example? Did they leave it at the airport? Did they hand it off to someone en route? In my heart of hearts, here's what I hope: I hope Lars dropped his family at the airport and recalibrated. That would be my version of a happy ending, that he began his life anew but found a way to hang on to Elsa.

But who can say? Sometimes people extricate themselves from bad situations, and sometimes they don't. As for the child, I hope that she is happy and that she has found herself a better pet. It wasn't her fault we didn't get along; I was in a bad place myself, and I take responsibility for my behavior.

I still see the Stager, you might be surprised to hear. She staged a few other houses in The Flanders, riding the success of the Sorkin-Jorgenson's speedy sale, deserved or not. I see her crossing over to Unfurlings sometimes at the end of the day. She stops at the farm stand to buy vegetables, and then takes long walks with a man.

Privately, I urge her to be careful. The cars come around the bend too quickly here, and the roads have not caught up with the pace of development. One of my sisters was squashed by a garbage truck at the very spot where the Stager now stands.

It's best to be mindful in this world. You never know what life has in store. A little counting of the daily blessings, an occasional prayer, a reverence for superstition—none of that can hurt. As Elsa will learn from her new British friends, on the first day of the month, to bring good luck, the first words she speaks will be "Rabbit, rabbit, rabbit."

ACKNOWLEDGMENTS

The three section headings are from *A Pattern Language*, by Christopher Alexander, Sara Ishikawa, and Murray Silverstein, with Max Jacobson, Ingrid Fiksdahl-King, and Shlomo Angel. If you haven't heard of this 1977 bible of architecture, find a copy and keep it by your bedside. Dip into it like poetry. It will change the way you think about the way you live. It may even make you want to dance in the street. *Home Staging for Dummies*, *Staging to Sell* by Barb Schwarz, and an amalgam of newspaper and magazine articles as well as websites and informal conversations with stagers and Realtors helped inform the sections on home staging.

Thank you to Melanie Jackson and Sarah Crichton for their loyalty, support, and belief in reinvention. Also at FSG, to Jeff Seroy, Lottchen Shivers, Nick Courage, Sarita Varma, Marsha Sasmor, and Dan Piepenbring, as well as the brilliant production and copyediting teams who saved me from humiliations large and small.

Lissa Muscatine and Bradley Graham at Politics & Prose, along with Barbara Meade, gave me a fresh start and an extended family of fellow book nerds, including Sarah Baline, Hannah Oliver (seriously, those hugs keep me going some days), and Mark Laframboise. Lars Townsend generously gifted me the gun in the refrigerator. And, Ron Tucker, thanks for the "b." Truly, I wish I could thank every single person I have worked with over these last three years, but the number is too great and every attempt at naming even those I have worked with most closely inevitably leaves someone out, so let me just say that these are truly the greatest, most scarily smart and well-read colleagues in the world, and I love you all. Thank you, too, to everyone at Modern Times Coffeehouse for the caffeine and good cheer, and to every customer I have accidentally disconnected on the phone or whose transaction has required a void.

David Groff offered encouragement and invaluable manuscript advice at a critical early stage, and the following friends and family helped in ways both tangible and not: Dylan Landis, Lisa Zeidner, Jean Heilprin Diehl, Paula Whyman, Leslie Pietryzk, Michelle Brafman, Mary Kay Zuravleff, Kitty Davis, Gary Krist, Susan Shreve, Howard Norman, Ally Coll Steele, Emma Coll, Max Coll, Rory Steele, Valerie Strauss, Joanne Reynolds, Lisa Mandel, Julie Langsdorf, Alexandra Viets, Geoff Coll, Jonathan Keselenko, Kara Sargent, Marian Keselenko, Mel Tomberg, and Steve Coll. Also thanks to the crazily talented trailer crew: John Becker, Matt Ong, Andrew Clark, Susan Derry, Maggie Erwin, Phil Hosford, Ally, and The Rabbit. And Paul Goldberg, thank you for the close read, the tight edits, and the recalibration.

A NOTE ABOUT THE AUTHOR

Susan Coll is the author of the novels *Beach Week*, *Acceptance*, *Rockville Pike*, and *karlmarx.com*. A television adaptation of *Acceptance*, starring Joan Cusack, aired in 2009. Coll works at Politics & Prose bookstore and lives in Washington, D.C.